# COMMUNICATION IN
# THEOLOGICAL EDUCATION:
# NEW DIRECTIONS

# COMMUNICATION IN THEOLOGICAL EDUCATION: NEW DIRECTIONS

EDITED BY

**MICHAEL TRABER**

## ISPCK
**2005**

**Communication in Theological Education: New Directions** –
Published by the Rev. Ashish Amos of the Indian Society for
Promoting Christian Knowledge (ISPCK), Post Box 1585, Kashmere
Gate, Delhi-110006.

ISBN : 81-7214-839-9

*Cover Design:* VIRENDRA SINGH

*Laser typeset at* **ISPCK,** Post Box 1585, 1654 Madarsa Road,
Kashmere Gate, Delhi-110006.

Tel.: 23866323,  Fax: 91-11-23865490.

E-mail: ispck@nde.vsnl.net.in    ashish@ispck.org.in

Internet: www.ispck.org.in

# CONTENTS

*Dedicated to*

**In Memory of
Rev. C.R.W. David (1932 - 2001) and
Fr. Joe Naidu S.J. (1941 - 1995)**

They were the pioneers who introduced
Communication Studies into Theological Education in
India

# Acknowledgements

The publication of this book, and the consultation on which it is based, were made possible by a grant of the World Association for Christian Communication (London), which is gratefully acknowledged. The book shows the active participation in the consultation by Dr Pradip N. Thomas, director of WACC's Global Studies Programme.

The United Theological College, Bangalore, was a perfect host to the consultation. Special thanks go to its Principal, Rev. Dr O.V. Jathanna, and to the chairperson of the Communication Department, Rev. Dr Joshva Raja.

# Preface

Communication is the prerogative of human beings. Being so closely linked to what it means to be human, communication cannot become the monopoly of any specific academic discipline, although if taken seriously, it can serve as a guiding principle for all disciplines.

Communication is an art in which one individual is revealed in another. It is an act of interdependence. While we reflect our individuality through communication, we simultaneously recognise the other's potentiality:

> Communication is stated to be established by discussion in the course of which individuals become convinced that their dissociation is caused by the accepted patterns of thought, whereas they are brought closer together by that wherein they differ and by that which constitutes their unique individuality (Rosenthal and Yudin 1967: 84).

Communication also serves as protection for both the self and the common bond. But sometimes it may remain on the periphery of the self, guided by the principle of 'be vocal, be victorious'. The only aim of communication, then, is to be 'victorious' over others. This attitude makes the communicator more aggressive but less creative, more logical but less imaginative, more analytical but less emotive. Thus, if we are to prevent communication from becoming a mockery of itself, what is required is a fair combination of both these aspects.

Indian political leaders, however corrupt, are generally regarded as possessing a 'special gift of communication'. Backed by state-owned media and political machinery, they often consider themselves to be above public criticism by virtue of their 'special communicating gift'. Is such a 'communicating gift' worth possessing? Does it lead to a new horizon for communication, particularly in the field of theological education? Where do these public leaders figure in the parameter of theological education? What sort of leaders does theological education produce, and with what kind of 'communicating gift'?

The underprivileged have always been stigmatised by society. They have been marginalised, even in the field of communication. They have a voice, but they have been made voiceless by disqualifying their participation in the 'art' of communication. For this reason, their communication has often remained one-way. Can there be a hierarchy in the field of communication? Can we afford to ignore the communication ability of the underprivileged? If the marginalised of society do not figure in the architecture of communication, then communication cannot claim a 'wholeness' for itself. Likewise, if communication in theological education has been designed for all, and if we are to find a new horizon for communication, then the underprivileged masses must find their proper place in it.

Silence is not a recent phenomenon in communication. In fact, it sometimes communicates more eloquently than words. Recently, silence was used to great effect by the opposition in the Manipur state assembly to register their protest against the ruling party. Although the place of silence in communication in theological education is yet to be determined, let us not allow silence to be silenced in theological education.

It is often said that women make better communicators than men. However, the issue is not how women become better communicators, but how they are used for the purpose of communication. When money is the prime driving force behind communication, women become merely commodities for communication. The ability of women as potential communicators is undermined when they are used as objects of communication. By allowing this to happen, we again make a mockery of communication.

If theological education is to find new horizons in communication, it has to work hard to prove its worth. It must be remembered that in this context, communication means to commune with the community at large with competence and compatibility. Here, the worth of communication lies in its uniqueness. Communication in education must therefore be made mandatory for all groups and/or disciplines.

Though communication is a discipline itself, it is interdisciplinary in nature. Its presence can be felt in all the disciplines that contribute to the theological education offered by the Senate of Serampore College. It is for this reason that the Senate decided that all candidates desirous of joining the teaching faculty of any theological college would have to have a working knowledge of communication methods.

We know, however, that often neither the traditional doctoral nor the MTh style of academic training assures that the successful candidates will know how to communicate the subject of their specialisation. We also know that they fail to communicate because they have not acquired the skills and methodologies of communication. The new MTh programme should therefore make a serious attempt to correct this lack by laying special emphasis on this area.

While the progressive outlook of the discipline may make communications better suited for exploring new horizons in theological education, it would require the cooperation of all disciplines. Every discipline has different methods/modes of communication. All these need to be integrated for optimum benefit.

In conclusion, I would like to propose that Communication Study be made mandatory for all those who wish to pursue higher theological studies, and that such study take into consideration the different methods of communication used by other disciplines.

— *Pratap Chandra Gine*

## REFERENCE

Rosenthal, M. and P. Yudin (eds.) (1967). 'Communication' in *A Dictionary of Philosophy*. Moscow: Progress Publishers.

# Introduction

At first glance this book appears to be of a specialist nature, appealing to men and women who teach communications in theological colleges. That indeed is its origin, namely, a consultation of theological educators and communication specialists that was held at the United Theological College, Bangalore, in August 2003. But its scope goes far beyond the narrow confines of practical theology. It is a book that tries to show that the mass media of communication are rapidly changing the environment in which faith is passed on and nurtured, and in which faith is professed and lived. This publication may well be read in conjunction with another similar book that tried to evaluate the influences of the *globalised* mass media on Indian cultural values.[1]

Pradip Thomas calls communication a 'confessional issue' for faith communities. This means that mass communication has to become part of a public discourse by which the nature and influence of communications are to be evaluated and judged from a religious/ethical perspective. Like gender discrimination, Dalit and tribal oppression and the exploitation of the natural environment, communication is now an issue that demands public debate, scrutiny and judgment. This, however, can only happen when the subtle and variegated facets of the modern communication phenomenon is studied in depth.

In this sense studying communication while doing theology is a new way of engaging in contextual theology. The socio-cultural environment in the last 30 years or so has been shaped by the mass

---

[1] Michael Traber (ed.), *Globalisation, Mass Media and Indian Cultural Values.* Delhi: ISPCK, 2003, p. 200.

media of communication in unprecedented but historically and geographically different ways. Theology has not only critically engaged itself with this new context but has also been enriched by it. That is amply described in the chapters that follow. But theology cannot, of course, be reduced to mere context. It also has a universal and universalising function. "If the message of what God has done in Christ is indeed Good News for all peoples, then the occurrence of grace in any setting" — including in specific acts and situations of communication — "has relevance for the rest of humanity."[2]

This new cultural context is the reason why many Christian theological colleges in India have introduced communication studies into their curricula. This speaks for the alertness of the churches and their concern not only for their own members but also for the people as a whole. The strategic importance of theological colleges is considerable. This is where the future pastors are being formed and from which the future educators and leaders of churches will have equipped themselves. They will spread the awareness that mass communication is too important to be left to the managers of television and radio stations or to the editors of newspapers and magazines. While the media are everybody's concern, they are of special concern to theologians whose work, in turn, can be enriched by them and other forms of communication.

Some readers may expect a good dose of media bashing in the chapters of this book. There is none of it. Making the mass media the scapegoat for all ills of society, as happens so often in Christian circles, would be a wrong approach. In fact there would be no point in studying the media at all. Instead of prejudging them, the contributors to this volume carefully consider the wider implications that the mass media have for life-in-common and life-in-faith. One conclusion from these chapters may be the support for the notion of an emerging 'communication theology', similar to liberation theology or Dalit theology. This type of reflection may surprise and enrich both media professionals and

---

[2]Robert I. Schreiter, *The New Catholicity. Theology between the Global and the Local.* Maryknoll, N.Y.: Orbis Books, 2000, 4.

communication scholars who rarely consider the wider cultural and theological implications of their work.

Although the mass media are rapidly changing our communication environment, creating a new mass-media-driven culture, it would be a grave mistake to put the mass media centre stage in theological education. The mass media are tempered, as it were, by interpersonal and group communication, which condition to a large extent the way the mass media are 'read' and interpreted. In addition, most theologically trained pastors or church workers will never appear on television or edit a newspaper or a popular magazine. But they will engage in face-to-face communication (as in counselling), or engage in group communication (committees, action groups), or address a worshipping congregation (sermons). In addition, there are specific 'cultural forms' of communication, different from region to region, which are usually categorised as folk media. The potential of folk media, as well as of music and visual art, for religious communications in India has hardly been explored. Understanding these non-mass-mediated forms of communication is crucial for any communication curriculum in theological education.

## FOUNDATIONS

The papers assembled in this book are arranged in three sections: Foundations, New Directions and Bible Studies. The first part combines mainly papers with new philosophical and theological insights into communications – as well as new communication perspectives relevant to theology. It starts with a short but pragmatic piece by Pradip N. Thomas, outlining the task ahead. This is followed by a chapter on the reasons for and the significance of communication studies in theological education. Traber's main argument is that the image or conception of the human being has changed. Humans are now seen primarily as communicators rather than rational animals (as was the case in the Age of Enlightenment). This view is supported by a new philosophical anthropology, which sees communication as constituting the authentic human being and by theological reflections about God as a communicating God.

Similarly, the church as *communio* consists primarily of communicating members. Finally, Traber describes the major shifts that have occurred in our cultures, culminating in a 'new culture' in response to the mass media.

Joseph Palakeel introduces 'theologising' as a key concept. Theologising presupposes an ongoing process of interaction between faith and life world, from which spring new meanings of feelings (rather than theories), relationships (rather than individual isolation), images (rather than just words) and rituals of community (rather than social mechanisms). These reflections lead the author to propose a communication theology that subsumes a symbolic-sacramental theology, an aesthetic theology and an ecological theology.

Theologising for Jose de Mesa is to dialogue between two poles: the Judeo-Christian tradition and the contemporary human experience. This dialogue consists of mutual interaction between the two poles. The starting point is the human experience, which connects with the faith *experience* of the early Christian communities. De Mesa's final section, on the salvific character of communication is, I believe, of special importance because it opens up a new vista about communication and theology. Salvation as total 'well being' is closely connected with divine-human and inter-human communications.

'The Unavoidable Dialogue between Theology and Communication' by Daniel J. Felton is the only chapter in this book that is not based on a conference paper. It is a summary of the author's dissertation as part of his Licentiate in Theology at the Gregorian University in Rome, and was first published in the journal *Media Development*.[3] The five relationships between theology and communication provide a map of the field,

---

[3]The journal *Media Development* of the World Association for Christian Communication (London) published a special issue in October 1989 on the theme Communication and Theological Education. One of the 15 articles in that issue is Daniel J. Felton's 'The Unavoidable Dialogue: Five Interfaces between Theology and Communication', pp. 17-23.

emphasising a comprehensive and systematic framework for further research and study.

'Lessons from Pastoral Practice' contains two contributions. Daniel Kirubaraj gives a brief summary of the empirical work he has done to ascertain the effectiveness of communication studies in Protestant seminaries in South India. Kavito Zhimo, a veteran teacher of communications in a seminary in Nagaland, pleads for a more contextual approach to the study of communications. This is no easy but nonetheless necessary task for a country like India, with so many different cultures, languages, religions and social settings.

## NEW DIRECTIONS

The five chapters under this heading deal with new realities in the field of communication or new perceptions of old realities (like cinema and music). It starts with a description of the immense and still growing power of those involved in information technology (IT) and the mass media. Pradip Thomas lists three reasons why we should be interested in the political economy of communication: a) the digital world has become the new power centre; b) in India these power centres are in the hands of a few business families; and c) a few international organisations (like the World Trade Organisation) make the rules and become power brokers. Digital technology is now all-pervasive and is the backbone of our new information and knowledge economy.

The next chapter deals with a different power: the power of the image. Artist and educationist Dr Solomon Raj gives a broad historical overview of the relationship of the church with visual art, including instances of iconoclasm. The author then, going beyond visual art, shows how symbolic language in general has been used whenever we speak about God and the sacred. He concludes that especially in India symbols and visual art have proclaimed the faith as eloquently as words.

Cinema is still India's most popular mass medium, yet it is the proverbial stepchild of communication studies in Protestant seminaries. Maybe the kaleidoscopic chapter by Suresh Kumar may inspire future teachers and students to engage with film studies in serious ways. The chapter shows the centrality of cinema for our cultures, with its dreams, myths, collective fantasies and fan clubs — in Tamil Nadu and elsewhere.

Hannibal Cabral, himself an eminent musical composer, analyses the religious role of music: It builds up community and makes people participants in it; it is the language of the transcendental; it creates identity and at the same time it can be understood and appreciated cross-culturally. And music, like religion, has feelings and speaks of experience. The chapter ends with concrete recommendations for the study of music in theological education.

Etienne Rassendren's chapter on Freedom Songs of the subaltern African-American people of the US is a finely honed analysis of cultural struggle and resistance. The author shows how the language of their white masters was 'stolen' and parodied to assert the black person's self. Rassendren also shows how the creators of the Negro spirituals appropriated the Judeo-Christian salvation story and inserted their own meanings about liberation and returning 'home'. Dr Rassendren poses relevant theoretical questions from the perspective of the subalterns (inferioritised).

## BIBLE STUDIES

The third part of this book contains three bible studies, which were given at the start of each of the three working days during the conference in Bangalore. Marlene Marak's reflects on some of the miracles of Jesus that were concerned with communication, opening up the blocked channels and thus restoring relationships — with God and with each other. They demonstrated an important aspect of God's Reign.

The second bible study deals with the thesis that behind every exhortation and statement of faith lurks a story. Dhyanchand Carr demonstrates this by recovering the authentic story behind some biblical passages. Carr asserts the "primacy of story over doctrine", which has profound implications for theology and religious communication.

Kuruvilla George reminds us that tears and lamentations are a universal language. It is the language of the weak and oppressed that God hears and understands. It is also a language that communication studies have largely ignored. Yet, Dr George concludes, "We are not fully fledged members of the human community until we break down and weep."

\* \* \*

In the end readers may ask, where is your new curriculum for communication studies in theological education? During the conference in Bangalore four regional groups produced drafts for a new communication curriculum on the BD level. One group represented the interests and priorities of North East India, a second group was from North India, and two groups worked out a curriculum from the perspective of South India. Alas, this volume offers no 'model curriculum', for there is no such thing as a single curriculum for use in Asia or even India. All this book can offer is a series of reflections and some principles that can guide teachers preparing themselves for, or already engaged in, the construction of a communication curriculum that must suit their students with their particular needs and in their particular circumstances.

*– Michael Traber*

# PART I
## FOUNDATIONS

## CHAPTER 1

# The Task Ahead

*Pradip N. Thomas*

Communication, like race, environment, gender and the Dalit cause, has now become a confessional issue for faith communities in India. Today, mediated communication

- has become an important source for societal values;
- has a highly influential role to play in setting the public agenda;
- is arguably the most powerful institution through which power is mediated in contemporary society;
- is being controlled by an increasingly small group of corporations via proprietary Intellectual Property Rights (IPR) regimes; and
- has led to the informationalisation of all life processes and to further amplifications of power through digitalisation and convergence.

As is always the case, it is the problems that loom large — and there are doubtless many limitations — direction, purpose, lack of training, lack of job opportunities, lack of fit between the needs of students and the curriculum and so on. Despite this, I am reasonably certain that history will vindicate this project. However, it is important to remember that just as the field of communications is undergoing change, so must our content and methodologies. We must also not forget the fact that communications in theological education is still a young subject, and that it will be a while before we can confidently claim that it has come of age.

In my view, there are about seven core areas that we need to deal with in relationship to communications and theology as a study enterprise:

1. There is a need to explore the interrelationships between religion, culture and communication, and between the Gospel, culture and communication. We may separate it for study purposes, but we must keep in mind the correspondences between the Gospel, culture and communication: how insights from culture can enrich our understandings of the Gospel, and those from the Gospels enrich our understanding of communications, and all of this can enrich our understanding of the life-centred vision of communication. At the same time, the non-correspondences and blind spots in these three areas can also become the source of reflection and action. Every media and non-media story — from Tehelka, to the features by P. Sainath, to those of Cyberabad and the IT economy — is a story that can potentially enrich our theology; and, in turn, some of the key values from the Gospels — love, compassion, solidarity, community, participation, liberation — cannot but be the scaffolding for our understanding and practice of communication. Theological reflection on these stories of communication should become one of the pillars of the programme.

2. In the context of validating and re-validating content, the curriculum needs to be exposed to and nurtured by understandings of the local and the global. By local I mean that it should be flexible enough to accommodate local communication and cultural concerns, be nurtured by context-based communication and culture, and be responsive to the communications concerns of the local church. This is a real challenge in the context of curriculum development. Do we understand the needs of local churches when it comes to

communication? How best can we create a study programme that equips seminarians to deal with local communication needs, and at the same time enables them to learn from global issues, such as the new challenges to religious worldviews from the informationalisation of life processes?

3.  It is necessary to ensure that for the content is grounded in an ethical understanding of communications —its relationship to philosophy, to theology, its roots in Biblical studies — enabling students to adopt an ethical stance on the way that they 'do' communications and approach communication possibilities and problems. There is a need for a life-centred communication ethics. This is a difficult, contentious area, but I strongly believe that the nurturing of an ethics of communication ought to be one of the pillars of a teaching programme.

4.  It is imperative that we grapple with communications as power, its various manifestations — local and global — and explore ways of redistributing that power, empowering people to communicate. We need to not only understand communications as power in the big picture — in terms of the new technologies, new pressures and new architectures of control that are being perfected — but also in terms of its exercise at the local level, at the level of church communications as it is practised today.

5.  Create the space to locate these issues within the context of subalternity and marginality, so that our theology and communications can help construct a politics of the possible. As soon as we deal practically with the mass media of communication we tend to be tempted by the glamour of technologies of power, which may put us into the very power structures we oppose. The test of the subaltern can prevent this.

6.  Ensure that the curriculum — be it journalism or the new media — is strong on communications practice, equipping the student with a skill that he or she can use. This is a tough proposition,

given the lack of resources, perhaps even staff, to deal with skills-related areas, but I think it is necessary.

7. Finally, we cannot forget that curriculum revision, irrespective of its institutional needs, fundamentally affects the future of students — and I am not sure whether we adequately take their views into consideration or prepare curricula that reflect their needs. I am not suggesting that the entire curriculum be prepared in an excessively participatory manner. But we would do well to remember that the success of the programme will be measured not only by the quality of teaching, teaching methodologies and the environments of study, but also on the basis of whether the course has succeeded in shaping a vocation, whether it has prepared a pastor or lay person to deal with the challenges of communication in the real world.

## CHAPTER 2

# Why Communication Studies in Theological Education

### Michael Traber

Communication is similar to the air we breathe or the water we drink. We take both for granted. Only when air and water become polluted do we really become conscious of them, and start worrying about these two necessities for life. And the result might well be that water and air may then become objects of study. So, too, with communication. Our ancestors did not worry about it as long as they felt they were in control, which they expressed in hundreds of cultural norms. Take one of those norms: truth-telling. When people still blushed when they were telling a lie and children covered their lips after lying, people thought they could deal even with lies and liars. But journalists do not blush when they type slanted stories into computers, newsreaders do not sweat when they speak lies into the microphone, and even if television anchor persons blush, we can't see it because of the heavy make-up on their faces. But when distortions and deceptions in the news media become too obvious we begin to worry, and communication becomes a focus of attention, even a subject of study.

After this negative remark, I would like to state that there are many positive reasons why communications should be taught in theological colleges, and most of the rest of this chapter deals with them. Before proceeding, however, I would like to briefly substantiate what I have said by referring to the United Theological College (UTC) in Bangalore. Founded as an ecumenical Protestant college in 1910, generation after generation of teachers and students never thought of studying communications in a systematic way. There were, of course, subjects like homiletics and religious instruction, but all other communication processes inherent in the study of theology were simply taken for granted. This changed in the 1980s. Some enlightened people began to realise that our cultural environment was changing. And as theologising always takes place in specific contexts, they started to prepare for the systematic study of that new context, the mass media of communication. After a planning process of several years, in 1992 communication studies became a compulsory subject in the curriculum of the Senate of Serampore College,[1] leading to the Bachelor of Divinity degree. Now communications at UTC (and other colleges) even has a department of its own.[2]

The first curriculum for BD students, though published in 1991, was actually worked out in 1989, two years *before* the World Wide Web made its first appearance. At that time there was no cable television in India, and in many ways Indian television was still in its infancy. In brief, the media landscape some 15 years ago was very different from what it is today. And yet we should not forget that, according to the National Readership Survey 2002, while exposure to television in urban areas was 52 per cent, in rural areas it was less than 32 per cent. The Internet in 2002 was used by slightly over four million people, of whom only 20 per cent used it at home, with the vast majority going to one of India's 100,000 Internet cafes.

After this rather lengthy introduction, we shall now consider a number of points that may be of relevance to our discussion about the development of communication studies in theological

---

[1]Serampore College, deemed university, is the coordinating institution for over 40 theological colleges in India. It prescribes the core curricula for its affiliated colleges and confers degrees.

[2]For information about the process of introducing communication studies to the Serampore curriculum, see Appendix III.

education. Our reflections start with the philosophical question of who we are as authentic human beings, and with the theological question of God as a communicating God. We then proceed to ask how communication constitutes community and the churches as social entities. The third part analyses the major shifts that have occurred in our cultural environment due mainly to the influence of the mass media, while the fourth section asks what possible contributions communication studies could make to a theology that relates to a new image of humans, and to the new context of our cultural environment. In conclusion I will list a number of points that are of special importance for communication studies in India.

## 1.  THE 'SPEAKING ANIMALS' AND THEIR COMMUNICATING GOD

Communication studies challenge theology with a new image of the human being, which is shaped by the presence of language. Humans are, by their very nature, communicators. Communication cannot be separated from their being. Reflection on this fact has led to the creation of a new philosophical and theological anthropology. I owe this insight to Paul Soukup, who writes:

> Where theology in past days characterised human beings as created, as sinners, as redeemed, as rational, as members of the Body of Christ, as free, as citizens, theology today sees human beings as hearers and speakers. Without denying everything else that human beings might be, the perspective of communication offers another vision. The world multiplies this vision in the media... and repeats it in language and art, enshrines it in culture, founds a universe upon it and takes it for granted, and finally offers every human being a home in the text of the world and in the word (Soukup 2001).[3]

---

[3] In writing this chapter I am greatly indebted to the seminal work of Paul A. Soukup SJ, the dean of the Communication Department of Santa Clara University (California). In numerous articles and book chapters, and in manuscripts still to be published, he has, over the last 20 years, developed a grid rather than a system for the various affinities between theology and communication science.

## A New Philosophical Anthropology

This new anthropology differs from the better known social or cultural anthropologies in that it is *not* primarily descriptive. Instead it reflects on human beings as they are constituted by nature and as sacred scripture reveals them. It is thus a cognitive anthropology, trying to answer the question: What ultimately makes us the way we are, and how does our being become truly human? I shall explore this briefly, first from a philosophical, then from a theological perspective.

The psychologist and communication scholar Paul Watzlawick (1969: 53) coined the axiomatic sentence: "One cannot *not* communicate." This echoes Plato's definition of the human being as 'the animal that speaks', which was later submerged in Aristotle's definition of the human being as 'the animal that thinks' (rational animal). Speaking and thinking, language and reason, are co-conditional; it is therefore meaningless to ask what comes first.

Humans are both creatures and creators of language. They are creating a highly sophisticated symbolic structure, based on sounds (phonemes) and minimal units of meaning (morphemes), with signs (e.g., a sound) and conventional codes (structures of meaning). The linguistic production of meaning is the very foundation of both communication and culture. Charles Morris (1975: 235, my translation) explains the centrality of language:

> Everything, which is characteristically human, depends on language. The human being is in a real sense the speaking animal. Speech plays the most essential — but not the only — role in the development and preservation of the human self — and its aberrations — as it does in the development and maintenance of human society — and its aberrations.

The broad purpose of language is human interaction. Language is what binds individuals together. It enables us to be-together in qualitatively different ways than animals. It thus reveals the essence of the human being: to-be-with-others, to interact-with-each-other, and to-be-in-relationship. Verbal language, viz. interpersonal communication, which I consider the primordial and, ultimately, only genuine model of all communications, enables us to become members of a group, of a community or society, and members of a shared culture.

Martin Heidegger (1971: 189) describes the centrality of language for the human being:

> Humans speak. We speak when we are awake and we speak in our dreams. We are always speaking, even when we do not utter a single word aloud, but merely listen or read, and even when we are not particularly listening or speaking but are attending to do some work or taking a rest. We are continually speaking in one way or another. We speak because speaking is natural to us. It does not first arise out of some special volition. Humans are said to have language by nature. It is held that humans, in distinction from plant and animal, are the living beings capable of speech. This statement does not mean only that, along with other faculties, humans also possess the faculty of speech. It means to say that only speech enables the human being to be the living being he [or she] is as human being. It is as the one who speaks that the human being is — human.

Needless to say that there are many other languages than the purely verbal and the verbal–visual language of script. Communication, in addition, consists of (*a*) the presentational language of our bodies, (*b*) the representational languages of things, visuals, icons and what we conventionally call symbols. Humans communicate (*c*) with music, which is a multifaceted language of its own, and (*d*) with silence. Humans technically construct (*e*) artificial languages like film and television, in which the audio–visual language, combining recorded sound and captured sight, plays an overpowering role. Audio–visual language is indeed a new language and thus a new type of communication that combines several different languages, making the process of communication extremely subtle. But I think it is of great importance not to see audio–visual language in isolation but in conjunction with other modes of human communication.

The philosophical base of all communications is inter-subjectivity for the purpose of conviviality (life together). The philosophical anthropology of the last few decades has replaced the notion of the autonomous individual, so dear to the Age of Enlightenment, with the concept of 'subject', which is defined in its relations to others, to its community and the historical–social realities that surround it. Communication, ultimately, is grounded in inter-subjectivity, which reflects the reality that humans are not just individuals but, as persons, essentially social beings. It has been suggested that the notion of inter-subjectivity, developed, among others, by Latin American scholars, is close to Asian anthropology, and in need of further development (Wilfred 2000: 82). In fact, Indian philosophy has gone a step further. Its theories of communication aim at the transpersonal, "in which oneness of the world is unambiguously perceived" (Dissanayake 1983: 29).

To sum up:

> Communication touches upon all that we are and all that we do. Communication … constitutes our inter-subjectivity. Through communication one becomes a full human and cultural being. Culture depends on the common sharing and participation by the members of a community. No community can be established or continue to exist without communication (Granfield 1994: 2).

After this brief sketch of a new philosophical anthropology, I will now outline some biblical–theological insights concerning God as a communicating Being.

## The Communicating God

Language, this unique gift to humankind, is reflected upon in the Bible, especially in the creation and covenant stories of the Old Testament and in the Logos theology of St John. God created the human being in his own divine image — as a couple (Gen.1: 22; 2:18, 21–22), and as part of the wider created order, in which humans 'name' reality (Gen. 2: 9, 19–20). The creator God is a communicating God, who in the cool of the evening converses with Adam and Eve in the garden of Eden (Gen.3: 8–11) and who, after the Fall, takes off the fig leaves from their bodies and, as mother God, clothes them with leather garments — God the tailor (Gen. 3: 21): a highly symbolic action.

When "in these last days" (Hebr.1: 2) God revealed himself in Jesus the Christ, we learn that God's very being — as far as we can understand — is communication and communion: the Father eternally 'speaking' the Son, in a dialogue that emanates the Spirit — a communion in perfect equality, so much so that the three persons share one nature. The divine image and likeness, in which humans are created, thus bears the trace-mark of the tri-une God, who is a community of love, expressed in tria-logue and communion. Being created in the Trinitarian image makes human communication with God possible and necessary, just as it enables and necessitates communication between humans. This, I think, is as far as we can go in theologising communication from a Trinitarian perspective. I agree with those who maintain that the Trinity is no 'model' of human communication (Amaladoss 2003: 68).

Communication, however, is not just a gift; it is also a challenge. It is wrought with crises and breakdowns. Genesis, which starts so hopefully, with humans being "very good" (Gen. 1: 31), soon informs us about communication breakdowns: Adam and Eve hiding when they hear the footsteps of the visiting God (Gen. 3: 8), Abel slaying his brother (Gen. 4: 1–16), the hubris of the city dwellers, constructing a tower "with its top in heaven" (Gen. 11: 4), whom God punishes by "confusing the language of the world" (Gen. 11: 9). Significantly, the breakdown of communication with God also leads to a breakdown in inter-human communications.

Much of the rest of the Bible, both Old and New Testaments, deals with God's efforts to restore communication *between* God and humankind and *within* humanity. The central theme is that of the covenant (Ex. 19: 1–7), in which God freely offers communication in the spirit of fidelity, reciprocity and mutual belonging, and which results in God having once again a dwelling place among his people (Ex. 40: 43f).

The divine self-communication reached its climax when the Word became flesh to initiate a new and final covenant with humankind. Thus Jesus announced the Good News of God's Reign, and implemented it symbolically by restoring divine–human and inter-human communication. It is noteworthy how several of his miracles healed blocked or interrupted communication, like blindness and deafness. In addition, the Good News of God's Reign was addressed first and foremost to those excluded and excommunicated by society: the poverty-stricken and those discriminated against by the dominant forces of society (Arens 1995: 56–64). Jesus even practised table fellowship with them (*convivium*), a symbolic action of great importance for the conviviality of God's Reign (cf. Luke 3: 29).

Finally, the outpouring of the Holy Spirit complements God's work in Jesus. The gift of the Spirit "reopens the channels of communication closed off at Babel, and re-establishes the possibility of easy and authentic relations among people in the name of Jesus Christ" (Martini 1994: 22). When the early Christians reflected on their experience of coming together, and of their power to communicate, they came to the conclusion that it was all due to the action of the Spirit of Jesus. And, according to them, the main categories of God's self-communication in the Spirit are: freedom, reconciliation, service (*diakonia*) and communion (Gal. 5: 2; 2 Cor. 5).

Pradip Thomas (1997: 40), reflecting on the primacy of the Word in the Christian tradition, points out some deeper communicative dimensions:

> The centrality of our faith hinges around our belief in the Word, that primary element of communications that in a sense animates all

human life.... The concept of the Word of God refers not merely to the written and tangible narrative expression of the life and teachings of Christ, but more fundamentally denotes a communicative encounter. It is linked inextricably with, and is fulfilled in, the Word becoming flesh, in the actual encounter, the event — the meeting of God with the human person. It is through this encounter that the revealed Christ becomes a part of each of us — what Swami Abhisiktananda describes as the meeting that takes place in the cave of the hearts — place of the ultimate encounter where the spirit of the human being becomes one with the Spirit of God.

This first theme of our reflections has shown how the humans, both from a philosophical and theological perspective, are essentially communicative beings, that is, beings for whom relationships with God and other humans are natural in the deepest sense of the word. We have also seen that communication — with the Trinity and with his human creatures — is part of God's nature. Our second reflection is on the nature of the church.

## 2.   THE CHURCH IS A SPIRIT-GUIDED COMMUNITY OF PEOPLE, COMMUNICATING THEIR FAITH

This definition of the church may appear commonplace or superficial. It is true that *communio (koinonia)* is only one 'model' (or analogue) of the church, and thus it is evidently one-sided. Avery Dulles, in a book entitled *The Church is Communications* (1971), lists five models of the Church:

1.   The church as institution, in which the hierarchy is the main communicator and its content is doctrine.

2.   The church as herald, whereby the entire church proclaims the good news of Jesus and speaks with a prophetic voice to the world.

3.   The church as a sign or sacrament, viz. the body of Christ, whereby God and the church continue Christ's presence in the world.

4.   The church as a communion, whose members are in dialogue

with each other and the world at large, communicating fellowship, life, truth.

5.   The church as a servant (*diakonia*) through actions for others, working for justice and love.

Soukup (2001) comments, "We can see here the value of no one model alone providing a complete description of the church; similarly no one kind of communication will satisfy the communication needs of the church." These five models, emphasising the communication dimensions of the Church, also underline the fact that "the church is multidimensional: human and divine, visible and invisible, institutional and spiritual. These different aspects" (in the words of *Lumen Gentium*, 8) "form one interlocked reality, which is comprised of a divine and human element" (Granfield 1994: 7).

Although no church council or magisterial document has ever mandated or prescribed one particular definition of the church, it is nevertheless a fact that the *communio* analogue became the central and most important ecclesial model in modern theology, particularly since the Second Vatican Council (which propounds it in one of its main documents, the Constitution on the Church (*Lumen Gentium*), but also in other documents like *Dei Verbum* and *Gaudium et Spes*.

Historically, the communion model is almost as old as the church itself:

Structurally, the early church was a communion of local churches *(communio ecclesiarum)*. Each individual church considered itself a communion of believers *(communio fidelium)*. Even though the Church of Rome acquired particular respect because of its association with the Apostles Peter and Paul, and eventually became the point of reference for the whole [Latin speaking Catholic] church, the relationship among the churches and with Rome was not understood in the sense of jurisdictional superiority or subordination. Communication among the churches was achieved by mutual exchange of information concerning their respective traditions of faith and ecclesial customs and by mutual reception (Pottmeyer 1994: 100).

However, the communion theology as espoused by Vatican II was not primarily concerned with church structures. *Communio* was the very basis of the Council's ecclesiology, subsuming other images of the church, including the Council's prominent expression, 'the People of God'. Breuning (cited in Kienzler 1994: 88) explains the centrality of *communio* as follows:

> If the church is *communio*, then the life form of this community does not exist alongside an external structure of order. Such an external order is vital for the organisational tasks of the church. But as far as its vital dimensions are concerned, it is not decisive in its life. Rather the form and formation of the Church must clearly be characterised by the ultimate reality of its *communio*.

Communion, community and communication comprise several dimensions and are found on the following levels:

– Communion with God, which is made possible through the Holy Spirit, by which believers have access through Christ to the Father.

– The eucharistic community, in which "Christ gave us the most perfect, most intimate form of communion between God and humans possible in this life, and out of this, the deepest possible unity among men [and women]" (*Communio and Progressio,* 11).

– The community and unity of the church: A unity in communion, "with radical equality in dignity and mission, which arises from baptism and underlies hierarchical structure and diversity of office and function, and this equality necessarily will express itself in an honest and respectful sharing of information and opinions" (*Aetatis Novae,* 10).

– "The communion of the faithful is the vision of a community of brothers and sisters in dialogue. That requires in the first place that we foster within the church herself mutual esteem, reverence, and harmony, through the full recognition of lawful diversity" (*Gaudium et Spes*, 92).

–   The communion of the church as Sacrament for the World: "The church does not exist for its own sake, but, by its very nature, it is intended to be the sign of salvation for the world. It follows that the *communio,* which is the church, must be a type, model, and example of the *communio* among all human beings and nations" (Kienzler 1994: 87). In addition, as a sign and instrument of unity and peace, the church's commitment to justice, peace and freedom for all human beings and nations is a fundamental perspective of the church.

Arens (1995:158) argues that the *communio* concept of the church is only credible if it is implemented in the church's praxis:

> The theological statement that the church is a *communio* must become visible in the church's structure and praxis, and must verify and prove itself in that structure and praxis. This occurs inasmuch as the church, as a community of testimony and confession, convincingly bears witness to Jesus Christ and, on the basis of mutually attained conviction, confesses Jesus Christ.

This vision of the church has a number of consequences. Among them are the overriding importance of dialogue and a reinterpretation of the concept of witness. Communication studies can shed some light on both these questions.

## Dialogue

All genuine communication is essentially dialogical. Communication is increasingly seen as a process through which sharing of meaning is made possible, and by which social relationships and, as a result, social institutions are created and maintained. It is a two-way process, interactive by its very nature. The very concept of communication demands participation. Dialogue is only possible in a spirit of equality. Further, dialogue, like love, is unconditional. Dialogue partners are accepted and affirmed in their basic otherness, as they are, not what they 'ought' to be.

Dialogue furthermore presupposes freedom. Coerced communication is a meaningless aberration of communication. A dialogical church must therefore be a place of freedom as well as a witness to the freedom that is part of the Reign of God — the "law of freedom" (James 1: 25). An atmosphere of fear — for example, fear of the authorities in church or state — is implicit intimidation, in which communicative freedom cannot flourish. But,

> We cannot be concerned with safeguarding individual freedom alone. Such freedom is always due to some other freedom. True freedom implies a view of society as a whole.... The issue here is to realise the freedom of all, which alone makes a free and just society possible (Collet 1981:19).

Finally, genuine communication presupposes what communication scholars call communicative competence. Children growing up in homes with computers and television normally acquire both technical and generic competence of the media in question. To increase critical competence is one of the aims of media education. Though communication competence is crucial for human development, it varies from age to age, from culture to culture, and according to discourse or subject matter. The question arises: if a church is dialogical, in which ways can she strengthen the communicative competence of its members and even of non-members?

*Dialogue as Self-Realisation of the Church* (Fuerst 1997) is the title of a critical study of the claims of a dialogical church.[4] It develops the following three theological criteria for the church (pp.131f):

• Commitment to the way of salvation, whereby God entered into communication with humans, accepting them as genuine partners in communication;

---

[4]The book in German is entitled *Dialog als Selbstvollzug der Kirche.*

- the dialogical way of life of Jesus with his disciples and the people, and his proclamation of a new dialogue under God's Reign; and
- the biblical assertion and praxis of the church as a community in the Holy Spirit.

## Witness

'Proclamation' is a term almost unknown to modern communication studies. But witness and witnessing are central, especially in media studies. Reporters in the field present themselves as eyewitnesses and programmes are cast as eyewitness accounts. Arens (1995: 88–89), a student of Juergen Habermas, describes witnessing in terms of the Theory of Communicative Action:

> A witness witnesses to what she has seen and what has become evident to her. In her (text of) testimony she communicates to others (the recipients of her testimony) that to which she bears witness, so that it might likewise become accessible and evident to them, so that it can be shared with them. Witnessing has its locations and its contexts. It is a political act that takes place in public. It thus can also be publicly called into question and disputed.

Witnessing intends to reach an understanding of a shared experience. It does not aim at a conceptual consensus but at an experience of something seen and heard, often a story. Witnessing, therefore, implies mediation in a communicative sense, namely, making accessible to, and sharing with others, stories about events and persons to whom they have no direct access:

> A witness makes a statement. In that statement she claims that what she testifies is true. She does so by putting forward her own person as a pledge of the truth of one's testimony… The action of the witness is aimed at bringing to bear the full weight of what is testified to, which is not accessible, except by way of the person of the witness (ibid. 94).

**Kerygmatic-missionary witnessing** comes closest to this view.

It is the first of four forms of witnessing. "All Christians who make the communication of the gospel their own and who make its content accessible and visible in their praxis, are bearers of kerygmatic-missionary witness" (ibid. 127). This witness is textually mediated, in an explicitly verbal manner, but is complemented by the authenticity of the witness' integrity and lifestyle. In this sense it can be said that *who we are* speaks louder than *what we say*. Witnessing is further accompanied by a multiplicity of other texts, derived from specific situations and locations. From these situations may arise the need for diaconal witnessing.

**Diaconal witnessing** takes place when "human beings give of themselves to others, stand up for them, stand by them in their distress, and help them" (ibid. 28). This type of solidarity with the oppressed, the suffering and needy, is that by which the solidarity of Jesus with the poor and weak is carried forward. Jesus' person and praxis are not necessarily articulated in words, and are not intended to have a persuasive effect, but they may become textual with questions, such as, why is a witness acting like this? Why does she care? The praxis of easing the suffering of human beings, and of liberating them through social service and political actions, borders on prophetic witnessing.

**Prophetic witnessing** begins with the denunciation of a situation of sinfulness and with the proclamation of a new, more just and humane order. Anyone acting prophetically bears witness to the praxis of Jesus, who condemned oppression and exploitation and confronted all injustice with God's liberating rule.

**Witnessing through suffering** is the fourth dimension of witness. It takes up the notion of the martyr as the church's privileged witness. The role of martyrdom for the early church can hardly be exaggerated: suffering and death for one's faith was a reality in the life of these communities, and martyrs were not only seen as continuing Jesus' sufferings and death, but also his resurrection. "Today those who witness through suffering are individuals, groups and communities, indeed entire local churches are persecuted on the basis of their praxis of faith" (ibid. 132).

The examples given show that "Christian witness, by definition, is not that of isolated individuals but of the community. The relationship of personal witness to the community...is fundamental to perceiving the meaning of Christianity and of the 'community of disciples'" (Antoncich 1994: 155). In this sense the distinction between evangelisation *ad intra* (within the church) and *ad extra* (outside the church) has become almost meaningless. Christian witness is ultimately the same, whether *ad intra* or *ad extra*.

This section may well be concluded with a statement by Roberge (1999: 7): "Every Christian is a communicator, a witness. Christians are the media of Jesus. Accordingly, they should be persuaded that before they say a word or posit an action, they, as Christ's media, already convey a message."

## 3. AT THE THRESHOLD OF A 'NEW CULTURE', CHARACTERISED BY THE MASS MEDIA OF COMMUNICATION

Theology at any time and anywhere is culture-bound, because it deals with human beings. Sathianathan Clarke (1997: 97), writing about Constructive Theology, states:

> Anthropos completes itself by the conceptual worlds that it weaves in order to frame its collective living both systematically and meaningfully. In this sense all communities testify to an ongoing process of what it means to be human. Because theology does involve human beings in changing cultural situations it will tend... constantly to construe what it means for a particular community to live collectively under God. A kind of dialectic dynamic is involved in theological activity: a movement towards creating contextual conceptual grids for collectively living sensibly, meaningfully and fruitfully under God....

Theology has began a dialogue with communication studies mainly because the mass media of communication have created a 'new culture' in industrially developed countries and are in the process of doing the same in much of the rest of the world. The aim of this section is to show how the contemporary world of mass communication affects human society in general and theology in particular. The following is a summary of some of the traits of this 'new culture' (adapted from Soukup 2002).

1. **Sources of knowledge.** In the past people knew mainly of what they had experienced personally, or what their neighbours spoke of, or what they heard at gatherings. Now we have access to a much wider world through processes of mediation. This is indirect knowledge, filtered through reporters, editors, media systems; yet it seems so natural that we sometimes forget that it is mediated.

2. **Use of time.** Time is finite, and we divide it according to duties, interests and leisure. Next to sleeping and working, the average person in industrialised countries spends more time with the media than with any other activity. The National Readership Survey 2002 says the average Indian with access to television spends one hour and 22 minutes daily watching television, about 20 minutes reading a newspaper and 30 minutes reading a magazine (www.thehoot 2002). The nature of people's leisure time has changed rapidly: people are progressively giving up community functions, church devotions, family games and even face-to-face communication in favour of watching television.

3. **Measuring importance.** Mass media tell people what is important in the world. They tell people not so much what to think, but what to think about. The more we read, hear and view certain topics in the media, the more we judge them important. This works the other way as well: We conclude that what does not appear in the media is unimportant. It is thus symbolically annihilated, like some ethnic groups, women and manual labourers. Similarly, God and the church may begin to lose their importance for some, especially young members

in our communication culture.

4. **Shifting places.** The electronic media are changing our 'sense of place'. There is a kind of virtual bilocation for those sitting at home and watching what is happening across the world. This ability to see beyond ourselves has led to the expectation to even see the private lives of politicians, actors and actresses etc., which may be a disrespect of others' privacy.

5. **Control.** In the past governments controlled what could be shown and heard on government-sponsored television and radio. Governments still issue licences for films that can be released. But the corporate structures of radio and television have wrested control away from governments and claim the right to broadcast what they think is appropriate. For the first time in the history of humankind, mass-mediated communication is now largely uncontrollable. And the Internet is a celebration of this freedom.

6. **Audience sophistication.** Audiences have become sophisticated in their media uses. They select programmes according to their own needs and preferences. Many audience members have their suspicions regarding the motives of producers, advertisers, government regulators, or anybody else trying to force ideas on them. This does not mean that they cannot be directed or even manipulated, but that they will move more slowly in the direction desired by programme producers. The church should expect the same sophistication and even suspicion in her own communications.

7. **Cognitive shifts.** Different ways and types of communication affect the way people think. This can be illustrated in the shift in theology from an oral heritage of scriptural narratives to a formulaic set of text-based, written culture. Now the way of organising knowledge is changing again to (what has been called) a 'new orality'. A mainly text-based theology is in danger of losing a large segment of those who now look to images and narratives as ways of understanding the world. In

addition, theology's emphasis of knowledge over practice is in danger of becoming irrelevant to the modern world.

"The current world of communication shows that theology and religious discourse confront a world dramatically different from what academic theology has inherited. This does not mean that academic theology lacks a place or a purpose. It does mean that theology should attend more to communication" (Soukup 2001). Attending to communication would mean becoming aware and systematically analysing new cultural trends (some of which have been listed above) that are increasingly shaping society. For such an analysis, the teaching of communication skills is not enough. What is needed are critical reflections on new discourses of our media culture, which are based on communication and mass media theories that communication science has constructed over the years.

## 4. THEOLOGICAL CHALLENGES FROM A NEW COMMUNICATION ENVIRONMENT

After teaching communication studies for some years at the United Theological College in Bangalore, I have come to the conclusion that what misdirects and obscures the approach to the mass media most is a rather extreme moralism. Moralism has little to do with media ethics; it is rather an assumption about the 'immoral' influences of the media and their 'bad effects' on society, particularly by the portrayal of sex and violence, and their display of 'materialism' and 'consumerism' in general.

### Active Media Users

In the moralistic approach there is an implicit belief in unverified presuppositions about media impact and media use. It further isolates the mass media from all other communication activities that affect our lives and moral judgements. What we perceive while watching television is not deposited on a *tabula rasa*, but on a mind and soul that has been informed and formed by other communication agencies, such as family, religious and educational background, interpersonal communications in a variety of groups, particularly reference groups. Media perception is further influenced by social structures and positions, the views we hold of society and social groups and the social actors represented in the media. Furthermore, media use takes place against the background of cultural norms and a host of cultural images that we carry with us. Media texts are always interpreted by a variety of contexts and are therefore inter-textual.

What is true, however, is that the power of the mass media increases when these backgrounds and influences lose their power. The decline of social institutions like the school, the church, the political party, etc., will strengthen the influence of the mass media. It is therefore not moralism, but the critical analysis of strategies on how to maintain and strengthen such social institutions that can provide the much-needed counterbalance to the mass media.

In any case, rather than being mere objects of the media, people using media include and incorporate in their uses their own world and world-views, both individual and social, secular and religious. The principle of inter-subjectivity with its web of relationships applies here as well – as it does to theological teachers and preachers.

Religions the world over, and Christianity in particular, have hitherto provided definitive meanings of life. This function has now, at least partly, been taken over by the mass media of communication:

> It is increasingly becoming a truism to say that the media account for a dominant share of our leisure time that is becoming, for many, the prime source of meanings...[The media] answer questions to life's large and small mysteries — our existential dilemmas and our personal/moral ones; they manufacture definitions of the world and provide the necessary frameworks within which we make sense of this reality and structure our responses to it (Thomas 1997: 31).

## The Meaning of Leisure

One reason for the relative effectiveness of the media is that exposure to media takes place primarily during leisure time. Sociologists list the occupation with media as leisure-time activity. Leisure is the time we have for ourselves and for family and friends. It is distinct from work and professional obligations. Leisure time allows for freedom: freedom to explore new possibilities, freedom to imagine a different kind of life, and freedom to imagine and dream of new horizons into which our human condition can be placed. Connected with all this is the 'liminal' (from *liminus*, meaning threshold).

According to Victor Turner, liminality is an intermediate space between two worlds: the world of every day programmatic routines and the world of the transcendent or cosmic meaning. The experience of liminality is thus a religious or semi-religious experience. Entering a transcendental sphere we may search for ultimate meanings and for God. This has been shown to apply to media like film, television and music in many empirical studies (cf. Albrecht 1982, 1993).

It should also be noted that the notion of leisure time includes private religious practices and public worship. Leisure is so essential for individual human beings and communities that God ordained the Sabbath as a day of rest and celebration (cf. Traber 1999). Some argue that today, more than at any other time, our personal experience of revelation, ultimate truth, moral purpose and individual reaffirmation is mediated by our media experiences. 'The media experience is the most common form of liminal experience in our more secularised societies" (White 1985: 815).

The new media environment challenges our print-based theology in yet another way, namely in the preponderance of images and musical sounds that characterise it, which is, I believe, of special significance for the teaching of practical theology in India.

## World of Images and Music

Advertising has transformed the outward appearance of our cities: we are literally walking from image to image. Enlarged and printed photographs, the world of cinema and, above all, the enchantment with television have made the lives of most people, and not just urban dwellers, largely image-bound. And as soon as we enter the Internet, we are once again confronted by images.

The ascendancy of the image does not mean that verbal texts will diminish or even disappear. But it does mean that there is a rather profound change in the perception of reality for people who live in cultures that are distinctly image-based. Images, or visual texts, have always been an integral part of human communication. The cave paintings are the first records of communications. Most small children, if given the resources, will draw images reflecting the experiences of what they see.

Images occupy a special place in some religions. Hinduism, for example, has developed visual languages of a veritable cosmic proportion, from a host of visual symbols to a universe of concrete representations. Christianity, on the other hand, is now essentially word- and even script-based, unlike the early Christian communities, particularly of West Asia. The immediacy of the image and its emotive character are now largely lacking in many, if not most, Christian churches. Images force us to be imaginative and creative in our explorations of the larger meaning of life. This is evident from the tradition of religious icons and Christian religious art. The quiet absorption or reflection on such images was thought to lead to a spirituality steeped in 'contemplation'. Today, these images have been largely replaced by the secular icons of media-based 'stars'.

Another change taking place in our media-driven culture is the overriding importance given to music. Recorded music of all kinds is now available almost everywhere and is amplified through increasingly sophisticated sound systems. What is most evident in this new musical culture is the Pop/Rock and Soul music of young people. In fairly rapidly changing fashions, pop music has become one of the defining characteristics of a youth culture, which young people hold in common, though there are subtle modifications from culture to culture (cf. Robinson 1991).

Peter Manuel (2001) argues that India has a distinct 'cassette culture'. Every conceivable kind of music is now being recorded and sold, from *bhajans* to classical music, and songs with socio-political content. A special place in the new cassette culture is occupied by Hindi film music, once the mainstay of radio, now available in a great variety of recordings. Its singers have obtained cult status. These films and their music are probably the most widespread and, perhaps, the most important media in India.

Bluck (1989: 30) observes that "our verbal language is becoming increasingly inadequate to describe the breath of our experience... The new literacy...is musical and visual rather than verbal, and for a word-dependent tradition like Christianity, that demands some urgent changes." Bluck (ibid. 31) believes that the "new literacy, musical and visual as it is, coupled with the new freedom that a more informal and varied communication climate brings, allows Christians to share their faith more clearly and fully". Sathianathan Clarke (1997: 96) sees Indian culture in general as "a multimedia configuration", and appeals to theology to critically but constructively engage in it:

> If Indian-Christian theology wants to critically reflect on communal social intercourse that is all-encompassing, it must give a fair hearing and sight to the imaginable expressions that lie outside the singular expression of writing. Theo-logia in India thus ought to become inclusive of theo-graphia and theo-phonia.

Pradip Thomas (1997: 35), referring specifically to theological education, appeals to theologians to comprehend the contemporary cultural context of faith.

> I do believe that if we are serious about exploring our commitment

to communications in theological formation, we need to affirm our willingness to explore the larger meanings of 'relatedness' and 'consanguinity'. We also need to begin to explore the new languages of thought and cultural expression, and to understand the scaffolding of popular culture and our media-saturated, socio-cultural context of faith.

These reflections on new cultural forms and a new cultural environment that are increasingly influenced by the mass media have not yet touched upon other factors that affect the development of a theology that seeks to be relevant and communicative (Felton 1989: 19). Questions that still need to be asked are: What is the nature of the theology that is to be communicated? Will theology become reductionist in the sense that theology drops what cannot be communicated easily or is not thought to be immediately relevant? What are the central concepts of communication and the main findings of communication science that a communicative theology explores? And what are the theological consequences when applying certain communication principles to the ways that theological content is disseminated?

There is an abundance of critical studies on the so-called Electronic Church, with its neglect of the central mystery of the Cross and its emphasis of the 'gospel of prosperity' (Gerbner et al. 1984). However, it would be wrong to seek the origin of this rather extreme form of religious communication in the 'character' of the electronic media according to the often-misunderstood formula of McLuhan, 'the media is the message'. In reality, the Electronic Church it is an extension of the Protestant revivalist movements in the USA (Hoover 1988), plus a giant business venture.

The way communication has shaped theology throughout history has been shown in a number of studies (O'Collins 1981). The contemporary Narrative Theology seems to have incorporated in indirect ways some of the exigencies of current European culture, such as the supremacy of the personal over the abstract and the experience over thought (Metz 1973). But the questions posed above still need to be addressed by systematic studies of contemporary cultures and contextual analysis in India and beyond.

## CONCLUSION

In conclusion I would like to list seven points, which I think are important for the construction of a curriculum in communication studies.

### 1.   Communication should be studied holistically

Non-mediated communications like interpersonal, in-group and inter-group communication form the very basis of a proper understanding of communication processes. The mass media, then, are only a small but important part of the human edifice we call communication. They have increased and intensified a host of other communication processes that characterise human life, because each media perception triggers off, on different levels, other types of communications, and together with them we negotiate meaning from the media text and various other contexts.

### 2.   Communication in a multicultural context

Although communication studies deal with some sets of universals (like humans as communicating beings), they should be grounded in a people's specific culture. Each culture and subculture has its own norms and forms of communication. Communication studies in India have barely started to explore the multifarious ways of communicating in this multicultural country. This is particularly true for Dalit culture and the tribal cultures of North East India. Communication curricula must be refashioned to reflect this cultural reality.

### 3.   Communication studies can illuminate aspects of theology, and *vice versa.*

The role of communication studies is similar to that of culture in general and the social context in particular, with which theology is interacting as a matter of course. But the notion of culture, usually associated with traditional culture, should include the new popular culture, which is emerging under the influence of the mass media. Theology may not be accustomed to relate to such modern hybrid cultures, yet they are a reality. Some of the characteristics of a culture driven by mass media have been described. But in reality we know very little of how Indian people interact with the mass media and in which ways the media have influenced their perception of themselves and of reality in general.

## 4.   Communication studies should teach practical skills

So far we have said nothing about practical skills in different kinds of communications, and in some curricula skills development is entirely ignored. But there is widespread agreement in India that skills development is an essential part of communication studies. The current BD curriculum of Serampore allocates about a third of the teaching time to the development of practical skills, primarily journalism, audio-visual techniques and computer skills. How they should be taught is, however, an unresolved question. Should we start with such practical training and then integrate it with communication theories? Or should skills development stand alone? What provisions should we make for the development of special skills, such as drawing/painting, musical composition/ performance and Indian dance? My inclination is to treat communication theories on the BD level in a practical fashion, perhaps as an extended course of Communication Education and Media Literacy, and increase and diversify skills development while reserving the grand theories for the MTh level.

## 5.   Communication studies in relation to other agents of ministerial formation

Another related task is the relationship between communication studies and Practical Theology as a whole and to the various subjects being taught in UTC's department of Christian Ministry, such as counselling, religious education and homiletics. Communication studies cannot be a substitute for such specialised pastoral subjects. But neither can the two ignore each other.

## 6.  Communication and creativity

When I first came to India I was convinced that radio and television broadcasting was not possible for the churches and hardly for Christians. Since then I have changed my mind. There is a wide scope for telling modern parables in all the media, provided we know the techniques of mediated story telling. We seem to have a very narrow conception of what Christian communication is all about. And we seem to lack the sheer willpower and courage to try. Communication studies in theological education should foster the creativity of individuals and groups, and not just by way of cultural entertainment on special occasions, but also in terms of the development of ideas. The question is, should we provide at least elective courses in creative writing and photography, to skills with which such creative processes often start?

## 7.  Communication for self-empowerment or disempowerment

This chapter has tried to demonstrate communication as a reality that embraces all of life, human thinking, human relationships and individual and collective actions. Communication is meant to be self-empowering, so that humans can become what they are. But this proposition is increasingly being questioned (Hamelink 1994). The structures of society and the church can have a silencing effect on people. Likewise, the mass media. They can disempower rather than self-empower.

Part of the meaning of communication studies in theological education, perhaps its most important aspect, is to teach and practise how communication power can be seized by the powerless. Intra-group and inter-group as well as organisational communications are the privileged sites where power can be usurped for the sake of transformation and social change. The mass media, particularly small media, alternative journalism and alternate media, can contribute to this process, but it must start with the powerless themselves who, of course, are part of our churches.

In our long journey through a vast new landscape we have tried to sketch a map. We started by looking at ourselves — as essentially communicating beings that mark the contemporary image of *anthropos*. We briefly reflected on the communicating God who acts in history by communicative actions. We dwelt on the meaning of the church, and found that it was *communio*. And we finally tried to understand the new culture, fashioned by communication and, particularly, by the mass media. These four movements, which are at the heart of communication studies, are an important part of the context of theologising in the twenty-first century. They are, increasingly, an important part of people's lives. The great lay theologian M.M. Thomas once said that Indian theology must be understood as "a product of the church's participation in the life and self-understanding of the people...seeking a new life" (Philip 1986: 149). Communication studies, I believe, can contribute to that new life.

## REFERENCES

Albrecht, Horst (1982). *Arbeiter und Symbol. Soziale Homiletik im Zeitalter des Fernsehens*. Muenchen/Mainz: Gruenewald.

_____. (1993). *Die Religion der Massenmedien*. Stuttgart/Berlin/Koeln: Kohlhammer.

Amaladoss, Michael (2003). *Theology's Responses to the Challenge of Communications*, in Joseph Palakeel (ed.), *Towards a Communication Theology*. Bangalore: Asian Trading Corporation, pp. 60-71.

Antoncich, Ricardo (1994). *Christian Witness as Communication*, in Patrick Granfield, *The Church and Communication*, Kansas City, MO: Sheed and Ward, pp.137-157.

Arens, Edmund (1995). *Christopraxis. A Theology of Action.* Minneapolis, MN: Fortress Press.

Bluck, John (1989). *Christian Communication Reconsidered.* Geneva: WCC Publications.

Clarke, Sathianathan (1997). Constructive Christian Theology: A Contextual Indian Proposal, in *Bangalore Theological Forum,* Vol. 29, Nos.1 & 2, pp.95-109.

Collet, Giancarlo (1981). Communication and Freedom: Reflections on the Task of the Church, in *Media Development,* Vol.28, No. 4, pp.17-19.

Dissanayake, Wimal (1983). Communication in the Cultural Tradition of India, in *Media Development,* Vol. 30, No 1, pp.27-30.

Dulles, Avery (1971). *The Church is Communications.* Rome: Multimedia International.

Eilers, Franz-Josef (1996). *Communicating in Community. An Introduction to Social Communication.* Indore: Satprakashan Sanchar Kendra.

Felton, Daniel (1989). The Unavoidable Dialogue: Five Interfaces between Theology and Communication, in *Media Development,* special issue (October), pp.17-23.

Fuerst, Gebhard (ed.) (1997). *Dialog als Selbstvollzug der Kirche?* Freiburg/Basel/Wien: Herder.

Gerbner, George, et al. (1984). *Religion and Television.* Philadelphia: Annenberg School of Communication, University of Pennsylvenia.

Granfield, Patrick (1994). The Theology of the Church and Communication, in Patrick Granfield (ed.), *The Church and Communication.* Kansas City, MO: Sheed & Ward, pp.1-18.

Hamelink, Cees (1994). *Trends in World Communication. On Disempowerment and Self-Empowerment.* Penang: Southbound/ Third World Network.

Heidegger, Martin (1971). *Poetry, Language, Thought* (trans. Albert Hofstaedter). New York: Harper & Row.

Hoover, Stewart (1988). *Mass Media Religion. The Social Sources of the Electronic Church.* Newbury Park, London, New Delhi: Sage.

Kienzler, Klaus (1984). The Church as Communion and Communication, in Patrick Granfield (ed.), *The Church and Communication*, Kansas City, MO: Sheed and Ward, pp.80-96.

Manuel, Peter (2001, 2nd edition). *Cassette Culture. Popular Music and Technology in North India.* New Delhi: Oxford University Press.

Martini, Carlo Maria (1994). *Communicating Christ to the World.* Kansas City, MO: Sheed & Ward.

Metz, Johann Baptist (1973). A Short Apology of Narrative, in *Concilium*, Vol.85, pp.84-98.

Morris, Charles (1975). Sprechen und menschliches Handeln, in H. G. Gadamer und S. P. Vogler (Hsg.), *Neue Anthropologie.* Stuttgart.

O'Collins, Gerald (1981). *Fundamental Theology.* London: Darton, Longman & Todd.

Philip, T.M. (1986). *The Encounter between Theology and Ideology. An Exploration into the Communicative Theology of M.M. Thomas.* Madras: Christian Literature Society.

Pottmeyer, Hermann J. (1994). Dialogue as a Model for Communication in the Church, in Patrick Granfield (ed.), *The Church and Communication,* Kansas City, MO: Sheed and Ward, pp. 97-103.

Roberge, Gaston (1999). *The Faithful Witness. On Christian Communication.* Anand (Gujarat): Gujarat Sahitya Prakash.

Robinson, Diana Campbell et al. (eds.) (1991). *Music at the Margins. Popular Music and Global Cultural Diversity.* Newbury Park, CAL.: Sage.

Soukup, Paul (1983). *Communication and Theology. Introduction and Review of Literature.* London: WACC/CSCC.

_____. (2001). Communication Theology as a Basis for Social Communication Formation. Unpublished manuscript.

_____. (2002). Communication Theology as a Basis for Social Communication Formation, in Franz-Josef Eilers, *Social Communication Formation in Priestly Ministry,* Manila: Logos Publications, pp. 65-92.

Thomas, Pradip (1997). Communication, Media Studies and Theological Education, in *Religion and Society,* Vol. 44, No 1, pp.27-42.

Traber, Michael (1999). The Meaning of Leisure. Unpublished Class Lecture Note.

Watzlawick, J. H. et al. (1969). *Menschliche Kommunikation: Formen, Stoerungen und Paradoxien.* Bern: Haupt Verlag

Wilfred, Felix (2000). *Asian Dreams and Christian Hope at the Dawn of the Millennium.* New Delhi: ISPCK.

White, Robert (1985). Formation for Priestly Ministry in a Mass-Mediated Culture, in *Seminarium*, Vol. 26, No. 4, pp.805-828.

**Documents of the Second Vatican Council and other official documents of the Roman Catholic Church:**

*Lumen Gentium,* Dogmatic Constitution of the Chucrh (1964), *Dei Verbum,* Dogmatic Constitution of Divine Relevation, (1965); *Gaudium et Spes,* Pastoral Constitution on the Church in the Modern World (1965), in Flannery, Austin (ed.) *Vatican Council II. The Conciliar and Post-Conciliar Documents.* Mumbai: St Pauls, 1999 (first published in Dublin, 1975).

*Aetatis Novae* (1992) and *Communio et Progressio* (1971) in Eilers, Franz-Josef (ed.), *Church and Social Communication.* Manila: Logos Publications, 2nd edition, 1997.

## CHAPTER 3

# Interfaces between Theology and Communications

### *Joseph Palakeel*

Statements like 'Christianity is communication' may indicate that there is much in common between theology and communication, but they do not advance the debate about that commonness. Christian life and ministry in the twenty-first century suggest that a purely instrumentalist view of communication is no longer sufficient to proclaim the Good News today. And the launching of a few courses in communication, for example, or training in new homiletics, or in a few audio-visual skills, would not make the Gospel the leaven in the multimedia culture. Theology and communication can no more be considered as competitors, nor communication as a mere handmaid of theology. Instead, both need to be seen as partners in dialogue. The partnership between theology and communication would need to go beyond a 'theology of communication' or 'communicative theology' and become a 'communication theology', which is based on a theology that is conversant with communication culture, and a study of communication with theological content. For this, the interrelation between theology and communication would have to progress to a more advanced stage, where communication is at the heart of the church's life as well as the core activity in theologising.

The interrelationship between theology and communications needs to be explored in detail. The attempt here is to search for common areas between theologising and communication when the two are juxtaposed in a transparent fashion. Interface means the point of interaction or communication between two entities, groups or subjects. An honest investigation necessitates that we look at theology and communication from both sides before arriving at any conclusions. However, theologians and church communicators will lay more stress on the implications of the communication revolution for theology and examine how communication insights can significantly challenge theologising.

It is necessary, therefore, to begin with a survey of the growing partnership between church and communication, elaborate the challenges posed by communication to theology and the questions raised by theology for communication, and determine the major points of common interest and benefit. A further look at theology is also warranted because today's communication culture challenges theology to renew itself, both in content and method. Rethinking theology with insights from communication would lead us to a communication theology.

## THEOLOGY AND COMMUNICATION

Over the centuries, the engagement between church and communication has been progressively increasing, with the church being a prime communicator using the best available means of communication to teach and preach. But while it was amongst the first to use the mass media of print and radio, the recent emergence of the electronic media has left it limping behind. The initial response of the church to the electronic media was one of suspicion, seclusion and censorship. As the awareness grew that these are "wonderful means" for the propagation of the Gospel, segregation soon turned into imitation and collaboration, sometimes based on critical understanding and discriminating service. This movement led to further appreciation of the media and the subsequent realisation that communication is an integral dimension of Christian life and mission. This attitudinal change has led to a behavioural change from isolation and critique to appreciation and immersion.

Now considered an essential dimension of Christian life and ministry, communication has been described by Pope John Paul II as the "modern Areopagus" and "the house-tops" from which the Gospel has to be proclaimed today.[1] Different episcopal conferences in various parts of the world are seriously discussing the impact of communication on the church.[2] The World Council of Churches, and especially the World Association for Christian Communication, have highlighted the importance of communication in today's culture. There is now a widespread awareness that the church should not only 'use' communication and make herself more 'communicative', but also enter into a serious dialogue with the communication sciences to draw insights for Christian life and ministry, teaching and theologising, because in the present circumstances "faith and culture are called to meet and interact precisely in the area of communication..."[3]

## Faith and Communication

The growing engagement of the church with communication realities has its effects on theology too. Today revelation is described as God's self-communication through the Son and the Spirit, both within the interiority of humans and in and through the world and history,[4] and faith as one's personal-existential response (self-communication) to God's self-communication. Likewise, theology as faith-seeking understanding (meaning and expression) is recognised as a communication activity, both as

---

[1] The Catholic Church has dedicated several documents to communication, among which *Inter Mirifica* (1965), *Aetatis Novae* (1992) and World Communication Day messages are prominent. For a full list see Eilers (1997 and 2002a).

[2] The Federation of Asian Bishops' Conference has several documents on church and communication. See Eilers (2002b and c). The Catholic Bishops' Conference of India (CBCI) held a discussion on the church and social communication in its meeting at Trissur, Kerala, on 7-14 January 2004.

[3] The Pope's message to the participants of a congress on the Church and Information Technology (IT) in Monterrey, Mexico, 1-5 April 2003. See ZE03040302, Zenith News, 3 April 2003 at www.Zenith.org

[4] Second Vatican Council, *Dei Verbum*, 2-4.

interiorisation (making sense) of the foundational experience of God, and as an exteriorisation of the meaning with and within the community of believers. Thus, we can say that communication is an integral dimension of theologising or, better still, theologising is communication.

Before analysing the implications of such a view for theologising a brief discussion on how communication challenges theologising and theology is in order. A fresh look at theologising in the light of these mutual challenges can help us redefine the nature and functions of theology on the basis of the common ground (interfaces) between the two.

## COMMUNICATION CHALLENGES TO THEOLOGISING

For the sake of brevity, we shall discuss primarily certain epistemological and semantic shifts brought about by communication, which are of significance to the method and content of theology. The way we gather, store, retrieve and process information has changed today, and with it our mental habits of knowing and making sense. Modern communication has a new grammar, syntax, logic and semantics adapted to the multimedia and multi-sensorial approach. The integration of images, sound and text with random (multi-sequential) access makes different levels and ways of knowing possible.

### From Word to Image

The evolving multimedia and digital revolution challenges first and foremost the methodological assumptions of theology (as well as other sciences). It has ushered in a new era in literacy, where text and image do not just co-exist (as in an illustrated book) but collaborate to produce meaning (Palakeel 2003: 37-43). Images often dominate in this type of communication, which can be understood by even the 'illiterate'. This means that the whole process of making meaning is being reconstituted.

The multimedia and multi-sensorial communication marks a definitive move from word (reading/writing, saying/hearing) to image (seeing and experiencing), with communication becoming more visual than verbal. Knowing today is almost equated with seeing. Although words are still used, the pride of place goes to the image. We find ourselves surrounded by a universe of images: photos, films, television, advertisements, billboards, road signs, illustrations. The image has become a component of our sensory experience, our thought processes, our feelings and even ideology. The invasion by images is so huge that it is almost as if visuals are now substituting language. Earlier, images served merely as illustrations of a dominant text. Today it is the function of the text to explain the images. This is because of the progressive realisation that the image can teach faster, more easily and efficiently, allowing a quick grasp in a single glance, often without analysis and explanation. Hence the transference of knowledge, be it theology or science, is effected predominantly through images. In other words, it can be said that with the emergence of the visual culture, the hegemony of the word has ended. The most demanding challenge that the practice of visual culture places before the church is to go beyond the 'word' (Kalliath 2003: 83-103).

## From Head to Heart

The shift from verbal to visual has certain major epistemological implications. There are predominantly two ways of knowing: the mythical way or primordial knowing, and the rational way or conceptual knowing. The period of myths and epics was characterised by the synthetic and intuitive ways of knowing, which were superseded by the Socratic method, Platonic 'myth-ology' and Aristotelian science. This move was crowned by Scholastic dialectics and the Cartesian quest for clear and distinct ideas. Ever since, mainstream education and progress have been marked by the triumph of the rational, analytical and conceptual ways of knowing and thinking. However, the primordial way of thinking has survived in oral cultures and in traditional arts and music. The audiovisual and multimedia communication has initiated a 'rediscovery' (not exactly a return) of the primordial ways of making sense. The audiovisual media discount linear, analytical and clear speech; instead, they take recourse to myths, stories and narrative. Meanings and values are transmitted through feelings and relationships rather than theories and direct statements. Linguistic signs no longer have priority in communication: we can now write by stringing together images, sounds and text. It is a new language with its own grammar and syntax, semantics and logic, which is often contrary to familiar logic.

Modern psychology and pedagogy have found that simultaneous presentation of verbal and visual stimuli that occupy more than one sense at a time enables better understanding. Although there are multiple intelligences, evidence is growing that the two predominant channels of the mind are the verbal and the visual (seemingly corresponding to the left and right hemispheres). The successful 'wiring' of both (known as *dual coding*) produces best results in learning and thinking (hence the shift in emphasis from IQ to EQ and SQ). Modern audiovisual communication is really based on the insight into the synergetic functioning of the mind's many channels.

Meaning construction and value formation are effected through feelings and emotions, relations and associations, as is best exemplified by certain advertisements. Theology, however, understood as a science or as a heuristic study or hermeneutics, is undoubtedly rational and verbal (logocentric) or conceptual and theoretical. The quest for maximum monosemy and clear and distinct ideas produce dogmatic statements and faith formulae, whereas religion itself and the Bible in particular consist of stories and narratives of primordial experiences, memories and witness. This necessitates a re-examination of the method and content of theology.

### From a Mechanistic to a Ritual Sacramental Perspective

The logocentric world-view was also mechanistic in that everything happened according to fixed laws and patterns. The shifts from word to image and from head to heart do not mean just a substitution of images and diagrams in place of word. It is true that images are replacing words; however, these are not just any pictures but symbolic images that are loaded with meaning. Thus we can see here the emergence of a new symbolic representation of reality where a complex syntax and semantics are at work. The visual thinking and representation of realities are more symbolic than verbal communication, which appears more natural to the *homo symbolicus*.

The visual thinking is founded on a sacramental perception of the world. The human being as spirit in the world, or as body-soul, or physical and spiritual being, perceives and understands everything in sensible and tangible ways. Even the Ultimate or Transcendent is experienced through the secular and tangible. We experience the Ultimate in liminal situations created by ritual-sacramental celebrations, in which the role of symbols, sacraments and rituals is obvious. Anthropologists testify to the existence of rituals and symbols, sacraments and ceremonies in all religions. Christianity, too, has this dimension, although it has been somewhat lost, primarily because of the focus on the pure word and the fear of multiplicity and plurality.

When sacraments and celebrations of faith were discredited or became obsolete in the Christian churches, humans started drawing their liminal experiences from secular events like mega shows, sports events and talk shows. Today, TV and sports events are being increasingly recognised as modern rituals. This suggests that there is a need to rediscover Christian symbols, myths, narratives and stories, parables and metaphors, as well as poetry and music, arts and architecture, and rituals and celebrations.

### From Monolithic and Hierarchical to Popular, Plural and Global

The multi-sensorial and multimedia communication, which is essentially symbolic, makes it possible to see reality from different levels and angles. For example, a book consists of 'figures' (printed letters, words, sentences), while in a film the visual and audio ambient convey meaning and understanding. This means the atmosphere, ambient, and manner and medium of presentation become relevant to the content. It thus presents a synthetic and global view that is interpreted by each viewer in her or his own way, leading to an inevitable pluralism and ambivalence. Traditional and hierarchical values and systems are often questioned and discarded while a more participatory production of meanings takes place — meanings that are significant and relevant to specific groups. The acceptance and promotion of these meanings give a boost to popular culture, popular religion and ways of life as opposed to high culture and mainline religious practices. Naturally, Christian tradition and theology get challenged, particularly the latter, which depends primarily on long established dogmas, theories and categories.

These are some of the major challenges that today's communication culture poses for theology. While not new to Christian theology, these and other developments point to the need for developing a new and different approach in theologising in order to make sense to people of the media culture. Christianity has ample resources to counter these communications challenges to meaningful human existence.

## THEOLOGICAL CHALLENGES TO COMMUNICATIONS

The colossal growth of communications naturally casts its shadows too. There is an inherent danger of godlessness or ungodliness in any purely human project as exemplified by Babel. Modern humans are getting lost in the Promethean quest for self-transcendence and new age gnosticism, in which they lose sight of the truly transcendent realities. Worldly gods like consumerism, individualism and fragmentation often have the upper hand in the human project. Christian faith and theology should play a prophetic role here. Faith should bring the miracle of Pentecost to the modern Babel.

## The Inherent Immanentism

The overemphasis on symbolic and ritual experiences and celebrations risks the hidden danger of a pseudo-religion or pseudo-transcendence, which is nothing but a disguised immanentism in the garb of transcendence that fails to put humans in contact with the mystery of the divine. As most new age tendencies reveal, this ends up in a sort of pantheism or gnostic self-redemption. Theology can help communication in this situation by articulating the minimal moments of liminality in the light of revelation to make the experience of the transcendent tangible and possible by awakening the interiority of the people and setting in motion a quest for God.

## Worship of False Gods

Immanentism results from a "failure to go beyond the apparent" or from "stopping with what is seen and heard because the things that are seen are beautiful" (Wis 13: 7). The beautiful images, enticing sounds and pleasurable sensations of the communication world are so attractive that people are enslaved by pleasure-seeking and consuming. This is idolatry in the strict biblical sense and calls for a prophetic intervention to awaken in people the desire to 'go beyond' the beautiful things to the author of beauty. In future, theologians and pastors should be able to use creative and innovative ways to stimulate the religious imagination of the people towards the transforming power of the Gospel. This will not be possible through abstract doctrines of faith but by fashioning stories of faith in parables and metaphors, art and music, rituals and celebration. Reclaiming the ritual-sacramental dimension of Christianity in a new way can be helpful. A symbolic-sacramental perception of the world and human life as the sacred manifesting itself in the secular can help us cultivate the habit of going beyond the beautiful and the pleasurable. Such a perspective involves an aesthetic approach to faith and practice, theology and life.

## Fragmentation and Individualism

Although by its very nature communication is oriented towards community and communion, it often promotes individualism and egoism. In spite of its global and plural approaches to reality, it can also cause fragmentation. We find too many small islands in the global village. The proclamation of the Good News, however, is to gather all nations into one.

Theology and communication thus challenge each other. They are mutually enriching and highly fecund. Communication challenges theology to explore anew the dynamism and enthusiasm of the Gospel.

## RETHINKING THEOLOGY

When we speak of interfaces between theology and communication, it is not enough to highlight the essential communication dimension of theology or list a few areas of collaboration or dialogue between them. Rather, the content and method of theology need updating, revision and renewal. Such an investigation necessitates a multifaceted discussion of theologising at the level of principles.

An analysis of the origin and growth of theology indicates that the shift from the simple faith of the Bible to the learned faith of the Alexandrians (Origen) was further stabilised by Augustine and finally crowned by Thomas Aquinas, who turned theology into a science. The modern rational and anthropological method, with its quest for clear and distinct ideas, completed this rationalistic turn of Christian theology. In this system doctrines and dogmas became the canons of faith with a single-voice and uniform confession. To this was added the preoccupation with orthodoxy (initially opposed to heterodoxy or heresy), which led to a mistaken notion of unity as uniformity and Catholicity as conformity.

Even the reformers' quest for liberating Christianity from philosophy through the ideals of *sola fides* and *sola scriptura* did not help much as they too fell prey to either rationalism or fideism of the times, and the tyranny of the text through printing, which led them to understand the 'Word' as purely conceptual and rational. The creeds and catechisms, the instructions and manuals are all based on the culture of word and text. Paul's assertion that "we walk by faith and not by sight" (2 Cor 5: 7) was taken literally, the presumption being that we just 'hear' God speak and abide by his Word and do not 'see' God. Consequently word and text became predominant in Christianity, and theology became notional and rational.

However, the communication revolution with its characteristic shift from verbal to visual challenges Christianity (more than other religions) to move from a 'proclaimed and heard' to a 'witnessed, seen and touched' faith in order to make sense of God today. Christian theologising should move away from its dominantly logocentric to an *iconocentric* perspective of God and the world. Such a perspective is not new to Christianity. The Bible is full of stories, poems and picturesque language. It does not contain theories and statements but witness and confessions. This is true particularly of Jesus' preaching and teaching. Above all, although the 'Word became flesh' is currently interpreted in a logocentric fashion, it is in fact the best form of iconocentric communication and hence the most pertinent model for theologising today.

It is exactly in this area that theology is most vulnerable vis-à-vis communication. In this context it must be said emphatically that more than depending on lessons from communication, theology needs to draw on its own inherent resources in synergy with communications. Since it would be difficult to elaborate on all aspects for reasons of space, I shall just outline the main thrust of such a theology that, for lack of a better term, could be called 'communication theology'.

## Theologising as Faith Seeking Understanding

One of the best definitions of theology is the one given by Anslem of Canterbury: Faith seeking understanding (*fides quaerens intellectum*). It gives theologising a dynamism of its own by placing 'seeking' at the centre. This leaves theology ever rooted in faith and the Christian tradition, while allowing ample space for *intellectus*. Theology thus becomes an ongoing process of self-understanding by faith. The many theologies we know originate from this understanding of theology. However, because of the preponderance of the Thomistic emphasis on the intellect, theology as *intellectus fidei* as well as *fides intellectus* has become a logocentric science. The preferred, if not chosen, medium is verbal expression. The tools are concepts. The focus is on truth. The handmaid is philosophy. Somehow we have tended to privilege abstract statements over narratives and to see revelation as a creed or a series of clear statements (Amaladoss 2003: 63).

The Bible as the written word and tradition is seen as the handed-down word for reading; and preaching-hearing (verbal expression) has become the privileged way of understanding and assent. All other forms of expressions are discredited as less worthy or unworthy of being theology. Where revelation is seen as a creed or set of doctrines, assent to a certain statement of truth is considered as the only way of believing. The consequence is uniformity of expression, an endless chase for clear and distinct concepts, dogmatic formulae and definitive statements of truth.

In this conception of theology, the word is considered the most refined expression of humans, as even God's word comes in human words. So revelation is understood as the word of God, and faith is described as assent to the word. Since logos meant word and reason, it was easy to go the rational way and "give reasons for the hope that is in you" (1Pet 3:15). Theology, consequently, is words about God or discourse on God. The word-theology of Protestants, based on the doctrine of *sola scriptura*, is the most refined form of a religion of the word or book. 'Understanding', however, is conceived in a purely notional and rational sense. But today, more than ever, there is a strong feeling that 'understanding' itself needs a new understanding. The emerging communication revolution challenges theology to revision its self-understanding.

## Theology as Faith Seeking Meaning

The entire exercise of theology (*habitus theologicus*) is under question. The verbal and conceptual expressions, taking pride in unanimity and uniformity, and faith as rational assent and verbal confession, have left modern humans untouched. This calls for redefining theology as faith seeking meaning and relevance in the given life-situation of every believer. As a meaning-making process, theology is "a continuous and renewed process of interpretation, systematic reflection, articulation and praxis after encountering a God who communicates himself with humans and their world" (Parappally 2003: 72-82).[5]

## Theologising as Faith Seeking Communication

Theologising, by its very nature and methodology, is communication. We can identify three sets of communications at three different stages of theologising, each with an *ad intra* and an *ad extra* dimension. The eternal self-communication among the persons of the Trinity *(ad intra)* overflows in time as God's self-communication *(ad extra)* to humans (creation-revelation-salvation), constituting the *principium* (source and foundation) of all theology. The faith response of the individual Christian (or theologian) involves both *ad intra* (reflection) and *ad extra* communication, vertically towards God and horizontally towards

---

[5]Parappally then goes on to elaborate how theologising involves *intra-communication, inter-communication, extra-communication* and *ex-communication.*

the community of believers. Theologising is thus an intensely personal experience of the foundational communication and a communitarian response and reflection on God's self-communication in rediscovering the meaning of the Christian revelation/faith experience. This communitarian faith-experience and reflection is to be shared, through dialogue and proclamation (mission), with the entire humanity. The communitarian communication of faith seeks expression (*ad extra*) to the entire humanity and world as an encounter and dialogue with all religions, cultures and social systems. In this perspective, theology extends much beyond an academic exercise into an intimate dialogue (exchange, communication, communion) of a Christian with oneself (*ad intra*) and the community, and with God and the world (*ad extra*).

Revelation and incarnation have always been considered acts of communication, although it is only recently that revelation was defined as God's self-communication. Many theologians, both ancient and modern, have highlighted the integral communication dimension of theology as well. The learned faith (as opposed to the simple faith) proposed by Origen and the subsequent Alexandrian theology implicitly points to the communication dimension of theology. Other important theologians of the early church like Ireneus of Lyons, the Cappadocean Fathers and St Augustine were also well aware of this dimension. There are 2,350 references to the theme of communication in Thomas Aquinas. Even the interpretations of the Trinity in terms of personal properties (Cappadoceans), relation (St. Augustine) and perichoresis (John Damascene) consider Father, Son and Spirit as persons in communication and communion.

We are also familiar with many recent efforts to rethink theological method from the communication perspective. Years ago, Karl Rahner pointed out that theology is all about communication. Bernard Lonergan considers communication to be the eighth functional speciality of theological method, "in which theological reflection bears fruit and without which the first seven are in vain". For Avery Dulles, the "communication dimension is inherent in theology"; thus "theology at every point is concerned with realities of communication"(Lonergan 1979: 355ff; Dulles 1992: 22). However, it must be added that they were all concerned with the method of doing theology that is *communicative* in a rational-cognitive perspective, whereas recent developments in communication challenge any genitive (theology *of* communication) or adjective (*communicative*) theology.

The emerging multimedia culture demands a new interpretation of Christian revelation (content) and necessitates new ways of doing theology (method), which appropriate the multifaceted richness of human communication as the core of theology. Theology is invited to theologise from the communication perspective, as opposed to the philosophical and linguistic-hermeneutical point of view. Thus communication challenges the method and content of theology.

## THEOLOGISING TO COMMUNICATE

Communication theology should take into consideration all the factors that we have discussed so far. It should emphasise visual rather than verbal thinking, primordial and experiential rather than notional and conceptual knowing; it should also take into consideration feelings and relationships in addition to thinking and theories; it should give due importance to ritual and sacramental dimensions and should be holistic and plural. At the same time, such a theology should be capable of leading people beyond the immanent and apparent to the transcendent, and make them look for ultimate values and meanings. It should thus be a global and plural (ecological) theology which is appealing and attractive (aesthetic), yet leads people beyond the secular to the transcendent (sacramental). All these characteristics can be found in a new form of a natural theology — called 'superbly natural' or super-natural theology — in a profoundly Christian (not general religious) sense.

### Super-Natural Theology

Communication theology thus has to be a *natural* theology. Saying this does not mean that the old debate on natural theology versus revealed theology is not relevant. Nor does it mean that it is the 'forecourt theology' or *preparatio evangelica.* When we speak of a natural theology in the context of communication we mean a theology that is *natural* to the human being, because the world of communications redefines theology itself in terms of its 'natural' methodology.

When revelation is considered as God's self-communication, any *ad extra* communication by him is revelation, be it in creation or in history of salvation. We have to concede that the God who spoke to our fathers in many and varied ways, continues to do so with us as well. This is not to rule out or reduce the importance of the unique self-communication of God in Jesus Christ. But it is unique not because it is a different type of revelation but because it is qualitatively the culmination or crowning moment of all other revelations. In fact, incarnation is unique because it is so *natural*. Becoming human was the way God felt was best suited for communicating with humans.[6] Thus the word-become-flesh is a communication 'technique' adapted to both divine and human nature. We can call it a *supernatural* — in the sense of a *superbly natural*— communication.

This view can be validated from various theological perspectives. This is the theology found in the Gospels, especially in John. The Antiochean *logos-sarx* (Word-Flesh) theology versus the Alexandrian Word theology is the oldest instance of such a theology. In our own times, theologians like Schillebeeckx and Rahner, and Barth and Juengel have spoken of the realism of incarnation as a theological paradigm. Barth's booklet, *The Humanity of God* (1967) and Juengel's great work *God as the Mystery of the World* (1983) show how God keeps communicating with the world using all human resources. God is acting in history not as an alien power but as part of it, using the natural and the secular. Thus we are becoming increasingly aware of the fact that there is no purely natural phenomenon, there is only graced nature. When the supernatural is infused into the natural, the natural becomes *super-natural* because it is able to communicate the supernatural to us without losing its own 'naturality' (e.g., the humanity of Jesus).

## Symbolic-Sacramental Theology

The realism of the incarnation is that the sacred manifests itself in and through the secular. It means that God's communication is symbolic and sacramental. Modern philosophy and linguistics testify that all communication is symbolic and mediated. We know, learn and understand by moving from the familiar to the unfamiliar. Thus knowing is metaphorical and analogical. From this modern understanding of the human being as *homo symbolicus,* and from

---

[6] Second Vatican Council, *Dei Verbumi, No. 2.*

all that is in the world as symbolic and sacramental, we are in a better position to understand anew natural theology.

To be able to discern the sacred in the secular, we need to necessarily have a symbolic/sacramental understanding of reality (and theology). In the formal ontological view, "a symbol is the supreme and primal representation, in which one reality renders another present" (Rahner 1966: 224). In this sense all beings are by nature symbolic because every being realises itself by expressing itself in an 'other'. The 'other', which is constituted as the expression of the original being, is its symbol. Thus all realities have a symbolic structure and meaning.

The dynamics of symbol or sacrament is that we move from/ through the familiar to the unfamiliar, from visible to the invisible. Here, what is seen and heard or experienced is just a visible, tangible medium through which we experience the invisible, intangible and incomprehensible. It is true that God is invisible, incomprehensible, veiled. But we can think and speak of God in his visibility through self-communication. The invisible God became visible in the humanity of God (Jesus); word became visible in the flesh. The sacred became present and manifest in the secular. This is what is meant by the sacramental-symbolic perspective. Parables and metaphors are the linguistic parallels of the sacramental symbolic structure and the modern communication media make ample use of them. When Jesus wanted to present the invisible Kingdom, he said, "It is like ....". Thus parables, metaphors, stories and narratives of faith make God transparent. The so-called infinite and qualitative distance/difference between God and humans is overcome in this way. This was the realisation by which Barth moved from his *Church Dogmatics* days, when he asserted that "God is God and man is man", to *The Humanity of God*. Luther's problem with the hidden-ness of God (*Deus absconditus*) also betrays a failure to understand the sacramental structure of revelation.

In Luther's tradition Barth opposed natural theology for fear that it would strip God of his transcendence and absoluteness, and images would end up in idolatry. It is true that the symbolic-sacramental or parabolic-metaphorical approach to God has the inherent danger of getting stuck with the medium or stopping with what is seen and heard — what is described as idolatry in the Bible. But with the incarnation God has demolished this fear. We have to go beyond the humanity of Jesus to see his divinity which, however, is even today experienced through his humanity. Those who see the man Jesus of Nazareth see the Son of God. Jesus said that those who see him also see the Father. This is the witness of the Apostolic Church. Hence our apprehension will become reality only if we hold on to what is seen, if we stop with the symbol and fail to transcend it.

It is here that theology should exercise its prophetic role of facilitating the process of 'going beyond' the threshold of the visible-tangible. This is what is actually happening in all symbolic, ritual and sacramental situations and celebrations. Even language has this dimension, i.e., meanings lie beyond the written/spoken signs. Parables and metaphors and stories and narratives are then the best forms of expressing the faith because they function purely by this pattern of transcending the symbols. In fact, such a theology is the only answer to the immanence and idolatry of the media culture.

**Visual and Aesthetic Theology**

Our discussion makes clear that theology has to reclaim the 'image effect', 'symbolic expression' and 'artistic conception' of the revelation-faith experience and the reflection on it (Elavuthingal 2003: 121-42). The rejection by theology of beauty in favour of truth and goodness was the beginning of the rationalisation of theology. But reflections on communications have shown that truth and goodness cannot be communicated convincingly without being accompanied by beauty. And beauty without a connection to truth and goodness becomes ephemeral and meaningless. Modern communication operates basically in the realm of beauty and pleasure, often without any proper roots in truth and goodness.

However, for life and experience to be meaningful, the harmonious coexistence of the three is essential. Theology has to step in here. But traditional theology operates in the realm of truth (orthodoxy) and traditional religion is more concerned with goodness (orthopraxis). The third transcendental, beauty, is very much ignored in theology, although the Bible is full of manifestations of the glory (beauty) of God, as Hans Urs von Balthasar (1982-1991) amply demonstrates. In the third millennium, theology is again invited to operate in the realm of beauty (*orthokalia*). A theology that integrates truth, goodness and beauty will be a (super)natural theology, founded on a new way of looking at God's presence in this world.

## Global and Plural (Ecological) Theology

Such a natural theology, which is both symbolic and aesthetic, should also be a global and comprehensive method of experiencing the divine manifesting itself through the word and spirit. Here the cosmological and anthropological visions of reality fuse into a theological perspective. Traditional natural theology was a part of the cosmological method (unmoved mover); the rational turn given to it marked the shift to the anthropological method. New methods like the transcendental or the more recent linguistic-hermeneutical turned out to be just forms of the anthropological. Today we need to integrate all three methods — cosmological, anthropological and theological — because in reality following just one method and excluding the others does not work.  What we need is a comprehensive or holistic/ecological method that would include God, the world and humans. Thus the challenge of communication to renew both the content and method of theology points the way towards a superbly natural theology, which is global and ecological, aesthetic and symbolic. Modern communications, with its thrust on ambience or atmosphere together with the figure, is proposing this way for theology to have a holistic and global perception of the human being. Once again the cosmo-theandric vision of the incarnation as found in Maximus confessor (and in Raimundo

Panikkar in a slightly different sense) assumes greater importance in this perspective. This realisation is manifest in the increasing use of the ecological approach in different areas of our life. Integrating this dimension into theologising would help us to resist fragmentation and alienation.

## CONCLUSION

It is important that the interface between theology and communication takes place in a spirit of collaboration or synergy. Only then would the outcome be a communication theology that is ecological, aesthetic, symbolic and natural. Such a transition would not only challenge the nature and functions of theology, but also lend a transcendental orientation and dynamism to the immanent and idolatrous adventurism of communications.

One of the dangers of such rethinking is loss of identity. It would therefore be necessary to safeguard Christian identity and specificity without sacrificing relevance. Otherwise Christian faith and practice will cease to attract people. Walter Kasper suggests a way out of this dilemma: "If the Church worries about identity, it risks loss of relevance; if on the other hand, it struggles for relevance, it may forfeit its identity" (Kasper 1976: 15-17). Balancing identity and relevance has been the task of theology at all times, and this has not changed in this millennium. Yet we need to lay more stress on relevance today, as theology appears to be much too preoccupied with identity. Our analysis of the interfaces between theology and communication shows that modern communications offer many insights on how to make theology authentic and relevant without losing Christian identity and specificity.

Modern communications are weaning people away from the dominance of the word and reason and opening a way for them to experience the world through the senses. Through the multimedia combination of sights, sounds and words, myths and stories, parables and metaphors, analogies and narratives are making a return without, however, undermining the role of word and reason. The image carries the meaning, sound gives depth and word gives interpretation. Thus we find that the much-discredited natural theology must make a return in a refined form to make theology conversant with the communication culture.

## REFERENCES

Amaladoss, Michael (2003). 'Theology's Responses to the Challenges of Communication' in Joseph Palakeel (ed.) *Towards a Communication Theology*. Bangalore: Asian Trading Corporation.

Balthasar, Hans Urs von (1982-1991). *Glory of the Lord. A Theological Aesthetics* (7 vols). Edited by J. Fessio and J. Riches. (Translated from *Herrlichkeit: Eine theologische Ästhetik* I-III, Einsiedeln 1961-1969). Edinburgh: T.&T. Clark.

Barth, Karl (1967). *The Humanity of God.* (Translated from *Menschlichkeit Gottes*, Zollikon 1956). London

Dulles, Avery (1992). *The Craft of Theology. From Symbol to System.* Dublin: Gill and Macmillan.

Eilers, Franz-Josef (ed.) (1997). *Church and Social Communication. Basic Documents.* Manila: Logos.

_____. (ed.) (2002a). *Church and Social Communication. Basic Documents 1998-2002.* Manila: Logos.

_____. (ed.) (2002b). *Church and Social Communication in Asia. Documents, Analysis, Experiences.* FABC-OSC Book 1. Manila: Logos.

_____. (ed.) (2002c) . *Social Communication in Priestly Ministry.* FABC-OSC Book 2. Manila: Logos.

Elavuthingal, Sebastian (2003). 'Art and Theological Communication' in Joseph Palakeel (ed.) *Towards a Communication Theology,* Bangalore: Asian Trading Corporation.

Juengel, Eberhard (1983). *God as the Mystery of the World. On the Foundation of the Theology of the Crucified One in the Dispute between Theism and Atheism.* (Translated by D.L. Gudder from

*Gott als Geheimnis der Welt. Zur Begründung der Theologie des Gekreuzigten im Streit zwischen Theismus und Atheismus* (Tübingen 1977, 1978). Grand Rapids: Eerdmans.

Kalliath, Antony (2003). 'Communication Theology, Intercultural or Inculturational' in Joseph Palakeel (ed.) *Towards a Communication Theology.* Bangalore: Asian Trading Corporation.

Kasper, Walter (1976). *Jesus the Christ.* New Jersey: Paulist Press.

Lonergan, Bernard (1979). *Method in Theology.* New York: Seabury Press.

Palakeel, Joseph (2003). 'Theologising with Insights from Communication' in Joseph Palakeel (ed.) *Towards a Communication Theology.* Bangalore: Asian Trading Corporation.

Parappally, Jacob (2003). 'Theologising as Communication' in Joseph Palakeel (ed.) *Towards a Communication Theology,* Bangalore: Asian Trading Corporation.

Rahner, Karl (1966). The Theology of the Symbol. *Theological Investigations,* Vol. 4, London : Darton, Longman & Todd.

## CHAPTER 4

# Theology and Communication in Mutual Interaction : A Reflection

*José M. De Mesa*

The basic condition for any interpretation of the Christian faith that is faithful to the Gospel is the meaningfulness of that interpretation. An interpretation is meaningful when it reflects and articulates real experience. The experience of our everyday existence in the world must give meaning and reality to our theological talk. To me, good theologising means making sense of people's experiences in the light of faith and of faith in the light of present-day human experiences. If this basic condition is not satisfied, that is, if human experience is not expressed in theological language, then such theological talk is meaningless, and the question whether the new interpretation is either right or wrong is *a priori* superfluous. All theological interpretation must, as a reflection on lived experience in the light of faith, have a meaning that can be understood by people. It is only in relation to human experience — the issues, questions or concerns of people in a specific cultural and historical context — that faith understanding has a chance of becoming meaningful.

## BASIC PRINCIPLE OF THEOLOGISING: MUTUAL INTERACTION OF TWO POLES

There is a basic principle of theologising, on the basis of which specific theological methods are worked out, that is being presupposed here. There are two constitutive poles, two indispensable sources, or two essential realities which need to be taken into account: the pole of the Judaeo-Christian tradition,[1] which is the tradition of experiences of a believing community with their God, and the pole of contemporary human experiences. Both are sources for making sense of or for finding meaning in what is going on today. The tradition provides us with faith interpretations by harnessing the wisdom and insights of past faith experiences, which we intentionally and consciously link to our present-day experiences. In this way we discover how our present is necessarily connected to our relationship with God, which Jesus Christ revealed in a definitive manner. Likewise, our contemporary experiences proffer fresh interpretations that incorporate new insights derived from human creativity and that provide new possibilities of re-appropriating the Gospel for our times.

Theology arises precisely from these two poles in dialogue with each other. Essential in this principle involving the two poles is the *mutual* interaction between them. The adjective 'mutual' is crucial, for in articulating a theology human experience throws light on the tradition and the tradition throws light on experience. Doing theology is not a matter of merely considering what we think our tradition is, but of correlating this tradition in such a way that it is formulated precisely in the light of our experiences. Nor does it consist of just reflecting on our experiences broadly and deeply to ensure a good grasp of what is really going on. The experiences must be viewed vis-à-vis our faith tradition. The mutuality of interaction between the two poles is a must if we are to avoid imposing the tradition on our experiences or merely using it to affirm what we think we have discovered from our experiences.

To illustrate, a theology of communication would arise from

---

[1] Some may prefer to use the term 'Gospel' rather than Judaeo-Christian tradition. But since it does not come to us apart from its cultural and historical expressions, it may be useful to employ the term 'tradition', which suggests that human beings have something to do with it. I find this helpful in avoiding the temptation of identifying particular cultural and historical expressions of the Gospel with the Gospel itself.

the mutual interaction between our contemporary experience related to communication and pertinent or corresponding aspects/dimensions of the tradition. The resulting theological reflection, it must be noted, would not be *the* theology of communication, but *a* theology of communication. No theology can claim to be the definitive theology. Given that our experiences continue to evolve and change means that our theology needs to develop and vary as well. So a theology of communication that is articulated at this time and in this circumstance is very much a contextual theology, rather than one that claims to be perennial. It is necessary to point out at this juncture that the mutual interaction is not simply an interaction between theology and the reality of communications today, but between the Gospel and communications. In fact, it is the role of theology to facilitate this interaction between the Gospel and the world of communications that we experience at this time.

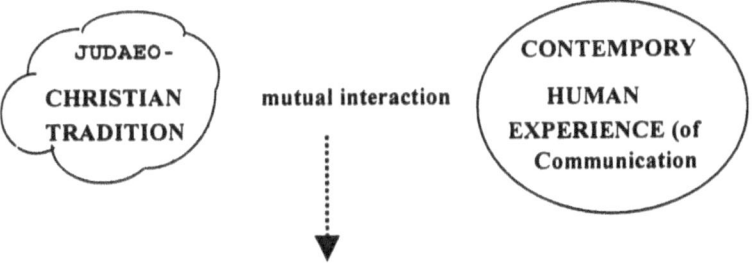

## A THEOLOGY OF COMMUNICATION

We have posited the interaction of the two poles as mutual, not a one-way affair from the tradition to experience or from experience to the tradition. There is a reason for this. If the dynamics of the interaction were to be limited to a movement from the Judaeo-Christian tradition to the pole of our present experience of communications, communications could easily be instrumentalised and be seen as an object to evangelise. The various media of communication, in this point of view, are profane, secular realities that need to be imbued with the spirit of the Sacred. They have nothing to contribute in the understanding of the faith. In this case the tradition, most likely regarded as fixed, is presented for acceptance in what is thought to be the most palatable way possible, not excluding the sophisticated use of such media. This more than suggests that meaningfulness can come only from this religious source, disregarding the workings of the Spirit in the ordinary experiences of life, in the mundane.

Conversely, if the process were restricted to the movement from the pole of our present-day human experience of communications to the pole of the Judaeo-Christian tradition, the latter may only be used to legitimise ideas earlier worked out from and positions already taken in the former. This will lead not only to a marginalisation of the Gospel, but also to the ideologisation or idolisation of communications. In effect, the pole of experience would become the sole arbiter of what is true and can be accepted in faith. In this situation information or knowledge that is communicated most attractively, efficiently and effectively becomes the gauge for what is right. The tradition is dismissed as symbolic of what is irrelevant or obscurantist. The two poles imply the need for any theology to manifest a double rootedness: to the Gospel and to the situation. Christian theology must be faithful to the Judaeo-Christian tradition *and* to contemporary human experience in an inclusive manner; that is, fidelity to the tradition in the context of human experience and to human experience in the light of the tradition.

## STARTING FROM THE POLE OF EXPERIENCE

In the mutual interaction between the two poles of theology, the starting point must be located in the pole of human experience. The Pastoral Constitution of the Church in the Modern World of the Second Vatican Council, *Gaudium et Spes*, beautifully articulates this point when it opens its vision of what it means to be Church in Article 1 of the document as: "The joys and the hopes, the griefs and the anxieties of the people of this age, these too are the joys and hopes, the griefs and the anxieties of the followers of Christ. Indeed, nothing genuinely human fails to raise an echo in their hearts."[2]

It can be validly argued that, since the interaction between the two poles is mutual, theological reflection can start from any pole. While this is true, there is also the consideration that in the recent past the dominant theology within Roman Catholicism prior to the momentous worldwide meeting of its bishops in the Second Vatican Council (1962-1965) was neo-scholasticism.[3] In this theology, insistence on the absoluteness of the revealed truths from God led to the identification of its culturally and historically bound expressions with revelation itself. Neo-scholasticism then developed a theological method that began with these absolute and immutable truths and ended with their application to whatever situation one found in the world.[4]

Under the influence of this theology, the notion that the church was the depository, guardian and communicator of divinely revealed truths, which were absolute and immutable, became widespread. Perhaps more than the theology itself, it was the accompanying assumption that it possessed the truth — the whole truth — that led the church to believe that since it had sole possession of the truth, it had no obligation to listen in order to learn. With a church that had nothing more to learn, it could only develop a 'teacher complex' according to which communication (as evangelisation/evangelism) is a persuasive monologue rather

---

[2]Quotations from Vatican II are taken from Walter Abbott. S.J. (1966).

[3]The theology developed in the eighteenth, nineteenth and early twentieth centuries within Roman Catholicism as it responded to the challenges posed by rationalism and the development of empirical sciences.

[4]The four steps of the methodology were: statement of the official teaching of the church, proofs from Scripture and Tradition, speculative elaboration and application to a specific situation. Cf. José M. de Mesa and Lode L. Wostyn (1991), Chapter 1.

than a participatory dialogue. Put in terms of the two poles of theology, since the church is responsible for the spread of the tradition,[5] it must persistently present as well as continuously expound, clarify and apply what is already known and fixed to an ever-changing world of communications. One can see here how theology influences the way of thinking of people in the churches, paving the way for peculiar perspectives regarding a given reality.

## USE OF CULTURAL THOUGHT PATTERNS AND AVAILABLE VOCABULARY

It is important to recall that, while theology as a specialised discipline has developed its own special patterns of thinking and its own distinct vocabulary to formulate what it wants to communicate, these are really drawn from everyday life, from ordinary ways of thinking and speaking. This is particularly true of the manner in which official theological statements or doctrines of churches have been expressed. We should remember that the New Testament was written not in esoteric Greek, but in *koine,* the vernacular of common people. Theological language may appear to be highly specialised to us, but it was not so for the Christians who thought and communicated in that fashion. Terms like 'Theology' (*theos-logos*), 'Christology' (*Christos-logos*),[6] 'Ecclesiology' (*Ekklesia-logos*), and 'Eschatology' (*Eschaton-logos*) may be daunting for the uninitiated in theology, but Christians belonging to the culture that was familiar with such *koine* Greek words most likely knew what they meant. What I am saying is, we have difficulty with such language because it is *not ours*! Consequently, if theology is about communication and communications is going to make sense to us today, it ought to use language (whatever its form) that is familiar, intelligible and meaningful to the people concerned.

---

[5]Tradition here represents the official teachings of the Roman Catholic Church together with scripture as interpreted by it.

[6]'Christ' is a cultural title or name given to Jesus to express his salvific significance in a given context. See Edward Schillebeeckx (1981), pp. 20-26.

In this connection we have an official acknowledgment from the leadership of the Catholic Church regarding the relativity of (theological) language to particular times and places. Its relativity stems mainly from its relatedness to definite contexts of culture and history, as well as from the fact that these contextual factors somehow limit the usefulness of such language when made to function in another cultural and historical situation. Way back in 1973 the Congregation for the Doctrine of the Faith issued the Declaration *Mysterium Ecclesiae* acknowledging that doctrinal formulations are historically conditioned in four ways:[7] by presuppositions (i.e., "the context of faith and human knowledge"); by concerns (i.e., "the intention of solving certain questions"); by thought categories (i.e., "the changeable conceptions of a given epoch");.and by the available vocabulary (i.e., "the expressive power of the language used at a certain point of time") of the culture in which they are composed. When we use these categories to analyse any theology, including neo-scholasticism, we can see how much it is historically and culturally relative. But being 'relative' is the way of all human understanding. It is 'relative' because it is *related to* a specific cultural and historical context, and 'relative' because it is also *limited by* that very context.

When communications-oriented theologians speak, then, of a theology of communication, it should not be surprising that they are attentive to concerns arising from our experience of communications today, employ presuppositions and thought categories derived from this world, and profit from the available vocabulary offered by the communications media.[8] This implies that a theology formulated from the vantage point of communications can legitimately utilise interpretative models and

---

[7] Declaration *Mysterium Ecclesiae* of the S. Congregation for the Doctrine of the Faith (11 May 1973). Cited from J. Neuner S.J. and J. Dupuis, S.J. (1982), p. 60.

[8] Dr Palakeel utilises the thought pattern and available vocabulary coming from communications in his presentation of a communications theology, something which is also evident in the paper (this volume) by Dr Michael Traber, 'Why Communication Studies in Theological Education?'

elements drawn from this very field. Theologian Alexandre Ganoczy, by way of an example, has made use of a thought pattern as well as of a vocabulary of a communications theory in order to articulate a sacramental theology. In elaborating such a theology, he writes that sacraments can be understood as

> systems of verbal and non-verbal communication through which those individuals who are called to Christian faith enter into the communicative process of the ever concrete faith-community, participate in it, and in this way, borne up by the self-communication of God in Christ, progress on the path of personal development (Ganoczy 1984: 156).

This is really not any different from the way the Graeco-Roman Christianity made use of the terms 'ratio', 'truth', 'revelation' of and 'assent' to such truth in faith. Following the Greek philosophical pattern of thinking that the human being is essentially *ratio-nal* in search of true knowledge or truth, what brings about fulfilment for the human being interpreted in this way is truth. Hence, revelation came to be seen in this context as God's revelation of truth and faith as the human response to the truths which God reveals. One also understands easily from this why the churches of the European West emphasised the need for orthodoxy or true (correct) knowledge in matters of faith.

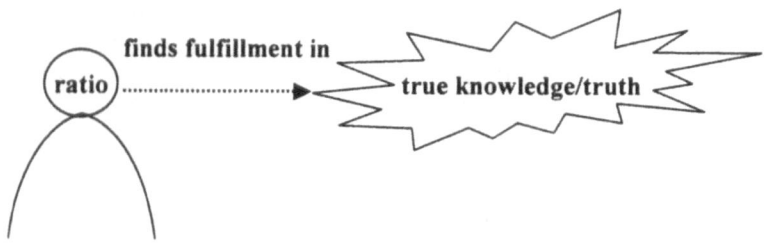

**CULTURAL PRESUPPOSITION:**
Humans are "rational" animals

Likewise, when it is presupposed today, as it is by personalist philosophy, that to be a human being is to be intersubjective, then the goal of people in this perspective is communion. As a consequence, revelation is understood as God's self-communication and faith as a person's entrusting one's whole self freely to God. This latter interpretation of the relationship between God and people arises from a cultural presupposition that to be human is to be intersubjective, to be in communication.[9]   It is clear that the Vatican II's document on 'Divine Revelation' is using personalist thought category and vocabulary when it describes faith as "an obedience by which man entrusts his whole self freely to God."[10]   Contemporary theologies of revelation and faith quite often present God's action in relationship with human beings as well as the human faith response in terms of self-giving or self-communication.

**finds fulfillment in**    **communion**

**CULTURAL PRESUPPOSITION:**
**To be human is to be intersubjective**

Three related remarks may, perhaps, be *apropos* here. First, a word of caution. The generations of Christians within the Graeco-Roman culture (Western European) should be looked upon as trying to communicate meaningfully to their contemporaries within a common cultural frame of reference of their time. The official

---

[9]This implies that the relationship between God and people can and should be expressed in ways that are in accord with particular cultures. See José M. de Mesa (2001).

[10]Article 5, the Dogmatic Constitution on Divine Revelation in Abbott (1966).

condemnations of the thought of Tomaso D'Aquino in the middle ages is a reminder that Christians of that time dared to comprehend and express (i.e., communicate) the Gospel in a way that made sense to their contemporaries, despite the objections raised by the religious authorities of the time. Criticising past theologies as narrow and lacking in insight is both misguided and unfair. It is misguided because the concerned generation of Christians was actually doing its best to respond to the challenges of the time. And it is unfair because we really cannot claim that we know and understand their situation better than they did themselves. We should bear in mind that looking at our past in terms of what we think are our predecessors' shortcomings rather than their desire to be equal to their challenges also makes us open to the same criticism by future generations of Christians.

Second, since we mentioned the role played by cultural resources in articulating theology, we need to pay attention to the importance and strength of culture. Culture is a way of feeling, believing, behaving and structuring life shared by a group of people, which has become 'second nature' to them through the process of socialisation. Language and other ways of communicating mentioned by Michael Traber[11] — the presentational language of bodies, the representational/symbolic language of things, music and even silence — are all culturally conditioned. And the internalisation of culture is so successful that most of the time we are not aware of such cultural conditioning. We *feel* culture rather than consciously speak of it. For this reason, it makes a lot of sense to describe culture as the "shared gut feeling of a people".[12]

Thirdly, in speaking about the impact of the mass media on culture, it may be helpful to consider culture as being likened to the sea. On the surface, there is much movement. But as one goes deeper, the movement lessens, with the least movement occurring at the bottom. Similarly, there is a lot of change at the ephemeral

---

[11]See Chapter 2 in this volume.
[12] From a conversation with Gerald Arbuckle, S.M.

level of culture, but less at its conjunctional level where many values are located, and least on its structural level where we find, as it were, the 'soul' of a people. With this in mind, we may ask to what extent mass media impact on culture and thus reflect on the influence of media on the indigenous culture.

## A MATTER OF SOTERIOLOGY?

Could it be that in making communication so central in understanding Christianity, not just as a theme, but as a basic pattern of thought and source of theological language, we are presenting 'communication' as a soteriology? The importance of this question is hinged, of course, on our conviction that the Gospel is about 'salvation'. But our uncritical dependence on handed down articulations about this reality may turn, if it hasn't already done that, the Good News into a situation where it is neither good nor news.[13]  Let us consider what is involved in a discussion of soteriology.

'Salvation' as a cultural theological term refers to the happiness and total well-being which God wills for humankind.[14] Precisely because it is a cultural interpretation, although this was not the way it had been presented often, it is better to refer to it here in quotation marks. This is to indicate that 'salvation' is but one way to talk about the reality it embodies and expresses. To be sure, the reality of 'salvation' has been interpreted culturally in different

---

[13]'Salvation' for many Christians is a supernatural reality that has very little connection with life in the world.  Moreover, preaching a gospel that threatens damnation to those who do not accept it can hardly come across as a hopeful message.

[14]"From the first to the last page of the Bible, it is clear that God's will aims at humans' well-being at all levels, aims at his definitive and comprehensive good: in biblical terms, at the salvation of man and women. God's will is a helpful, healing, liberating, saving will.  God wills life, joy, freedom, peace, salvation, the final, great happiness of human beings:  both of the individual and of humankind as a whole.  This is the meaning of God's absolute future, his victory, his kingdom, which Jesus proclaims: human beings' total liberation, salvation, satisfaction, bliss" (Küng 1976: 251).

ways, but always in terms of contrast experience. The description of a positive situation in contrast to a negative one has yielded in the history of theology different cultural ways of talking about it. Jewish Christians talked about it in terms of *yasha* (space), whose opposite is *tsarar* (being constricted). Greek Christians who experienced *apoleia* (destruction), spoke about *soteria* (wholeness). Roman Christianity interpreted this reality as *salus* (health), because it saw negative conditions as *infirmitas* (sickness); and Anglo Christianity perceived it as *salvation* since its opposite is *damnation*. Lately, confronted by *dominación* or *opresión*, Latin American Christians proclaimed the *liberación* brought by Jesus Christ.

By extension of this thought structure of contrast experience, we can easily see how *peace* is 'salvation' where there is war or conflict, how *joy* is 'salvation' when people are experiencing loneliness, how *acceptance* is 'salvation' where there is rejection, or how *justice* is 'salvation' if people are being unjustly treated. We remember, too, how the Bible talks about 'salvation' in terms of *life* as the opposite of *death*. If communications, as Dr Palakeel (2003) has suggested, is about intimate dialogue, exchange, communication and communion, it obviously counters alienation, indifference, isolation and antagonism. Surely, it is possible in the context of communications today to legitimately speak of this well-being coming from God as *communion*, or at least explore its potential to express what Christians deem as 'salvific'.

In any discussion of the soteriological, we would be well advised to keep in mind that 'salvation' is both historical, and therefore fragmentary, as well as eschatological when such gift from God becomes fulfilment. This complete happiness and total well-being is understood within the Judaeo-Christian tradition as a future reality when gauged in terms of realisation. But when seen as fragmentary and provisional, albeit real and concrete, 'salvation' is part of our present experience. In this sense we are *already* saved, but *not yet* saved fully. 'Salvation' is already being experienced partially, but will still be experienced in its completeness. This means that 'salvation' is really in the present and not just a future hope. Consequently, 'communion', when used as a possible interpretation of human well-being from God, will also be characterised as somehow being already experienced now and yet looking forward to its complete realisation.

'Salvation' as human happiness and well-being affects all the different dimensions of our humanity. For it to be real, we should be able to experience 'salvation' in our corporeality and its links with the natural world, in personal intimacy with others, in institutions and structures of society which give us social identity, in culture which provides us with a way of life, in harmony of our convictions and behaviour, and in hope which provides meaning to life (Schillebeeckx 1983: 731-43). Otherwise, the Christian preaching of 'salvation' will remain a mere abstraction for people of flesh and blood, with no connection to their experiences in life. These same areas of our being human would need to be reflected upon in the light of our present experience of communications. We need to ask and elucidate how *communion* is being realised in these different dimensions of human life.

With the question of soteriology, we are led back to the whole point of theologising, whether this be in the context of a search for knowledge ('salvation' as knowledge, *gnosis)*, a hunger for *liberation* ('salvation' as liberation, *liberación*), or a yearning for *communion*: to facilitate the experiencing of God in our human situations, to sensitise people to God's active presence in their midst. In a sense the question of 'salvation' is at the heart of what is theological. For is not theology about that which 'we have seen, have heard, have looked upon and touched with our hands' (i.e., what we have experienced and has transformed us) and which we proclaim to the world — the life-giving (i.e., communicating in order to be in communion) Word who is God?

## REFERENCES

Abbott, Walter S.J. (ed.) (1966). *The Documents of Vatican II.* New York: Association Press.

De Mesa, José M. (2001). *Inculturation as a Pilgrimage.* Chicago: Catholic Theological Union.

De Mesa, José M. and Lode L. Wostyn (1991). *Doing Theology: Basic Realities and Processes.* Quezon City: Claretian Publications.

Ganoczy, Alexandre (1984). *An Introduction to Catholic Sacramental Theology.* New York: Paulist Press.

Küng, Hans (1976). *On Being a Christian.* New York: Doubleday & Company, Inc.

Neuner, J. and S.J. Dupuis (eds.) (1982). *The Christian Faith in the Doctrinal Documents of the Catholic Church.* Bangalore: Theological Publications in India. Fourth edition.

Palakeel, Joseph MST. (2003). 'Theologizing with Insights from Communications' in Joseph Palakeel (ed.) *Towards a Communiction Theology.* Bangalore: Asian Trading Corporation.

Schillebeeckx, Edward. (1981). *Interim Report on the Books "Jesus" & "Christ".* New York: Crossroad.

_____. (1983). *Christ: The Experience of Jesus as Lord.* New York: Crossroad.

## CHAPTER 5

# The Unavoidable Dialogue

### (Five Types of Relationships between Theology and Communication)

### *Daniel J. Felton*

A review of the literature on the dialogue between theology and communication quickly reveals a growing interest in 'connecting' these two disciplines.[1] Given the fact that Christianity is essentially a religious tradition about communication,[2] it is not surprising that "many major contemporary theologians such as Schillebeekx, Lonergan, Tracy, Ellul and Bastian are taking up questions of communications either explicitly or implicitly and are using the language and concepts of the communication sciences..." (White 1983: 7).

At the same time, communication science, even though a fairly new academic discipline, continues to develop itself as an interdisciplinary science. In fact, theology, like communication, is not a single discipline. Both are interdisciplinary, and thus share a "similar stance relative to *method*, to the perennial *one-and-the-many* relationship, to *practice*" (Phelan 1981: 20).

History also plays a significant part in bringing these two fields together. "At the major turning points in the history of Christianity

---

[1] For a helpful bibliography and review of the literature on theology and communication, see Paul A. Soukup (1989).

[2] For a discussion of Christianity as communication see Robert Kress (1985: 161-203); and Johannes Heinrichs (1981: 1-2).

— usually coinciding with periods of great social change and the introduction of new methods of communication — theological discussion of modes of communication have leapt into the forefront"(White 1983: 8). Avery Dulles also addressed this point as he explored how "the changing styles of communication affect the church's understanding of its own nature, its message, and its mission" (Dulles 1971: 5). Tracing the historical development of theology and communication from the oral tradition of the first generation of the Christian era, through the era of the written word, manuscripts, the Reformation age of print and into the twentieth-century communications revolution of the electronic media, Dulles points to the intimate historical relationship between theology and communication.[3]

Another 'connecting' point is located in the current study of *communication and culture* as a forum for understanding how religious meaning is created, reinforced and changed in human experience and societal structures:

> At minimum, tying communication science to theology responds to these signs of the times. In such a study we recognise the powerful influence of communication and use this knowledge not only to speak to the world but also to inform theology. In addition, communication also helps to explain some of the current movements in theology and spirituality by situating them within the broader context of a global 'communicative culture'. The relationship of communication science to theology is an important one, justified by far more than communications popularising or disseminating function in relation to the conclusions of the theological enterprise (Soukup 1986: 78).

This 'tying' together of communication and theology takes into consideration theology, cultural forms and communication. Unfortunately, what is lacking in all these theological, historical, cultural and communication 'connections' is a more systematic

---

[3] Another historical mapping of communication and theology is presented in Paul A. Soukup (1986: 79-82).

study of theology and communication. But this certainly does not imply that seminary theology and philosophy courses are not reflecting upon communication. Nor does it imply that

> theologians have not reflected upon communication. Indeed they have — many theological concepts and models (from the Alexandrian Logos theology to Augustine's inner world to the *communicatio divinis* and so forth) attest to that fact. However, recent attempts to integrate communication study with theology have not borne the fruit they might. This results as much from the nature of the communication concepts employed as from the ways in which theologians employ them (Soukup undated).

There are many reasons why there has been no systematic theological study of and reflection upon theology and communication. One of these is the failure of some of those involved in this study and reflection to appreciate and understand the various *types of relationships* between theology and communication, thus adding confusion to an already complex topic. Knowledge of fundamental approaches, concepts and terms used to discuss the relationship between theology and communication is essential to all theological study and reflection upon this subject. I therefore examine here five distinct relationships that exist between theology and communications, highlighting the distinctive features of *each* relationship through a 'horizon analysis'.

> For Bernard Lonergan, the term horizon literally denotes
>
> the line at which the earth and sky appear to meet. This line is the limit of one's field of vision. As one moves about, it recedes in front and closes in behind so that, for different standpoints, there are different horizons. Moreover, for each different standpoint and horizon, there are different divisions of the totality of visible objects. Beyond the horizon lie the objects that, at least for the moment, cannot be seen. Within the horizon lie the objects that can now be seen (Lonergan 1972: 235).

In other words, 'horizon' is the maximum field of vision from a determinate viewpoint, and it is within this vision that the "scope of our knowledge and the range of our interests are bounded" (ibid.: 236).

I therefore explore the five relationships between theology and communication by ascertaining the 'determinate viewpoint' (stance), 'horizon' and the 'objects between the determinate point of view and the horizon' of each relationship. This analysis will help to clarify the terms and categories that are used to discuss the 'maximum field of vision' and the 'line' at which theology and communication appear to meet in each type of relationship. It is important to note that these relationships are examined with an emphasis on their *theological* relevance.

## FIVE RELATIONSHIPS BETWEEN THEOLOGY AND COMMUNICATION

The five relationships being examined here are: theology *and* communication; *communicative* theology; *systematic* theology *of* communication; and Christian *moral vision of* communications. Certainly, these five relationships do not exhaust all the approaches or the relationships that exist between theology and communication. However, they do represent the 'key' relationships that guide a significant portion of the theological study and reflection presently taking place.

Each of these relationships contains its own concepts, categories, interests and terms. Furthermore, each relationship is characterised by a distinct determinate viewpoint, horizon and objects in-between. Any approach to the theological study of theology and communication will necessitate a familiarity with each of these distinct relationships.

### 1.  Theology *and* Communication

In the relationship between 'theology *and* communication', we find ourselves standing in the science of communication and looking at the horizon of theology. In this case the two intellectual disciplines are juxtaposed, each a coherent whole striving for intelligibility. As such, the interest of theology in this relationship is limited mostly to 'borrowing' those known object of communication science (theories, methods, models, constructs, etc.) that can be of aid in illuminating its own study and reflection upon religious faith.[4]

Underlying the interaction between theology and communication in this model of 'Theology *and* Communication' is a presumption in favour of theology's ability (both theoretically and practically) to borrow known objects of interest from a human science to understand itself and the reality of religious faith. There are those who resist such a 'borrowing' because theology is discourse on God. But most would accept the presumption that one can borrow (sometimes implicitly, other times explicitly) concepts and models from communication science to clarify and express religious faith. Concomitantly, the acceptance of this presumption is based upon the theologian's understanding of theology, systems and 'borrowing'.

What is theology? We define theology as "the study which, through participation in and reflection upon a religious faith, seeks to express the content of this faith in the clearest and most coherent language available" (Macquarrie 1977). The discipline of theology, in its intention to "participate in and reflect upon religious faith", recognises the formative factors of culture and reason in its pursuit of intelligibility and clarity. In this case, there are times when theology borrows from culture and reason theories, models and constructs of communication as an aid to its own internal illumination of reflection upon religious faith.

---

[4] Frequently, the actual 'borrowing' from one system into another assumes a 'mutually critical correlations' model of exchange. H. Richard Niebur develops what might be called mutually critical correlations between sociological and theological understandings of the reality 'church' in his book, *The Purpose of the Church and Its Ministry* (1956: 17-27). This model is also operative in David Tracy's presentation of fundamental, systematic and practical theologies, as well as in his theological understanding of both 'church' and 'world' and an assumption of mutually critical correlations between them; see Tracy 1981, especially chapter 2.

There are theologians who understand secular disciplines, culture and reason as *theological* expressions and realities for the study of religious faith. In this case, theology borrows from the discipline of communication, from culture as the expression of contemporary forms of communication and from reason as helping to make communication intelligible, because there exists a need to explicate and correlate *both* theological and communicative understandings of the reality of religious faith.

Paul Soukup (1983), in his book, *Communication and Theology*, has made a comprehensive review of the literature that implicitly or explicitly links theology and communication. He identifies four major topics that constitute the subject area of the formal interchange between the two disciplines: religious self-understanding, attitudes toward communication, the Christian use of communication (including the kinds of strategies appropriate to the churches), and communication ethics and advocacy.

These are, for Soukup, the primary areas of theological reflection upon theology and communication. Furthermore, Soukup distinguishes six communication analogues or images that are 'borrowed' (implicitly or explicitly) by theology from the field of communication as an aid to illuminating the topic under consideration. These six communication analogues or images are: linguistic, aesthetic, cultural, dialogic, broadcast and theological (ibid.: 13).

Soukup points out that when theologians have employed communication in their reflections, they have usually chosen (borrowed) one of the six communication analogues or images mentioned above. At the same time, Soukup also points out the 'limits' in theology's field of vision when looking at the horizon of communication:

> the images of communication common in theological discourse are only part of the communication picture. And, because the images are often used for illustration, they fail to contribute to an ongoing theological reflection. That is, the theological role of the

communication image or model is to justify or augment an argument constructed upon other premises (ibid.).

In this instance, Soukup maintains that

as in any borrowing of terms, the end result is both narrower than the original and slightly distorted...yet another danger inherent in the use of any communication image is that the model from which it is drawn has its own presuppositions and built-in limitations...(ibid.).

Soukup is arguing in favour of maintaining the *integrity* of communication whenever the theologian enters into the science of communication as his/her determinate viewpoint. In other words, the theologians must *respect and be knowledgeable* of the reality of communication that is being borrowed and applied to theological reflection. For example, Soukup locates the six communication images (general organising perspectives) employed by theologians within the broader perspective of five communication constructs (meta-theories of communication systems and methods). The five constructs are discourse, contexts, texts, the taken-for-granted and communicative competence, and they

stand in some contrast to those images of communication common in theological writing (language, art, dialogue, transport, culture). They have been developed as tools to aid the understanding of the communication process from different perspectives: philosophy, psychology, semiotics and sociology. Because of this they complement the images of communication by providing a framework of questions with which to interrogate any particular image (ibid.).

Any theologian who enters the field of communication with the purpose of importing communication images into theological reflection will need to know about these constructs as a means of insuring the integrity of the image or model of communication that is to be borrowed.

Paul Soukup's work is but one attempt to articulate an understanding of the 'objects that lie between' the determinate viewpoint of communication and the horizon of theology. However, his contribution is monumental in its ability to organise a vast amount of material in the fields of theology and communication.

### Framework for future study

The following framework outlines some questions that are important to any study of and reflection upon the relationship of 'Theology *and* Communication'.

1.  What is the nature of the 'borrowed' communication? The communication that is being borrowed by theology was taken from communication science. What are its central theories, concepts and images? Who are the representative figures (authors) connected with this communication?

2.  What is the theology underlying the communication? Theology borrows communication theories, constructs, etc., from communication science for its own internal illumination and systematisation. What is the nature of the theology that seeks to be illuminated by this communication? How is theology illuminated and systematised internally by this communication construct?

3.  What are the theological consequences of 'borrowing' this communication? When there is resistance to the idea of theology borrowing from communication theory, construct, etc., there is a fear of the consequences of its application to theology. What would these consequences be?

4.  What are the practical issues? How would the illumination of theology affect concrete and practical theological problems, questions and issues?

### 2.   *Communicative* Theology

In the relationship represented by '*Communivative* Theology' we find ourselves standing in the field of communication looking at the horizon of theology. Unlike the relationship between 'Theology and Communication', communicative theology does not seek, first and foremost, to borrow objects of interest and knowledge from communication for its own *internal* illumination and systematisation. Rather, the interaction between theology and communication is concerned primarily with how theology as discourse on God is communicated in the clearest and most coherent language available.

Furthermore, communicative theology is not just interested in an interaction with communication study as it is reflected in society; it is at the same time interested in its own contemporary theories, models, methods, etc., of communication within theology. Often these somewhat pragmatic interests in communication turn to culture in an attempt to understand the cultural forms of contemporary communication that impart theological relevance.

The relationship represented by communicative theology raises a basic semantic question, the core of which is captured by Anne van der Meiden when he asserts that "a communicative theology is not a theology 'of' communication; it is a communication-centred and -oriented theology. There is no 'theology of communication' because communication is included in the term" (van der Meiden 1981: 43-47). Accordingly, Meiden advocates a communicative theology that would develop the following fields: knowledge about the communicating human being; media knowledge; problems of decoding a message; effects of bringing the message across; problems of encoding a message; the world of the communicative media; and the task of helping people to process media contents. All of these fields are concerned with matters of communicating theology, as well as with how theology is formed and shaped so that it is communicative.

A communicative theology is more than selecting the best medium to disseminate theological content. In addition, it necessarily considers the cultural influence of contemporary communication on the ways in which we think, speak and write; the culturally accepted places for finding the subject matter for speaking about God; the impact of a communication environment upon religious sensibilities and responses to the world; the way communication has altered the relations among the various institutions of society, including the role of the family and the church; and the impact of the communication industry upon religious experience.

These considerations do not exhaust the possible ways in which culture influences contemporary communication, and consequently, communicative theology. However, it does recognise the significant impact of culture and cultural forms upon the development of a theology that seeks to be relevant and communicative.

Another aspect of communicative theology examines the dimension of communication *within* the theology that seeks to be communicated. In other words it looks at how the content of theology self-consciously uses and is formed by communication constructs.

In this sense, the models, constructs and methods of communication science are explored within the theology that seeks to be communicative, i.e., symbolic theology or symbolic communication. As such, the theology is self-consciously informed by communication both as a process (how it develops its content as a communicative theology) and as a product (how the content of the theology is to be dismissed).

*Framework for future study*

The following questions are important for any further reflection upon the relationship of theology and communication in communicative theology:

1.  What is the nature of the theology to be communicated? Theology looks to communication to aid its own communicability. What are the central categories, concepts and images of this discourse?

2.  What is the nature of the communication being explored by
    theology?  Theology explores theories and methods of
    communication to aid its own development as a communicative
    theology.  What are the central concepts of communication
    being explored by theology? Is there a model of communication
    self-consciously contained in the theology?

3.  What are the theological consequences of applying this
    communication to the development of a communicative
    theology or as a way of disseminating theological content?
    Will the application of this communication construct, image,
    theory, etc., change the theological content?  How will the
    theology be more relevant, communicative and understood?

4.  What are the practical issues?  How will this communicative
    theology affect the concrete practices, activities and decisions
    connected with communicating theology?

## 3.  *Systematic* **Theology** *of* **Communication**

In a 'Theology *of* Communication' one is always standing in the
theory and practice of theology looking at the horizon of
communication.  In this instance, communication turns to theology
for an understanding of itself, as well as a theological explanation
of present communication practices and policies.  A '*Systematic*
Theology *of* Communication' seeks to build a theoretical,
systematic theological study of the phenomenon of communication,
either as a specific discipline or at least as a discipline within
the sphere of systematic theology (e.g., Christology, Ecclesiology,
etc.).

From the earliest days of Christianity to the present times there
has been an operative theology of communication alive within the
Christian church, albeit for the most part in an implicit form.  In
more recent years, the theological study of communication has
become much more explicit in its examination.  This movement
from implicit to explicit theological reflection has been prompted
by many factors, including recent church documents citing the

need for an explicit theology of communication, the introduction of a new method of communication, and the appearance of communication science as a distinctly emerging field.

One response to this movement has been an attempt by certain theologians to develop a systematic theology of communication with its own components, methods of observation, enquiry and verification. This approach often extrapolates the disciplines already connected with a systematic study of Christian religious faith. Such an extrapolation commonly draws upon the implicit theology of communication found in a theology of revelation, trinity, incarnation, doctrinal development, etc.

A further characteristic of this approach to a systematic theology of communication is the assumption that theological categories can be imposed upon communication as a way of defining how the world *should* be communicating. These theological categories address questions that tend to be existential rather than contextual (practical). It presumes a 'conversionist' understanding of Christ and culture,[5] and therefore imposes its theological perception of the world on communication as a way of understanding the realities of communication.

Since this theology is still in its infancy, perhaps it is more appropriate to speak of the individual theologians who are attempting to systematise a theology of communication. Given the fact that there are a number of theologians addressing this area, it is not surprising that we have a plurality of *theologies of communication.*

John Mills suggests three basic topics for a theology of communication: creation, human nature and incarnation (Mills 1981: 68-76).[6] Another approach is presented by Gaston Roberge

---

[5] A conversionist's view of history finds the human person actively involved in the making of history, transforming human life in and to the glory of God. See H. Richard Niebur (1951: 194-96).

[6] This example is presented as it is cited in Paul Soukup (1983: 25).

who centres his theoretical framework on the opening lines of the Letter to the Hebrews: "God has spoken to us through his Son." Consequently, his theology of communication includes: Christ is the image of the unseen god; man is the image of God; we are turned into the image that we reflect; theophanic images and idols; iconosphere (Roberge 1982-83: 378);[7] speech-less, word-less and sign-less communication; and effable presence (ibid.: 137-45).

Another biblical framework is offered by Robert E. Webber. His systematising of a theology of communication is eminently biblical and doctrinal in nature. His theology is divided into the following parts: 1) The Basis of Communication: God and Creation; 2) Models of Communiction: History, Language and Vision; 3) Models of Communication: The Incarnation; 4) The Breakdown: Man and Sin; and 5) The Restoration: Christ and Redemption (Webber 1980: 69-139).[8]

Critics of this theoretical approach emphasise the need to build a theology of communication from a theological reflection upon contemporary communication problems and questions being discussed in *practical and pastoral contexts.*[9]

Another concern takes into account the extremely broad and somewhat chaotic nature of communication science theory and conceptualisation at this time. Given the fact that a 'Theology *of* Communication' has communication as its horizon, there exists presently a natural resistance to any theological systematisation.

*Framework for future study*

The following framework outlines some questions that are

---

[7] Roberge (1982-83: 378) states that 'Man, himself an image, lives in a milieu that is a complex image. The bio-sphere of faithful man is an iconosphere.'

[8] This summary is from the work of Emil Santos (1986: 30).

[9] For a helpful presentation of how one builds a theology from the starting point of *contexts,* see Robert J. Schreiter (1986).

important to any further reflection upon the relationship of theology and communication in a *systematic* theology *of* communication:

1. What is the nature of the communication to be systemised? Given the wide range of communication study, what is the theory or construct of communication that a theoretical theology of communication is attempting to systemise?

2. What is the theology underlying the communication? This approach often extrapolates an implicit theology of communication from a theological concept of discipline. If an attempt is being made to develop a systematic theology of communication, what is the theology that is systematising communication?

3. What are the consequences of developing a systematic theology of communication? There are those who resist the theoretical, systematic approach to a theology of communication. What are the elements in this approach that are being resisted?

4. What are the practical issues? A theology of communication provides a system of theological reflection. What are the practical and pastoral issues in communication that can be addressed by this particular systematic theology of communication?

## 4. *Pastoral* Theology *of* Communication

In a '*pastoral* theology *of* communication' we find ourselves standing in the field of pastoral theology looking at the horizon of communication. The starting point is often a relevant issue or problem that has arisen within communication. At other times it is a theological reflection upon communication that generates a pastoral plan, strategy or goals. In either case, the determinate viewpoint is pastoral theology and the horizon is communication.

A *pastoral* theology *of* communication addresses specifically the horizon (reality) of communication *practice*. This entry point is somewhat different from the more theoretical, systematic starting points of the previous three relationships examined here.

Pastoral theology is a branch of practical theology that seeks to understand the implications of faith for the pastoral activity of the church at any given moment. It is concerned with all endeavours, tasks and functions of the church which make up its total pastoral activity, e.g., ministry of various kinds, catechesis, preaching and counselling. A *pastoral* theology *of* communication, then, seeks to give expression within theology as a whole to the questions and issues raised by communication practice, activities and decisions, and reflects upon scripture and tradition to formulate pastoral communication goals and plans for communicators and their communications activities.

The methodology of these two tasks might involve an examination of the different models of the church, of the emerging patterns of communication in local Christian communities, or the evolving cultural forms of popular communication and religious language — always for the purpose of establishing principles for the church's relevant and effective communication of the Gospel.

One example of an attempt to develop a *pastoral* theology *of* communication can be found in the Latin American church:

> In the Latin American church there have been notable attempts to develop a more or less comprehensive theological reflection on communication. After a long series of seminars on the subject, the Department for Social Communication of the Latin American Bishop's Conference (DECOS-CELAM) came up with a document after a Congress held at Piracicaba in Brazil in 1981. Entitled *Hacia una Teologia de la Comunicación en América Latina,* the document got its inspiration and orientation from the CELAM documents of Medellin (1968) and Puebla (1979). The second and third parts deal with the *Reflexión Teoliogica sobre la Comunicación* and *Pastoral de la Comunicación.* This treatment speaks clearly of the method used, in which an analysis of the situation in Latin America goes side by side with doctrinal considerations. Like Medellin and

Puebla as a fruit of these reflections concrete pastoral directives are traced.[10]

The DECOS-CELAM document is a good example of how a *pastoral* theology *of* communication brings together the practical issues and questions connected with communication and pastoral theological reflection upon communication. The document points out that initially the mass media were greeted by the church as the modern solution to the problem of evangelisation — as a pulpit for the masses. However, over a period of time, problems were regarding to the impact of the mass media on the Gospel message and its reception by the mass media audience. Furthermore, the structure of the mass media industry favoured the values of a consumer society and powerful élites, which were contrary to and inconsistent with those of the Gospel.

As a result of theological reflection upon mass media, the DECOS-CELAM document proposed that 'group media' represent a more suitable approach to evangelisation in Latin America than 'mass media'. Group media support the emerging communication patterns consistent with basic Christian communities and a pastoral preference for the poor. Slowly, but surely, in the process of evaluating the communication actions of two decades in evangelisation, a theory of communication has evolved (and continues to evolve) which now guides and directs the pastoral theology and practice of communication in the Latin American church.

This examination of a *pastoral* theology *of* communication would be incomplete without addressing the place of communication in ministry formation programmes and theological

---

[10] The *Pastoral Instruction on the Means of Social Communication, Communio et Progressio* (1971), speaks of the need for pastoral theology to address the whole question of social communication in Christian education (nos. 102-113). More recently, the Congregation for Catholic Education has issued an instruction entitled, *Guide to the Training of Future Priests Concerning the Instruments of Social Communication,* London (Catholic Truth Society) 1986.

studies. New theologies of communication, emerging patterns of communication within the church and new cultural forms of communication can all have an impact on models of ministry and ministerial formation. The task of formation has proven to be quite difficult as

> both communication education for pastoral personnel and theological education are in a period of transition, and it is not clear to those responsible for planning programmes of pastoral studies *how* communication education is to become an integral dimension of theological/pastoral studies (CSCC 1984).

There is basic agreement, though, that the communication education of pastoral personnel is more than "simply encouraging a more intensive use of media (unfortunately, a typical approach) or training church personnel in the techniques of 'the new media' (the fallacy of the two-week course tacked on to seminary programmes)' (ibid.).

Instead, communication education in pastoral studies and formation programmes seeks a *habitus theologiae*. That is

> The habitual mode of religious interpretation of life experiences which a formation in a particular theological perspective inculcates. It implies a theology which is concerned about pastoral communication and has therefore appropriated concepts of contemporary communication theory and practice which reflect contemporary cultural contexts. But this discussion focuses on the personal formation in theology. That is, it is concerned not with giving pastoral personnel pat answers...to every particular question but fostering a habit of theologising about situations they face. Such a *habitus theologiae* would lead pastoral and apostolic people in the church toward the attitude of inculturation and evangelisation (more pastoral terms for communication) (ibid.: 5).

The development of a suitable 'theological habit' is vital to the formation of all pastoral personnel. It is for this reason that all ministers engaged in communication activity should have sufficient training and formation in *both* theology and communication, so as

to allow for an adequate understanding of the implications of faith
for the communication activities of the church at any given
moment.

*Framework for future study*

The following questions are important to any reflection on a
*pastoral* theology *of* communication:

1.  What is the nature of the question or problem of
    communication that is being raised for pastoral theological
    reflection?    At times, communication looks to pastoral
    theology for an explanation of its communication action. What
    is the question being addressed in this situation? Describe the
    communication activity that is at issue. What is the cultural
    context for this communication concern?

2.  What is the current pastoral theological reflection upon this
    communication problem or question? Often, the process of
    trying to explain a communication action initiates pastoral
    theological reflection on the church's approach to this
    communication matter. How is pastoral theology expressing
    the problem or issue at hand to theology in general? Is there a
    pastoral strategy or goal that addresses the question being
    posed by communication? In the process of structuring reasons
    to explain a pastoral decision, a 'theology' is generated often
    regarding the particular communication-related problem. Is
    there an operative implicit or explicit theology of
    communication evolving in response to the issue being raised?

3.  What are the consequences of raising the communication
    question, both for pastoral theology and theology in general?
    There are times when a practical concern looks to pastoral
    theological reflection for an answer, but finds that there do
    not yet exist solid theological grounds for answers and
    decisions.    What are the implications of this for the
    communication action being questioned? Where does the
    discussion stand for developing a theological basis for the

pastoral practice being questioned?

4.   What are the practical questions?  New theological insights into communication have implications for pastoral communication activity.  Given these new insights, how will current pastoral practice change?  What new models of pastoral ministry are emerging and, consequently, what will be the new educational needs for the pastoral minister in theology?  How will the church be more relevant and effective in its actualisation of the Gospel?

## 5.   Christian *Moral Vision* of Communication

In a 'Christian *moral vision* of communication' one is standing in the field of moral theology looking at the horizon of communication.  In this instance, the field of communication is primarily the horizon (reality) of communication practice and policy-making.  As such, communicators and recipients of communication practice and policy-making turn to Christian ethics for moral principles to guide, justify and critique communication practices and decisions from the perspective of what is morally right or wrong. Accordingly, the focus of a Christian *moral vision of* communication is twofold.  It addresses the moral dimensions of communication practice and policy-making *within* the church; and it addresses the ethical issues affecting human communications *in general.*

The distinctly Christian moral dimension of the relationship between theology and communication has long been, and continues to be, a familiar entry point for Christian churches into the development of a theology of communication. However, in recent years, the focus of the entry point has shifted significantly as these churches seek to provide a Christian moral vision for new modes and patterns of communication emerging within the Christian churches and contemporary culture. For example, for the Catholic Church the primary entry point into a theology of communication has been centred for centuries on those aspects of communication which may "influence the belief and morality of human beings and therefore their chance of salvation" (Biernatzki 1978: 8).

For the most part, the initial attitude of the Catholic Church towards new modes and emerging patterns of communication has been negative and distrustful. In contrast, the period immediately following the Second Vatican Council was characterised by a 'change of attitude' towards modern *means* of social communication. Accordingly, post-conciliar documents such as *Communio et Progressio* (1971) and *Evangelii Nuntiandi* (1975) stressed mass media as a gift from God in accordance with his providential design and plan for salvation. These documents represent a new moral vision and point to an attitudinal shift of the Catholic Church towards social communication and the mass media during the 1960s and 1970s. Underlying this new attitude was an implicit theology of communication.

More recently, the Christian churches have manifested yet another shift in their moral view of communication. The enthusiasm of the 1960s and 1970s has been tempered by a more critical evaluation of the new modes of communication, especially new media technology. This reassessment has sought a more systematic ethics of media to respond to the moral questions and issues being raised within communication practice and policy-making. A number of factors, both religious and cultural, have contributed to this shift in attitude.

Two contemporary trends in particular seemed to be greatly influencing the development of a Christian *moral vision of* communication for the 1990s. The first trend was related to a more critical reflection upon the new means of communication and the need for a systematic media ethics; the second trend addressed the moral dimension of new emerging patterns of communication in Christian churches and in society.

However, a more critical acceptance of new media technology and related issues has raised a number of broader moral issues and questions for communicators working within contemporary church media practice and communication policy-making. These moral issues and problems are generated from such areas as news in the religious media; youth, evangelisation and the media; church responses to cable television; the family, religion and the media; coming to terms with video culture; freedom of expression in the church; the church and the right to information; advertising and the Christian imagination; religious programming for children; and the electronic church.

Given the moral issues connected with these topics, communicators within the church are turning to moral theologians for ethical principles and for systematic moral reflection to guide and critique their communication practice and policy-making. Concomitantly, moral theology, while reflecting upon communications both within the church and within society, at times addresses particular aspects of communication and media from a Christian moral theological perspective. This moral guidance is often addressed not only to communicators involved with church communications, but also to all those who are professionally involved in communications and, more specifically, to Christians who are professionally competent in the field.

At the same time, a more critical acceptance of new media technology, practice and policy-making is taking place in the secular media. In fact, many of the moral issues and problems troubling the church are ethical concerns for the secular media as well. These include ethical questions concerning conflict of interest, truthfulness, privacy, social justice and confidentiality in journalism and the reporting of news; subjects and techniques of advertising; élite ownership of media and maintenance of status quo; and the problem of violence in the entertainment media. Responding to these ethical concerns, Robert Rutherford Smith asserts: "There is a need for a systematic theory of media ethics based on something more than current journalistic fashion or the latest exposé of media malpractice" (Smith 1979, quoted in White 1980).

Both religious and secular communication, then, are raising questions of a moral nature and are seeking to be informed by a systematic communication ethics. To date, there has been little dialogue between moral theologians and media professionals in addressing this common need.

A Christian *moral vision of* communication that is relevant to our times will need to develop a more systematic moral theological reflection upon communication ethics and the moral issues facing communicators involved in church communication, as well as all those professionally involved in communication.

There is another trend that is related to an emerging pattern of communication within the church and the world. The 'New World Information and Communication Order' (NWICO) proposed by UNESCO asserts that communication is a basic human right and responsibility. To violate this human right is to violate the human person. With an emphasis both on the communicator and the recipient, the NWICO calls for democratic and participatory communication:

> Communication today is increasingly seen as a process through which the exchange and sharing of meaning is made possible, and by which social relationships and, as a result, social institutions are created and maintained. It is a two-way process, interactive by its very nature. The concept of communication demands participation (Traber 1985: xii).

So far, the "church has made little or no explicit contribution to the international discussions leading toward the proposals for a New International Information Order. This is surprising and regrettable considering the many issues of social justice and personal morality that are implied in the NIIO concepts."[11] Christianity does, however, assert that communication is a basic human right and, as such, "the Christian seeks to establish a pattern

---

[11] 'The Church and the New International Information Order', *Research Trends in Religious Communication* 1:2 (no date given): i.

of communication in which the free, creative expression of the person is recognised, respected and invited. It is a recognition that every person is an active participant in building a culture".[12] In this instance, the Christian churches connect communication with moral principles based on the dignity of the human person.

The development of a Christian *moral vision of* communication will therefore need to address the social justice and moral issues connected with NWICO. Communicators and recipients will turn to Christian moral theology for guidance in the justice issues connected with how the Christian churches deal internally and externally with communication as a human right, as well as participatory and democratic communication. At the same time, Christian moral theological reflection will continue to address professional communicators, perhaps contributing to the development of ethical norms for a NWICO.

Robert White, reflecting on how Christian communicators can contribute to the NWICO, speaks of the importance of developing models of democratic, participatory communication within Christian churches:

> Yet the professionals have a right to demand of the Christian church, "Show me some practical working models of what you are talking about. Especially show me the way the churches run their own media and the way that they structure their own patterns of communication." It becomes obvious that the church cannot tell media professionals or policy-makers to develop more democratic communications if the church is not doing this itself (White 1985: 116).

These two factors — the need for a systematic ethics of communication and the movement towards a more participatory democratic communication — will greatly influence the development of a Christian *moral vision of* communication. As these moral issues and problems are addressed by moral theological

---

[12]'Christian Alternatives to Media Control', *Research Trends in Religious Communication* 4:1 (1983): 1.

reflection, an implicit or explicit theology of communication will most likely evolve as well: "For ultimately, the question of whether a particular way of expressing the word is faithful to Gospel values and does bring forth authentic Christian community rests upon a process of theological reflection" (White 1983: 10).

*Framework of future study*

1. What is the nature of the communication practice or policy-making that is prompting moral questions to be raised? Communicators and recipients of communication are raising moral issues and questions within the context of communication practice and policy-making. What is the practice or policy of communication that has raised the questions? What are the theories and methods of communication practice and policy? Who is raising the moral questions?

2. What is the nature of the moral issue? Communicators and recipients turn to moral theologians for guidance in their communication practice. What are the ethical presuppositions of the moral question being asked? How do these presuppositions affect the moral analysis of the issue? What are the moral principles guiding the ethical analysis? How are these moral principles applied to the communication practice or policy?

3. What are the implications for moral theology of raising ethical issues and questions connected with communication practice and policy-making? There has been little dialogue between moral theologians and the various disciplines of communication. Is the discipline of moral theology able to enter into such a dialogue at this time? What has delayed this dialogue? What would be the resistance to moral theologians contributing to a systematic ethics of mass communication? What shifts or adjustments are necessary for moral theology to respond to the moral questions being raised in the field of communication?

4. What are the practical issues? What are the implications for communication practice or policy-making of applying these moral principles? Do the findings of research and moral analysis confirm or contradict the ethical presuppositions that prompted the moral question to be asked in the first place? How would these findings change pastoral practice and policies within the Christian church?

## CONCLUSIONS

Our analysis has shown that each of the five relationships that exist between theology and communication is *distinct,* possessing its own determinate viewpoint, horizon and focus of interest. Accordingly, each relationship provides a distinct entry point into the systematisation of theological study and reflection upon communication. A thorough understanding of *each* one of them is therefore essential to any theological endeavour to systematise this field of study and reflection.

Given the distinctive nature of each relationship, the question remains as to what extent the five relationships are compatible or incompatible. Even though we have not specifically examined how the five relationships interact and relate to one another, it does seem reasonable to propose that the five relationships are compatible with one another. This compatibility is based upon an inner cohesiveness that is sustained by each relationship's *theological connection to communication.* These theological connections include the borrowing of communication theories and concept for theology's self-illumination, the study of communication as a process and product for a relevant way to communicate theology and the raising of theoretical, practical and moral communication questions for consideration in systematic theology, pastoral theology and moral theology.

Any attempt to systematise this area of study and reflection will need to understand the distinctness of each relationship's theological connection to communication, as well as the internal relatedness of this common theological connection among the five relationships. Furthermore, our examination indicates that there is a distinct yet mutually complementary interaction among the five relationships. Each has its own uses and limitations, strengths and weaknesses. However, considered together, the different relationships depend upon one another's uses and strengths to provide a sense of completeness to their own development, as well as for comprehending the total interaction between theology and communication. In this instance, a horizon analysis of the five relationships would enhance an understanding of how these relationships complement one another.

Given the various interactions between theology and communication within each relationship, as well as the inter-relatedness of all the relationships, it would be most advantageous for the person studying communication to have sufficient training in *both* theology and communication.

## REFERENCES

Biernatzki, W.E. (1978). *Catholic Communication Research: Topics and Rationale.* London: The Research Facilitator Unit for Social Communication.

Catholic Truth Society (1986). *Guide to the Training of Future Priests Concerning the Instruments of Social Communication.* London: Catholic Truth Society.

Christian Alternatives to Media Control (1983). *Research Trends in Religious Communication* 4:1.

Christians, Clifford G., Mark Fackler & Kim B. Rotzoll (1987). *Media Ethics: Cases and Moral Reasonings.* Second edition. New York: Longman.

CSCC (1984). Developing the Communication Dimension of Theological Education. Unpublished position paper. London: CSCC.

Dulles, Avery (1971). *The Church is Communication.* Rome: Multimedia International.

Heinrichs, Johannes (1981). Theological Reflections on Communication. *Media Development,* 28: 4, 3-9.

Kress, Robert (1985). *The Church: Communion, Sacrament, Communication.* New York: Paulist Press.

Lonergan, Bernard (1972). *Method in Theology.* Minneapolis: The Seabury Press.

Macquarrie, John (1977). *Principles of Christian Theology,* 1. New York: Charles Scribner's Sons.

Meiden, Anne van der (1981). Appeal for a More Communicative Theology. *Media Development,* 28: 4, 43-46.

Mills, John Orme (1981). Towards a Theology of Swimming in the Deep End in E. Hofmann and J. Mills (eds.) *Multimedia International Yearbook.* Rome: Multimedia International.

Niebur, H. Richard (1951). *Christ and Culture.* New York: Harper and Brothers.

_____. (1956). *The Purpose of the Church and Its Ministry.* New York: Harper.

Phelan, John. (1981). Affinity and Conflict Between Theology and Communication. *Media Development,* 28: 4, 20-24.

Roberge, Gaston (1982/83). Semiological Reflection on a Theology of Communication. *Communicatio Socialis Yearbook,* Indore: Satprakashan Sanchar Kendra, 137-145.

Santos, Emil (1986). Toward a Theology of Pastoral Communication, Part IV. Unpublished doctoral dissertation. Rome: Pontificia Università Salesiana.

Schreiter, Robert J. (1986). *Constructing Local Theologies.* Maryknoll, N.Y.: Orbis Books.

Smith, Robert Rutherford (1979). *Questioning Media Ethics.* Edited by Bernard Rubin. New York: Praeger Publishers.

Soukup, Paul A. (1983). *Communication and Theology: Introduction and Review of the Literature.* London: WACC and CSCC.

_____. (1986). Communication, Cultural Form and Theology, *The Way* Supplement 55 (Spring).

_____. (1989). *Christian Communication: An Annotated Bibliography.* Westport, Conneticut: Greenwood Press.

_____. (undated). Communication Theories for Theologians. Unpublished paper.

_____The Church and The New International Information Order (undated). *Research Trends in Religious Communication* 1: 2.

Traber, Michael (1985). 'Foreword' in Philip Lee (ed.) *Communication for All.* Maryknoll, New York: Orbis Books, ix-xiii.

Tracy, David (1981). *The Analogical Imagination.* New York: Crossroad.

Webber, Robert E. (1980). *God Still Speaks to Us: A Biblical View of Christian Communication.* Nashville: Thomas Nelson Publishers.

White, Robert A. (ed.) (1980). The Ethics of Mass Communication. *Communication Research Trends* 1:1 (Spring).

_____ (1983). 'Preface: The Growing Dialogue between Theology and Communication' in   Paul A. Soukup, *Communication and Theology: An Introduction and Review of the Literature.* London: WACC & CSCC.

_____ (1985). 'Christians building a New Order of Communication' in Philip Lee (ed.), *Communication for All.* Maryknoll, N.Y.: Orbis Books, 105-17.

# CHAPTER 6
# Lessons from Pastoral Practice
## (A) Asking the Pastors
### *J. Daniel Kirubaraj*

Communication scholars from both East and West view communication studies in theological education as a basic necessity for the church. Carlos A. Valle (1995) contends that the present communication culture challenges not just theological education but the entire ministry of the church. Theological reflection on communication helps us to 'understand' the importance of 'faith practice' and the relational nature of God and human beings. The prime objective of introducing communication in theological education in India was to "critically reflect on communication in the context of theological studies to bring about a change in the attitude and behaviour of theological students and in the very manner of studying theology" (Philip 1988: 128).[1] To do this in the present social, economic and pluralistic religious context (Soukup 1983: 17), communication studies has to look far beyond the traditional preaching and teaching aspects of communication and be a part of other branches of theological studies, e.g., biblical, theological, historical and practical (David 1988: vii). The several new means of expression, with their new social, political and religious aura, claim new theological reflection.[2]

---

[1]Theological Education meets the needs of the few preoccupied elitists and fails to meet the needs of the church with her few ordained ministers (Philip 1988: 128).

[2]For example 'Cyber Theology', a field of study chosen by another research scholar in Indian context.

The presupposition[3] upon which communication study is accommodated into pastoral studies[4] seems to lack concrete "ways to express theology" (White 1983: 9-11), especially from the common people's point of view. The struggle of solving the problems of communication and theology thus falls in the fold of theological education and claims meaningful use of the mass media.

The present assumption that church communication is meant for preaching the Gospel with reference to the Great Commission (Matt. 28: 18-20) raises three questions relating to: a) whether the church can exploit the new communication technologies, b) the controversial nature of their language and 'neutral' transmission, and c) the paradox in scholarly opinions on media effect[5] (Soukup 1983: 74-75). To overcome these problems, the study of communication in theological education would have to find ways of fusing theology with communication and come up with a sort of 'Communication Theology'. Only such an attempt might help find a solution to the ongoing struggle between religious, ethical, technological, cultural and contextual values.

Since the study of communication in theological education is a religious activity, it needs to meet the principles of communication set by Jesus Christ and maintain "Christianity as a communication religion" (Palakeel 2003: 9). It warrants the church to share the truth and life with the new generations, in the new and changing contexts of time, space, symbols, culture, and media technologies (Periannan 2003: 193).

---

[3]That the use of mass media would help theological institutes to unite themselves to teach traditional theological content in a better manner and to a larger audience.

[4]With emphasis on the theoretical study of mass communication.

[5]Some claim that the media effect is greater upon human thought processes, global unity and development. Others are sceptical of this view and define media as a mirror that reflects society.

### THE INFLUENCE OF COMMUNICATION STUDIES ON THE PASTORAL MINISTRY

As part of my research on the influence of communication studies on pastoral practice, studies, I did a systematic survey of 99 pastors who had studied communications on either the Bachelor of Divinity (BD) or the Master's level (MTh) in Protestant seminaries of South India.[6] The following is a summary of the findings, organised alongside the seven modules (subjects), which have initially been taught on the BD level.

### Module 1: *Introduction to Communication*

The objectives set for the module warrant a knowledge and understanding of the complexities of human communication; principles and types of communication; ability to analyse the nature of social communication, especially in the Indian context; and promote the communication skills of students of theology. Ever since communication studies in theological education was introduced into the curriculum, the Senate of Serampore College has made this module compulsory for BD students in all theological colleges.

The findings of the study reveal that while all the pastors covered in the study acknowledged the importance of the study of communication in theological education, only 25.7 per cent of the 99 pastors felt that it had helped them in their pastoral ministry. However, 35.2 per cent agreed that it promoted a critical understanding of media in society.

### Module 2: *Mass Media and Issues in Communication*

The second module aims at making students aware of mass communication and its vitality in issues relating to social, political

---

[6]The thesis, 'Communication for Community Action: An Explorative Study of Communication in Theological Education in South India', by J. Daniel Kirubaraj, has been submitted to the Senate of Serampore College in partial fulfilment of the degree of Doctor of Theology (2004).

and economic changes. The students are expected to identify the range of media importance, to be exposed to media skills and to understand critically contextual communication issues, interpreting them from the perspective of social change.

From the data collected and analysed, 67.6 per cent of the 99 pastors supported the need to study social, political and economic concerns to determine mass media. But only 35.2 per cent out of 99 respondents said that they had gained a critical understanding of media in society. About 61 per cent of the pastors supported the study of media and culture theories, while 71 per cent out of the pastors felt the need to understand communication as tool for social change. Special skills training for social change was strongly advocated by 79 per cent of 99 pastors.

### Module 3: *Preaching as Communication*

The third module reflects the traditional Christian understanding of 'preaching' as communication, but involves a deeper learning of the neglected communication elements, e.g., the content, context, nature and barriers involved in preaching, based both on theory as well as skills for effective communication. Most but not all theological colleges teach this module, which is felt to be essential in preparing for the church ministry.

Out of 994 pastors only 31.4 per cent felt that the study of this module has any impact on the church ministry, though 70.5 per cent insisted that studying this module was necessary.

### Module 4: *Indian Christian Spirituality: Communication Perspective*

The rationale and aims of this module position the Christ-event as the ground for the communication between God and the people, asserting the relevance of Christian spirituality in the Indian context and cultural milieu. It postulates an inclusive cultural heritage from the communication perspective and expects the learners to achieve a proper blend of 'life and spirituality' from within Indian modes of action, i.e., add deeper meaning to Christian spirituality through struggles in the global communication context "to meet the needs of the poor, oppressed and marginalized in the day to day social strata" (David, 1988: 142-143). This module is very rarely taught in theological colleges, though the concept of Christian spirituality is often referred to in all disciplines of Indian theological education in India. It has a deeper application in Dalit, Feminist and Ecological Theologies. However, it does not seem to have envisioned a genuine theoretical and practical convergence from communication perspective.

Our field survey revealed that out of 99 pastors, only 25.7 per cent believe that this module is of practical use in dealing with practical social and faith concerns. Nevertheless, 75.2 per cent stated that its study needed to be promoted.

## Module 5: *Interfaith Communication*

The different facets of religious pluralism, and its political and economic implications, make this module an inevitable area of study in theological education in India. The communication role of pastors for a tolerant and peaceful world through dialogic, interfaith and participatory communication against faith-based barriers and evolving new communication methods are the broad objectives in this module. Its specific objectives are to bring about a 'truth'-based harmony among people and identify and change the exclusivist Christian communication approaches into relevant and meaningful Christian witness.

Our data reveal that out of 99 pastors, only 16.2 per cent felt that this module helps students in community-based communications. However, 63.8 per cent of the pastors see the need to promote interfaith communication.

## Module 6: *Narrative Theology*

As a module, Narrative Theology is based on traditional and historical modes of human communication practised all over the world, with a special emphasis on India where religious values are passed on by epics, drama, dance, poetry and story-telling. The narrative is an ancient form of human communication that fits well with the biblical story and links Kingdom values with the present human world. The objectives of this module are to stimulate theological students to critically analyse the new and old patterns of story-telling, to interpret and reinforce the value of human–divine stories, and to retain counter-culture values and theological insights in their ministry (David 1988: 194-95).

Our study reveals that 79 per cent of 99 pastors felt the need for strengthening students' communicative abilities in relation to Narrative Theology. However, only 28.6 per cent recommended skills training for producing narratives in films and for operating a video camera.

## Module 7: *Christian Communication for Community Action*

The seventh module of the BD curriculum is based on the rationale that the Kingdom values are applicable to both individuals and the community as a whole. These values relate to both the 'here and now' as well as to 'future' human experiences, with salvation being the ultimate goal of a change that aims at liberation from all kinds of oppression and at a joint human experience of a new humanity. The module thus makes the Kingdom values the criteria of responsible communication, thereby setting the agenda for dynamic coexistence. To that end, the ultimate aim is to enable every congregation to become an action-oriented community with a commitment (praxis) to group action. The objectives of this module are to inspire theological students to promote genuine human development at micro and macro levels; to handle common communication problems in this process and instil Kingdom values through group action to bring about social change (David 1988: 226-27).

Of 99 pastors, 49.5 per cent felt that the theoretical learning imparted by the module was useful for instilling Kingdom values in society, while 66.7 per cent gave more weight to its ethical perspective. In terms of understanding communication as a tool to introduce Kingdom values into the structural, economic and social aspects of the church, the need for having the module as part of the BD syllabus was expressed by 50.5 per cent of the pastors.

## COMMUNICATION THEOLOGY: A PARADOX

The study of communication in theological education seems to revolve around several paradoxes. To mention a few: Kingdom values such as truth, peace, justice, equality and human dignity have to compete with the affluent world of freelance evangelists, who use the mass media to perpetuate the gospel of prosperity, making money, power and popularity of central importance. In contrast, pastors of mainline churches seldom use media technology and struggle to achieve successful communication using traditional liturgies and preaching.

Another disadvantage faced by pastors is the vast difference between the atmosphere in seminaries and that in churches, especially those in rural areas. The use of new information technologies in urban congregations separates the urban from rural congregations. In most cases, rural congregations have to be content with the physical presence of the pastors, traditional church communications and little or no media use.

In seminaries, there is very little freedom for theological students to choose the modules and methods of learning communication, which are still biased towards Western theoretical and ideological precepts. This makes communicating the Gospel from the Indian perspective difficult.

The study of communication in theological education expects the learner to implement several unidentified interfaces of theology and communication due to its contrasting philosophical and scientific features. It thus lacks clarity on what communication is and on how to theologise it from within other existing strains, such as the social and structural problems involved in the pastoral ministry. This struggle seldom has the capacity to resist the force of media power in the socio-political, economic and technological contexts of our world. These observations are well supported by several scholarly works.

## Some Suggestions for Curriculum Revision

Some of the issues raised in the responses by pastors need further reflection and articulation. From my own work on communication in theological education, of which the pastors' response is only a small part, I can suggest the following recommendations for consideration in curriculum revision:

- Provide space for students to reflect on the present curriculum and its relevance to the pastoral ministry.
- Provide space for students to choose what they want to learn, e.g., theory or skills training, as well as how and where.
- Adopt more clarity in theoretical insights over the interfaces of theology and communication.
- Make 'co-learning' possible by promoting closer interaction between the teacher and students.

## REFERENCES

David, C. R. W. (ed.) (1988). *Communication in Theological Education: A Curriculum.*

Bangalore: Board of Theological Education of the Senate of Serampore College.

Palakeel, Joseph (2003). "Communications and Theological Formation' in Joseph Palakeel (ed.) *Towards a Communication Theology.* Bangalore: Asian Trading Corporation.

Periannan, Sebastian (2003). 'Communication Theology for Formation and Mission' in Joseph Palakeel (ed.) *Towards a Communication Theology.* Bangalore: Asian Trading Corporation.

Philip, T. V. (1988). 'Two Central but Forgotten Aspects of Theological Education' in H.S. Wilson (ed.) *The Church on the Move: A Guest to Affirm Biblical Faith*. Madras: CLS.

Soukup, Paul. A. (1983). *Communication and Theology: Introduction and Review of the Literature*. London: WACC.

Valle, Carlos A. (1995). *Challenges of Communication*. Delhi: ISPCK.

White, Robert. A. (1983). 'The Growing Dialogue Between Theology and Communications' in Paul A. Soukup (ed.). *Communication and Theology: Introduction and Review of the Literature*. London: WACC and Centre for the Study of Communication and Culture.

# (B) Make Communication Studies Relevant to India's Diverse Cultures

## Kavito Zhimo

The revolution associated with information technology and globalisation and the new and harsh religious climate created by Hindutva organisations have introduced a new meaning and posed new challenges to our pastoral ministry. Theological institutions and colleges are often questioned about their relevance to the ministry of the church in the current socio-cultural and political context. We shall therefore first look briefly at this issue from the perspectives of theory and practice to answer some of the questions about the role and contribution communication studies can make to theological education and to the pastoral ministry.

Firstly, the mushrooming of theological colleges in the country, especially in Nagaland and in south Indian cities like Bangalore, is a matter of serious concern for the churches. For example, Nagaland state alone has about 32 theological colleges, of which about 25 are in the city of Dimapur.[1] Every year, over 200 students pass out with BTh certificates, about 100 with BD and MDiv degrees and about 20 with MTh degrees from colleges all over India. The question is: where do these graduates go after completing their studies? According to the 1997 census, Nagaland has around 1,269 Baptist churches (congregations), but almost half of them do not have theologically trained pastors. Is the explosion of theological colleges in the state, as elsewhere in

---

[1]Dimapur is the only commercial town of Nagaland. It is linked to other parts of the state by road, railways as well as by air.

India, adding to the already severe unemployment problem in Nagaland?

Secondly, in the current system of theological education, there is a lack of fit between theory and practice. Many students with first class degrees do not fit into the church's ministry because what they learned during their three to four years in the seminaries was mostly theoretical, with little relevance to pastoral practice. Theological education should gird and shape the objectives of church and mission.

Thirdly, communication studies is one of the youngest disciplines in theology. Except for colleges affiliated to Serampore University, in most other theological colleges communications is not even part of the curriculum. Moreover, as my own experience and that of others shows, teachers and students of other disciplines tend to narrowly identify communications studies with practical skills alone. In fact, skills development is only a minor part of the communications studies curriculum. The question is, do the communication courses offered by seminaries relate sufficiently and realistically to our pastoral ministry? This leads us to the issue of 'contextualisation'[2] and appropriate use of theory.

Fourthly, one of the major concerns of academicians in the field of communications is to develop appropriate theories in which to ground the subject. It is generally acknowledged that there is a strong Western influence in our communication theories, which holds little relevance for our cultural values. Dissanayake comments that the major drawbacks of communications studies in India are its Western-oriented curricula, Western teaching practices, and a Western approach to communication research. He observes that Western authors have written 75 per cent of the textbooks used in Asia (Dissanayake 1988: 3). In addition, those

---

[2]The term contextualisation has grown very popular in theological circles. It has to be understood as a situational methodology that is meaningful in one's cultural context, where the gospel can be communicated in a way that is relevant to the recipient's life situation.

teaching communications at the postgraduate level have been educated in the West and remain wedded to their acquired Western approach. If this is the case, then communications studies in India will have to examine the nature of the courses offered by theological colleges, even in such subjects as journalism and mass communication. Obviously, there is an urgent need to produce communication theories that are more appropriate to our own social, cultural and pastoral context.

In the past few decades, South Asian communications scholars like Neville Jayaweera, Wimal Dissanayake, J.S Yadava and a few others have attempted to develop Indian theories of communication. They believe that communication theories should have their roots in the cultural ethos of Indian philosophies. It is obvious that without developing such theories, research cannot be carried out within one's own cultural setting(s). As Krishna Sondhi aptly points out, "Theory guides research and research refines theory" (Sondhi 1985: 21). What is lacking in India is a communication theory that could guide researchers to develop meanings and values based on his/her own cultural ethos. This does not mean that we should reject theories and models that come from the West. These could still be part of the dialectical enquiry we would have to undertake in our search for Indian communication theories. By developing such theories, communication studies could become genuine and acquire new meanings. Most Western theories and models cannot lead to the kind of research that is required in India, a country where communication is conditioned by castes, tribes, and different religions and cultures. Therefore, a critical examination and analysis are needed to develop appropriate communication theories, models and paradigms to make the study of communications more meaningful and research more appropriate.

The following are five suggestions that I think might facilitate effective communications for the pastoral ministry in India:

1.  Communications studies or courses should be more contextual and relevant, not only for India as a whole, but also for

individual cultural regions. This should be possible even if the Senate of Serampore retains its uniform curriculum.

2. Studies on traditional communication skills need to be formulated. The importance of folk-tales and songs, folk dance and music, and folk culture in general needs to be researched and taught to the student of communication. Gaining insights and skills in how people at the grassroots communicate with each other and celebrate their life together and with other communities would help us develop new types of pastoral communication.

3. Communications students should, at the same time, become familiar with the theories and practices of the mass media of communication. Based on this knowledge, they would be able to educate people about the ways in which media function and the value system inherent in them. Some kind of pastorally-grounded media education should become a permanent feature of the church's ministry. This calls for a new commitment, new resources and a new type of witness and involvement in the life of the people.

4. When we talk about communications we do not merely mean an academic discipline but also their relevance for the Christian ministry, namely communicating Christ through words and deeds in the reality of India. India is a country with a great diversity of cultures, languages and regions; it is also the birthplace of many major religions. No theory of communications in India can be separated from the diverse traditions that are woven into its cultures and religious practices. In a country like India, the inclusion of communications studies in theological education is both crucial and challenging and requires courage and creativity.

5. Students of communications should make a difference in their communities and societies by supporting truth and disclosing falsehood. The World Association for Christian Communication (WACC) has given us a concise guide for what it means to be engaged in communications. WACC's Christian

Principles of Communication assert that communication should create community — a community of peace, eliminating all the obstacles that prevent any group of people from becoming fully human, including those based on caste, race, class and gender. Christian communication should liberate people from the grip of power holders and media manipulation. It should support and respect culture by defining and redefining people's basic socio-cultural identities, acknowledging their human dignity and all religious values. Above all, Christian communication must be prophetic, serving truth and challenging falsehood (see WACC 1997: 6-9). These principles are amazingly relevant for our current situation in India.

## REFERENCES

Dessanayake, Wimal (ed.) (1988). *Communication Theory: Asian Perspectives.* Singapore: AMIC.

Sondhi, Krishna (1985). *Communication and Values.* New Delhi: Somaiya Publications.

WACC (1997). *Statements on Communication by the World Association for Christian Communication.* London: WACC.

# PART II
## NEW DIRECTIONS

## CHAPTER 7

# Taking Stock of IT Developments and the Political Economy of Communications in India : Implications for the Curriculum

## *Pradip N. Thomas*

In 1845, when Karl Marx was in his twenties, he and Friedrich Engels wrote *The German Ideology*. There is a celebrated passage in this text which has been the inspiration for many generations of scholars involved in writing on critical political economy of communications, from the late Dallas Smythe and Herb Schiller to contemporary scholars such as Dan Schiller, Peter Golding, Graham Murdock and Robert McChesney.

> The class which has the means of material production at its disposal has control at the same time over the means of mental production, so that, thereby, generally speaking, the ideas of those who lack the means of mental production are subject of it .... In so far as they rule as a class and determine the extent and compass of an epoch, it is self-evident that they .... among other things .... regulate the production and distribution of the ideas of their age: thus their ideas are the ruling ideas of the epoch (Marx and Engels 1970: 64-65).

In an era dominated by a turn to cultural studies, this passage and the tradition of political economy in general have been critiqued for their over-emphasis on economics at the expense of culture — and, as a result, text and context, discourse and representation have displaced the analysis of the relationship between structures and ideas. While any simplistic notion of determination needs to be discounted, the relationship between media structures and ideas is crucial to understanding the nature of power in our world today. We do need to acknowledge that audiences are active and not passive recipients of media content, that each one of us is capable of creating oppositional discourses. But the exercise of power by individuals, one must admit, is on a different plane from the exercise of power by a Rupert Murdoch (who directed 157 of his editors to take a pro-war line towards Iraq in 2002) or, for that matter, Silvio Berlusconi, the prime minister of Italy, who has turned all media into his media, or our own Marans, Mappilais and Birlas, who continue to act as foot-soldiers for economic liberalisation in India.

## THE MULTIPLICATION OF IT POWER IN INDIA

There are three reasons why we need to become conversant with the political economy approach:

1. The media and media products as commodities have become a potent source of power, values and profit in today's world. That power has been multiplied in a digital world. The logic of information has invaded every conceivable sphere of production and has reproduced it in its image. As markets penetrate into the deepest rural hinterlands, and as information becomes an essential raw material for all productive processes, key to the manufacture of genetically modified food (GM) and retroviral drugs for AIDS, as to surveillance, it is necessary that critical communication scholars begin to engage with the cybernetic moment, explore its centrality to economic and cultural globalisation, the creation of value and the overall implications of this for society.

2. The media environments in which we live are being increasingly controlled by a shrinking coterie of mughals and corporations. The de-regulation of media environments has

led to the transformation of old media giants into new media giants. While competition remains a rallying call for the proponents of economic liberalisation, it has not led to the establishment of a level playing field. All signs point to increased concentration. Read the business pages and you will quickly realise that the Tatas, Birlas, Ambanis and others among our revered business families, own vast media real estate, inclusive of both old and new media. Take, for instance, the Tatas. By taking over VSNL the Tatas have reinforced their already established presence in the telecommunications sector. They now have substantive interests at every stage of the telecommunications value chain — in cellular, basic, long-distance services, and are also poised to take over national long-distance services in the country. The conglomerate's telecom interests are represented by five companies — Tata Teleservices, Idea Cellular, Tata Internet Services, VSNL, and Tata Telecom. In IT, seven companies dominate the field: TCS, Tata Infotech, CMC, Tata Elxsi, Tata Interactive Systems, Tata Technologies and Nelito Systems. Tata Consultancy Services (TCS) happens to be the leading software company in India and an exporter of Indian software. Over the period 2002–2003, TCS posted revenues of Rs 5,012 crore (US $1.04 bn). It was India's leading software exporter in 2003-2004, with revenues of Rs 5,503 crore (US $1198.9 m) (see www.nasscom.org). The Tatas also own control systems — Tata Honeywell and Nelco — as well as have interests in publishing — the Tata McGraw Hill Publishing Company and Tata Infomedia. These companies are part of a mighty stable of 80 companies involved in engineering, materials, energy, chemicals, consumer products, communication and IT and the services sector (www.tata.com). Witness also the consolidations taking place in our cable industry or in the ownership of FM radio.

What are the consequences of concentration, conglomeration and inter-sectoral ownership in a country like India? How does it impact on media diversity, media democracy, and the play of opinion that is an important condition of democracy? We also need to acknowledge the abiding relationship between the state and the media. While there are points of conflict, the direction is towards greater accommodation and correspondence.

3. Global media governance structures (the World Trade Organisation [WTO], International Telecommunications Union [ITU], Internet Corporation for Assigned Names and Numbers [ICANN], World Intellectual Property Organisation [WIPO]) that are responsible for the making of key policies — the liberalisation of AV trade, spectrum allocation, Internet governance, intellectual property rights — are, for the most part directed by US and EU interests and beholden to private sector interests. The inability of global civil society to contest the nature and practice of global media governance has led to the rise of knowledge monopolies and to intellectual grabs that are analogous to the land grabs of the colonial era. Today all information, digital and non-digital, is becoming converted into property available for a fee. Intellectual Property Rights (IPR) have become the means for sustaining and extending the market for knowledge as property. Consequently, there has been a shrinking of ideas in the public domain. The enforcement of copyright has become big business in India as Hollywood, software manufacturers and the music industry enforce their writ on Indian cultural industries.

## OLD AND NEW CONCERNS

So what are some of the areas of concern typically explored from a political economy of communications perspective? Here are eight major concerns, some of which have the foci of substantial research:

1. The analysis of media ownership and control.
2. The study of the production, distribution and consumption of

media content.

3. The exploration of media/digital divides as a reflection of other divides.

4. The study of global media governance structures and their impact on local media.

5. The analysis of instruments such as the IPR tool kit in relation to the media.

6. The exploration of the political economy of cybernetics.

7. The nature of media reform.

8. Audio-visual trade.

To some extent, what I have dealt with so far, is the political economy of the 'old' media. Old media was characterised by discreet technologies, separate regulatory mechanisms and separate policies. New media is an altogether different ball game. It has many features, the key shared feature being the digital code. Digitalisation has led to convergence — and to marriages between previously separate technologies. We live in an era characterised by what the Intellectual Property (IP) critic Robert Boyle has termed the 'homologisation' of information. Almost all information, whether it be biological or non-biological, has become digitised. The digital code has become the mother of all productive applications across a number of sectors.

Information Technology (IT), at a very mundane level, functions as a transport mechanism for carrying information — just as roads carry vehicles, cables, electricity and waste pipes. However the analogy ends here because unlike roads, cables and pipes, IT is not just about flows; it is also the basis by which ideas are turned into commercially viable products and into intellectual property. The universality of the digital code enables networking, convergence, translation, blurring — and it is this quality, the inter-functionality of code, that is at the very heart of the vast changes taking places in the networked societies within which we live. It has also given rise to numerous ethical dilemmas as human biologicals and human biological information are turned into property to be exploited. Robert Boyle (1996) cites the example of a patient's contestation over genetic material removed from his own body without his explicit knowledge as an example of the real challenges facing Intellectual Property Right (IPR) in a world characterised by blurrings between the private and the public that have come about in part due to the fluid translations between computer-mediated information and genetic information. In 1976, doctors at the University of California Medical Centre, while treating John Moore for hairy cell leukaemia, isolated a cell line taken from Moore's spleen. In 1981, a patent was taken out for this cell line taken from Moore's T-Lymphocytes (white blood cells) by the University of California, with Moore's doctors cited as its inventors. Moore took them to court for the wilful exploitation of his genetic material without his consent, but the court ruled that since *a*) he had voluntarily consented to the removal of his spleen, and given that *b*) excised cells were subject to restricted property rights, and *c*) in the interests of furthering public research, he did not have rights over his cell lines as genetic information. As Boyle has noted, John Moore might have been the author of his destiny, but not of his cell line!

Not only has there been a colonisation of production by information, and the generation of substantive economic value grounded in information-based applications and processes, information has also invaded and embraced everyday life — the spheres of work, leisure, the daily rhythms of existence, relationships, understandings of the self and the beyond. In other words, information has not only given rise to a coherent, globally applicable world-view, it has also become the principle of organisation at the core of a variety of societal institutions: education, health, civil society, the economy. There have been many marriages between IT and biotechnology, IT and military technologies, IT and financial technologies, IT and surveillance technologies. And many mergers and alliances: IBM, Compaq, Hitachi and Motorola are not just IT companies; they

are now truly trans-sectoral multinationals involved in all
productive areas that have an IT dimension — from bio-informatics
to information warfare. It is for this reason that we need to
conceptualise information in terms of not discrete technologies
but as a 'totality'.

Dan Schiller's (1994: 102) observations on the pervasive,
cumulative and penetrative logic of information is a useful
introduction to the reality of convergence and the informational
mode of production:

> The transition to an information-intensive economy....does not
> depend on a narrow sector of media-based products. It is, rather,
> coextensive with a more or less thoroughgoing socio-economic
> metamorphosis across a vast and still undetermined range....The
> convergences and overlaps between genres traditionally of interest
> to communications research — television shows, newspaper
> reports, computerised data streams — and genes now subjected to
> unprecedented manipulation and control via bio-engineering,
> compel considerations as part of a single conceptual and historical
> process.

In other words, Schiller maintains that the many marriages of
convenience that have taken place between information
technologies and a host of other technologies such as
biotechnologies, nanotechnologies, surveillance technologies and
military technologies — make it imperative that the study of the
political economy of communication engages with issues and
concerns outside its 'traditional' remit. This is by no means an
impossible task given the normally interdisciplinary nature of
communication research. However, it is not made any easier by
the fact that the commodification of information is an extensive,
continuous, cumulative and rapid process, transforming all
previous productive processes in its image.

The question then becomes one of prioritisation: What are the
cross-sectoral information applications that impact most on life
processes and affect the survival chances of ordinary people? What

emerging structures are supportive of these new economic interests? How and in what way do information technologies impact on these processes? What are the ways in which new property regimes underwrite these developments? And what needs to be done to democratise these technologies and adapt them to the needs of development rather than to predatory forms of accumulation?

Today, computers are not merely used by bio-technology firms to store, analyse and retrieve data; they are being used to model, design, simulate, image products, processes, and re-programme life itself. Without digital technologies it would have been close to impossible to decipher the billions of bits of data being generated on the human genome. The social critic Jeremy Rifkin (1998: 181) has observed that the operational language of the computer has become the "...common language that is creating a seamless web between the information and life sciences and making possible the joining together computers and genes into a single, powerful, technology revolution".

## A NEW INFORMATION AND KNOWLEDGE ECONOMY

The ownership of information is already a critical and contentious area in global cultural, economic and trade policy. Databanks on biological and physical information along with archives on culture and society increasingly are being privatised. Global intellectual property regimes support the creation of enclosures via archives and databases. Together, they can be used to create formidable fortifications around knowledge that is only made available for a fee. Even the large public databanks in the USA that ostensibly are public repositories of knowledge, cannot be accessed by the ordinary citizen — in fact there are highly restricted access procedures that, in the post 9/11 environment, will become even more rigid.

All the major cultural industries are not only content producers but are also increasingly involved in production and distribution.

These TNCs are not only owners of the software, but also own the hardware and the backbone, the information highways. Sony's digital archives, as well as the archives owned by AOL-Time Warner, News International, Disney, Vivendi and Hollywood, are a source of revenue that is protected by copyright. Similarly, IBM and Microsoft's armoury of patents is used to maintain their dominance in hardware and software. These repositories of cultural and technical knowledge are complemented by a variety of databases on human and non-human biological information, physical information on sea and land resources, sociological information on populations, military databases, and so on. The National Library of Medicine's (US) database on the world's genetic information — the largest of its kind — and its Protein Identification Resource database on amino acids; the US pharmaceutical giant Merck's Merck Gene Index; the European Molecular Biology Laboratory; the databases owned by Human Genome Sciences and Incyte Pharmaceuticals; Celera Genomics; the Genome Database at Johns Hopkins; germplasm databases owned by seed companies such as DuPont (USA), Pharmacia (Monsanto-USA), Syngenta (Switzerland), Groupe Limagrain (France), Adventa (UK/Netherlands), Dow (USA) and the public seedbank Consultative Group on International Agricultural Research (CGIAR, Rome); and NASA's earth observation database on the atmosphere, biosphere, oceans and land surfaces are among companies that have knowledge of, and have patented a large share of the earth's resources. For instance, Incyte has won 500 patents on full-length genes and has applied for 7,000 additional patents on genes. While some of the larger countries in the developing world have begun to create their own databases — for instance, the National Bureau of Plant Genetic Resources in India — the very fact that USAID has contributed to 40 per cent of the costs of setting it up "in return for which American scientists have access to seed and data for research" (*New Scientist* 1992: 8), and the fact that companies like Hoechst (Germany), which owned 86,000 patents in 1995, had already screened 90,000 soil samples from India (Mooney 1996: 151), indicate the extent to which aid and bio-prospecting have reinforced the terms of neo-imperial conquest.

While modern molecular biology is centrally dependent on computing for the analysis, storage and retrieval of increasingly vast amounts of data, and bio-computing covers a wide range of information-processing options — simulation, graphical user interfaces and databases, among other applications — these information interfaces are by no means unique. Information technology and biotechnology have become a key aspect of modern military technologies exemplified by the 'smart bomb', biological and chemical warfare and the continuous remote surveillance of societies in different parts of the world. Electronics, sensors, computers and software, genetic engineering and the development of new materials are meant to enhance the prowess of the new age soldier in an era of informational and biological warfare. The adaptation of cybernetic principles to understand neural processes and human biology has led to fields such as artificial intelligence and to the development of biometric systems used for authentication and identification and for genetic profiling, an obsessive feature of life post 9/11. These new processes and applications are just a handful among literally hundreds of applications that have come about as a result of the advances and correspondences between biotechnology, nanotechnology, materials technology and their interfaces with information technology. The seemingly disparate uses of IT across a range of new applications hides a pervasive 'ordering logic' built on the cybernetic principles of control, command, intelligence and communication.

For those of us whose parameters for the study of a critical political economy of communications were mainly based on an interrogation of the politics, structures, processes, systems and rules pertaining to the extension, maintenance and dominance of the cultural industries, there is an absolute need to address not only the traditional structures of cultural and economic dominance in our globalised world, but also the new sources of global cultural, economic and political power and the instruments being used to reinforce this power. In other words, the lessons of the AOL–Time Warner merger and its decline may, in the long run, be of less significance than IBM's massive investments in the life sciences. And rather than deal with communication policy issues per se, it is imperative that we turn our attention to the source of property power in the knowledge economy.

## IMPLICATIONS FOR COMMUNICATION STUDIES

What are the implications of all this for the curriculum of communication studies? Firstly, there is a need for us to acknowledge the fact that communication is God's greatest gift to humanity. We are what we are and who we are because we communicate. And yet we recognise the fact that communication is not free, that it is difficult for ordinary people to access this gift or to make good use of it because it has become property, owned by those whom Isaiah (5:8) refers to as the people who "join house to house and add field to field". How do we begin to interrogate the sources of property power in the knowledge economy — the structures, the systems and instruments of intellectual property that have become the means of maintaining corporate dominance in the new economy'?

Secondly, curriculum revision offers us an opportunity to 'take sides'. Challenging the ubiquity of this global communication order is a call to discipleship. The Gospels, especially St. Mark, offers insights into Christ's own campaign strategy in Galilee, Capernaum, Judea and Jerusalem directed at de-legitimising the dominant social order and freeing people from the constraints of censorship and controlled communication. This is exemplified in Christ's confrontation of the symbolic power of the Jewish order and the political power of the stewards of that order. He challenged these symbols and the wielders of authority to use their power to humanise the debt system, to listen to people, to opt for justice and compassion rather than domination. How do we begin to explore old and new de-humanisations — the loss of freedom, creativity, control, autonomy, the new stratifications that have begun to define the resource rich and the resource poor?

Thirdly, a political economy approach to understanding global and local communications will help in an education process — the understanding of communication as a confessional issue, "a matter of faith, a test case for churches and Christians" as Rob van Drimmelen has referred to it in another context. The monolithic structures and one-dimensional visions of globalisation and the means and ends employed to usher in this brave new world are diametrically opposed to the vision of, and means and ends implied in God's promised Gift of Life to the whole of created order. This life-centred vision of created order is under threat from forms of governance, production and consumption. Rampant forms of censorship, the privatisation of communication, concentrated forms of ownership and trade-related regulatory measures have fractured the recognition of communication as a human need and a social necessity. The right to communication for all people is affirmed by the story of Pentecost — when the impulse towards a monolithic civilisation, best illustrated in the image of the Tower of Babel, is short-circuited by the restoration of communication for community. Just as the churches have committed themselves to covenanting on the debt crisis and globalisation, militarisation, biodiversity and racism, there is a need for a covenant on global communications, arguably the most potent source of power in our world today.

Fourthly, the adaptation of a political economy approach offers us the possibility to explore 'Christian responsibility' in communication. How does one begin to explore the basis for life-affirming technologies? How can the great wealth of old and new technologies be used to make a difference in the lives of ordinary people? How can a critical pedagogy be crafted to take on board some of these issues? The global communication order is the source of both symbolic and real power — power that results from the creation and manufacture of wants and desires, the ownership of the culture industries and the production of economic and cultural values. In Christ's time power was wielded by the Romans, by the keepers and stewards of the temple and an acquiescent, sometimes apathetic public, and he spent a lifetime trying to understand the manner in which this power was employed in order to make power and its exercise into a positive force for community — the power of love against the love of power.

And finally, how can we incorporate some of the new, emerging challenges that have been engendered in the interfaces between science and IT? What is the meaning of transcendence and immanence in the context of new technologies and virtual environments? How does one fathom the continuity of God in human and technological evolution?

Curriculum revision is as much a pilgrimage for teachers as it is for their students, for the seminary as much as for the Senate. Political economy offers some tools for this pilgrimage. It is by no means an all-sufficient substitute for understanding communication. For that, we need theology and cultural studies as much as political economy and appropriate communication skills. Is it a risk worth taking? Is this what is required? Are we ready for the consequences? Are we ready to accept that to be critical scholars of the media is an important aspect of ministerial formation? I will leave these questions in the hands of the reader.

## REFERENCES

Boyle, J. *A Politics of Intellectual Property: Environmentalism for the Net*, pp.1– 23), http://www.wcl.american.edu/pub/faculty/boyle#

Boyle, J. (1996). *Shamans, Software and Spleens: Law and the Construction of the Information Society*. Cambridge, Mass. and London: Harvard University Press.

Is India selling its seed bank short? (1992). *New Scientist*, Vol. 135, No.1838, 12 September, p.8.

Marx, K. and F. Engels (1970). *The German Ideology*. Edited by C. J. Arthur. London: Lawrence & Wishart.

Mooney, P.R. (1996). The Parts of Life: Agricultural Biodiversity, Indigenous Knowledge, and the Role of the Third System. *Development Dialogue*, 1-2.

Rifkin, J. (1998). *The Biotech Century: How Genetic Commerce Will Change the World.* London: Phoenix, Orion Books Ltd.

Schiller, D. (1994). From Culture to Information and Back Again: Commoditization as a Route to Knowledge. *Critical Studies in Mass Communication.* March, pp. 93-115.

Van Drimmelen, R. (1998). *Faith in a Global Economy: A Primer for Christians.* Geneva: Risk Publications, WCC.

*www.nasscom.org.* NASSCOM announces top twenty IT software and service exporters in India.

*www.tata.com/0_companies/index.htm*

## CHAPTER 8

# Images and Religious Imaginations

## *P. Solomon Raj*

Christianity, like many other religions, has been propagated mainly by word of mouth from generation to generation, with people sharing their faith by witnessing to one another. But along with the spoken word and printed page, the so-called plastic arts like pictures, wall paintings and sculpture, and the performing arts like song, dance and drama, have played an important role in Christian communication all through the past 2000 years of the Church. The Bible is a gallery of icons of God and his people — 'word images' made by the Semitic people of the Old Testament.

The greatest affirmation of the Christian creed is that God in Jesus Christ has become incarnate — the word became flesh — and, as St John says, the spoken word has become a perceptible form that we can see and touch with our own hands. In this way, God reaches us both by his spoken word and the image.

Our hymns have wonderful word images that we can perceive in our hearts. Take, for example, the great hymn: '*O, Worship the King/ All glorious above ....*' Here we see God who is riding a chariot and raising thunderstorms, with light as his robe and space as his canopy. Many hymns draw their images from the Old Testament and the Psalms. For example, this hymn of Robert Grant's is a paraphrase of Psalm 104. So when we talk about our faith, we use the language of pictures.

## THE CHURCH AND ITS VISUAL ART FORMS

The Christian Church inherited from Judaism a strict commandment against making graven images. This has impeded the free expression of our faith in handmade graphic pictures and, to some extent, in certain kinds of word pictures as well. But even this Old Testament prohibition, attributed to Moses, was not rigidly enforced until a later stage of Israel's history (Newton and Neil 1996). Solomon's temple had its golden cherubim guarding the symbolic dwelling place of God. These are, of course, either wooden figures overlaid with gold or figures that have been cast.

It is evident that Christians, even in the early days of their faith, used painted pictures, rock scribbles and wall paintings, as well as cryptic signs and drawings when they were being persecuted by the Roman emperors, not only to identify each other but also as secret confessions of their faith. A well-known example is the figure of a fish, which is IX-OVS in Greek. The faithful knew the Greek letters in the word fish stood for their creed: 'Jesus Christ the Son of God and Saviour'. The church historian R.H. Bainton (1974: 52) draws our attention to another second-century catacomb drawing showing the face of Christ with a round circle or 'nimbus' around it, flanked on either side with the Greek letters Alfa and Omega. Bainton tells us that three cultural elements had already joined together here in this simple rock figure — Syriac, Greek and probably Asian.

The earliest pictures of Christ show him only as a beardless young shepherd, sometimes with a lamb, or as a figure from the story of Jonah or from the sacrificing of Isaac, but not in the likeness of Christ himself. However, there were legends that St Luke painted the first picture of Baby Jesus and Mary, the *theotokos* — the bearer of God. Other legends claim that there were two images of Christ that he himself had given, which were called *achairo poe-atos*, not made by hand. One was the napkin given to Prince Abgar of Edessa, and the other the handkerchief of St Veronica.

But these are only traditions; the catacomb drawings are history. After the Roman persecutions ended and Christianity became the state religion under Emperor Constantine in the early fourth century, the secret and cryptic picturisations of Christ also came to an end, and the Byzantine artists began to portray him as the great Pantocrator, the ruler of all, sitting in council with angels and saints and martyrs. This fearsome yet benevolent Christ filled the cathedral domes of the Eastern orthodox churches and even some of the smaller churches. He thus became the emperor who ruled the universe, looking down at the worshippers from the high ceilings of cathedral domes.

The Greek and Russian icons were often used to communicate the teachings and key doctrines of the Christian faith. One of the most famous Orthodox icons is the fifteenth-century trinity icon painted by Andrei Rublev of the Kingdom of Kiev in Russia. It shows three angels visiting Abraham (the theophany) and partaking of his hospitality. Many such confessions of the church are passed on from generation to generation via pictures. The doctrines of the two natures of Christ and of the pre-incarnate existence of the logos, the meaning of the bread and the chalice — all these are permanently preserved in the ecclesiastic arts of that period. These pictures served not only the catechetical and didactic purposes of the church in those days, but also the sacramental and liturgical needs of the believers.

In those days, wall paintings and picture scrolls were considered the poor man's Bible — the *Biblia pauperum*. This was true even during the age of reformation and afterwards. However, the picture tradition of the church and the use of icons as useful aids to worship created a huge controversy in the eighth century. This so-called iconoclastic controversy was partly theological and partly political in nature. Some of the Byzantine rulers like Leo III were afraid of the neighbouring Muslims rulers and tried to prohibit the use of icons in worship (see Baggley 1987). But by then the great paintings and wall-sized mosaics of the saints, the *Pantocrator* and the *theotocus* had already filled many cathedrals. The faithful treated them as windows to heaven or as doors of perception (Raj 2002).

Though the iconoclastic controversy, which broke out around 726 AD, lasted for about a hundred years, it was subsequently resolved by the church at a council held in Constantinople. Based on the following arguments, the council decided in favour of using icons:

- Since God became man in Jesus Christ, when we make icons we are not depicting God, but picturing the incarnate Christ. In other words, if we deny the use of icons, we are denying the incarnation.
  - \* With the event of God the logos becoming human, all matter is blessed and redeemed and nothing is unholy.
  - \* The unseen God can reveal himself in images as well as in the spoken word.
- When we venerate the icons, we are not venerating the material, the wood, the paint and so on, but the prototype in the icon.

Thus the use of icons was restored and that was called the triumph of the orthodox, which is now celebrated on the second Sunday in Lent in many churches.

This was followed by 600 years of the so-called dark ages during which Christian faith was kept alive by the monastic orders and their creativity. One exception to this may be the medieval mystery plays performed in the streets: these were a lay initiative. But in the renaissance period — throughout the middle ages, in fact — image-making and the construction of the great Romanesque cathedral continued, with Michelangelo and other great artists keeping the art tradition of the church alive.

## SYMBOL LANGUAGE IN THE COMMUNICATION OF THE CHRISTIAN FAITH

Throughout the centuries, the Christian church was well acquainted with the language of symbols, as were the prophets of the Old Testament (Raj 2002a: 32f). Symbols like Jeremiah's pot or the rotting girdle are well known in the prophetic tradition of the Old Testament. Prophetic language is basically a picture language. It conveys the message in pictures and it conceals as much as it reveals, so that those who have ears will hear, and those who have eyes will see. "Amos, what do you see?" asks the Lord. The message therefore comes as something that can be seen and not just heard (Amos 8.2). Thus we see symbols like the nimbus, (the light of glory) around the heads of saints, the *hasthamudras*, the symbols of the sun and moon, the flowing river, the wide open eyes, the small mouths and the big ears (God's people must speak less and hear more), and figures of the good shepherd. We also see the fish and the bread and the cup which Christian artists have always used to communicate faith.

As the gospel travelled to many lands, artists have also used the symbols of the host culture, infusing them with Christian content. For example the lotus, which is an Indian symbol, has been used by Christian artists to convey the message of the soul emerging from the darkness of sin into the light of Christ — from death into life through the resurrected Christ. As we can see in many icons of Christ, the *pathaka hasthamudra* or the *abhaya hastha* was borrowed by Byzantine artists to convey the doctrine of the twofold nature of Christ by joining the thumb of the right hand with the forefinger. And we have already mentioned the second-century rock picture of the catacomb which made use of elements from three different cultures to depict Christ. This is symbolic language.

## IMAGES AND THEOLOGICAL EDUCATION

One definition of theology is that it is a process of understanding the faith in relation to our reality in order to live the mystery of both reality and faith. Theology is thus more than just a set of dogmatic discussions. Why should our theological dissertations need so many references and long footnotes to convey the message, when Christ has showed us the way to a theology of the birds of the air and the flowers of the field? Christ's teaching was always woven around images like the lamp and the lamp stand, the bushel and the bed, the mustard seed, the fig tree and the little lump which leavens the whole bushel-full of meal.

## CHRISTIAN ART IN INDIA

India is full of ageless artistic wealth and beautiful imagery. But the church in India was by and large very reluctant to use any of its art forms, whether plastic or performing. In fact, words like Ishwar or guru are still not accepted by many of the Indian churches. Symbols like the lotus do not seem to have much appeal and are rejected because of their pre-Christian associations with Hinduism. My own church forbids the placing of a crucifix on the altar. Only a plain cross can be used. Flowers and oil lamps are considered to be forms of idol worship. Some Indian artists like Jyothi Sahi have used a *pipal* leaf motif or the figure of a dancing Christ on the cross. But this was seen as too strongly associated with the figure of the dancing Shiva, despite our familiarity with the Sydney Carter hymn 'The Lord of Dance', referring to Christ and his word.

The problem is that we fear syncretism, even though the history of Christianity is marked by inculturation. Starting with St Paul, wherever the gospel was preached the church used the local idiom and imagery to communicate its message. Part of the problem also lies with the early missionaries, some of whom, like Roberto de Nobili, got so carried away with indigenisation that they called the Bible the fifth *Veda*. They also gave a new interpretation to *yagnopaveetha* and *vibhuthi* to appease those who wanted to remain at a safe distance from anything that looked or sounded 'Hindu'.

Interestingly, during the eighteenth century, when Indian

culture underwent a renaissance, many Hindu artists from Santhi Niketan took up the theme of the cross and human suffering as their subject matter. Jamini Roy, K.M. Panikar, Vinayak Mosoji and others, all painted pictures on the cross theme. Though the classical canons of Indian painting did not accommodate anything distorted, ugly and disproportionate, the humanist ideas of this period opened the eyes of these artists to the reality and the tragedy of human suffering.

In conclusion, we have seen that in the history of the church and its mission there has been a theology of art or a theology of images. For some obvious reasons the emphasis has moved away from visual images to word images. The economy of salvation includes word and flesh as it was revealed in the incarnation of Jesus Christ. Pictures have proclaimed our faith as eloquently as words. This is why we can talk about theology as art, and of faith celebrated and experienced with pictures.

## REFERENCES

Baggley, John (1987). *Doors of Perception — Icons and Their Spiritual Significance.* London/Oxford: Mowbray.

Bainton, Roland H. (1974). *Behold the Christ.* New York: Harper and Row.

Newton, Eric and William Neil (1996). *2000 Years of Christian Art.* New York: Harper and Row.

Raj, Solomon (2002). 'Fine Arts and Christian Worship' in *Thinking Aesthetically.* Chennai:    Satyanilayam Publications.

_____. (2002a). *Artistic Creativity and Prophetic Gift.* Chennai: Satyanilayam Publications.

## CHAPTER 9

# The Kaleidoscope of Cinema

*A. Suresh Kumar*

There is a close relationship between cinema, culture and society. In today's context, cinema not only defines culture, but also shapes its future trends. In traditional societies like India, where the performing arts and visual entertainment have a long history, people have developed a very strong relationship with cinema. In this connection, it is important to note the various relationships that exist between cinema and the facets of our life.

## FILMS AS DREAMS

Film theorist Edgar Morin (1956: 213) writes of film as a form of dream. Film director Louis Feuillade, too, believed that the film is essentially a dream (Lacassin 1967: 250). In a similar vein, Charles Pornon calls cinema "the machine for producing a dream" (Morin 1956: 16). All those who have written on cinema, from theoreticians to critics, filmmakers to film fans, have mentioned, in one way or another, the kinship that exists between the film and the dream.

Taking this link to its logical academic conclusion, art historian Walter Abell says: "Psycho-historically considered, art is one of the cultural symbols into which society projects existent states of underlying psychic tension.... Thus, we are led to conceive the higher forms of cultural expression in any society as manifestations of a 'collective dream'" (Abell 1966: 21). Freud wrote that

...what characterizes the walking state is the fact that thought takes place in concepts and not in images. Now our dreams think essentially in images; and with the approach of sleep it is possible to observe how, in proportion as voluntary activities become more involuntary ideas arise, all of which fall into the class of images... Dreams then think primarily in terms of visual images... what are truly characteristic of dreams are only those elements of their content which behave like images, which are more like perceptions, that is, than they are pneumic presentations... we shall be in agreement with every authority on the subject in asserting that dreams hallucinate — that they replace thoughts by hallucinations (Freud 1965: 85).

All films (and more so silent films) are essentially visual. They express themselves through images, and the hallucinatory nature of film has been cited by many theorists. The film possesses an extraordinary capacity for creating a sense of 'reality' that is "challenged by very few tested viewers". Film gives the viewer an impression of "being there living", which is unparalleled in any of the arts, including the theatre (Metz 1965: 76).

In the 1950s two American researchers discovered 'accidentally' that dreaming occurs primarily during certain periods of sleep. These 'dream stages', observably distinct from the other sleep periods, are characterised by several automatic, physiological responses on the part of the dreaming human which have since been measured in experiment after experiment. The dreamer 'watches' his own dream as if it were being projected onto a screen in front of him. The awakened dreamer recalls hallucinatory 'dramas' (and films are usually dramatic in structure and content), which the dreamer accepts as being 'real'.

The dreamer is absorbed into the content of his dream; the comparison with a child watching television, television being essentially visual (a sort of technological stepchild of the film), is not without point. The absorption of the film viewer into the film itself is conditioned not just by filmic content, but also by the particular psychological circumstances under which films are watched. Like the dreamer, the film viewer in his fixed seat is physically inhibited; only his eyes are in motion. The film viewer enters a state of relaxation; the spectator's musculature and the muscle tonus, particularly in the neck and facial region, slacken. The change in the dreamer's physiological state during REM (Rapid Eye Movement) dream stage sleep is dramatically reflected in brain wave (electro-encephalographic or EEG) measurements.

In this regard, a series of experiments with film viewing have yielded intriguing results. Watching any sort of projected filmic material modifies EEG measurements for all subjects. Regardless of visual imagery or dramatic content, all films produce these modifications. The viewer's musculature relaxes measurably. This eliminates the 'blockages' that produce fast, irregular alpha wave readings during normal wakefulness, and the alpha wave measurement slows down as a result. This corresponds precisely to the physiology of REM sleep (Cohen-Seat 1954: 20).

Exposure to any kind of film projection may trigger a crisis in a person with brain damage; the projection of a film at increased speeds can cause malaise or migraines in normal subjects; seizures occur regularly when epileptics are watching film projections. Reading a novel, looking at paintings, hearing a symphony, or viewing a theatrical performance differ from film viewing in that none of these experiences produces demonstrable physiological changes or modifications in EEG readings. The physiological effects of film viewing induce a unique psychological state, in which the film viewer normally accepts the film material as reflecting "what he believed, what he anticipated, what he thought" (Gernelli 1950: 136).

Thus, the human dream had mastered 'parallel editing' long before Edwin S. Porter introduced it into the cinema. The sensation Freud describes as being common to dream reports is also suggestive of a cinematographic device which was particularly important in the silent era: the 'super-imposition', whereby a simultaneous juxtaposition of visual material was achieved (Spottiswoode 1965: 165). Freud observed that "our dream-thoughts are usually represented in visual pictures which appear to be more or less life-size".

The film is the dream of the masses — masses which, however, may not be anonymous and unidentifiable. The popular French and German films of the 1920s were produced for and attended by a specific group that can be defined, not according to class or age, but by nationality. If it can be shown that the films were produced for a specific national audience, and were popular with it, then the analyst can interpret them, at least in so far as he has mastered the relevant national history — the stuff out of which group national psyche is formed.

## FILM AS MYTH

Film bears kinship not only to dreams, but also to myth. As Parker Tyler (1947: ix.) comments in *Magic and Myth of the Movies*:

> ... the true field of movies is not art but myth.... Assuredly myth is a fiction, and this is its bare link with art, but a myth is specifically a free, unharnessed fiction, a basic prototypic pattern capable of many variations and disguises, even though it remains imaginative truth. The individual's psychic state while viewing a film resembles the hypnotic.

Gustav LeBon (*Psychologie des Foules,* 1895) and Sigmund Freud (*Massenpsychologie und Ich-Analyse*, 1921) are in agreement that the psychological conditioning which induces the integration of the individual psyche into group psyche is a sort of hypnotic contagion (see Tyler 1947). If the movie theatre is the psychoanalytic clinic of the average person's dreams, that person is 'average' only in being an individual absorbed into the group. If "the film seems to be a new means for conducting humanity towards the recognition of the unconscious", it is then the group subconscious that is revealed in popular films (Tyler 1947: xiv).

Cinema is a highly valuable cultural institution for the elaboration of social reality through popular narratives, which allow for the creation of a symbolic universe marked by coherence and meaningfulness. Cinematic heroes and the narrative world in which they are developed fulfil a mythic function, for they help to create a world that is meaningful and purposeful for us. In this sense, myth is a primary form of communication, which facilitates our ability to understand the world around us and our place in it. It helps us to establish a map of our world, a compass for safe passage through unknown, uncharted seas. Through the mythic process, the world is seemingly punctuated with familiar landmarks, even when the terrain is new and unfamiliar. Thus, the different forms of popular media are indeed contemporary vehicles or carriers of myth. Writing particularly of the television medium but with implications for the cinema as well, Roger Silverstone (1981) observes that the medium as a powerful cultural institution is preserving, in form and function, much of what we had previously granted only to oral traditions in preliterate societies; and secondly, that its forms establish this cultural continuity. Story-telling and myth making are universal characteristics of cultural expression. As mythic expression, the filmic narrative involves the 'writing' of history or the telling of a people's story in their own images, embodying their own unique perspectives. Fundamentally, narrative is a cultural artefact that accounts for or provides legitimacy to a people and the (selectable-selected) options they take in order to define their existence.

Two issues are of significance here: the fundamental relevance of the mythic structures of the Hollywood-type traditional film narrative to the development of Indian cinema; and the dangers of using the mythic traditions of another culture without serious reformulation or redefinition for use within one's own cultural traditions. Although the study of the narrative developed within a marked emphasis which sought out universals, that is, to find all the world's narratives in a single narrative, the formalist endeavour to systemise the study of literature offered some concrete ideas on the nature of narrative. By narrative we mean the structures which govern how a story can be told. Of importance is the fact that the narrative is shaped by the socio-cultural context within which it arises. The formalists de-emphasised subject-matter or story (what the narrative was all about), laying more stress on the structural elements and their peculiar relations in the unfolding of the story.

The formulation of positioning in society occurs primarily to ensure the reproduction or continuation of the social system through its paradigms of sexuality, economic activity and its signifying practices. In essence, control and regulation of these important activities towards the ideological goals of the dominant society assumé high priority in the social agenda. The system of power is maintained or reaffirmed through the positioning of sexual and racial identities and through the fixed positioning demarcated in the system of social relations structured around categories such as male/female, white/black, producer/consumer and active/ passive. The symbolic code is derived from those psychoanalytic mechanisms that structure the unconscious of culture. It establishes the necessary conditions within which the text is produced and confirms not only the position of the viewer but also the intelligibility of the text. The distribution of relations of power and social positioning is symbolised by the key signifier of the phallus. The history of the institutionalised film industry reveals definite paradigms of power based upon race and sex. The cinematic delineation of power along racial lines is related intricately to the development of an ideology of colour that became characteristic of Western societies after the opening of the New World and gave rise to a mythology of colour based on the idealisation of the signifier 'white' and the subsequent denigration of 'black'.

## CINEMA AS COLLECTIVE FANTASY

Cinema is a prism that reflects dominant psychological concerns, certainly the conscious ones but especially the hidden, unconscious concerns of the millions of men and women who constitute its faithful and devoted clientele. Cinema can thus be approached as a collective fantasy, a group daydream, as opposed to the individualised fantasy incorporated in a work of literature, a painting, or the so-called art-film.

The balance between imagination and reality, the intermixture of fantasy and experience, are infinitely more complex in cinema. Like other high-fantasy products, such as children's fairy tales and adult daydreams, films emphasise the central features of fantasy: the fulfilment of wishes, the humbling of competitors and the destruction of enemies. The stereotypical twists and turns of a film plot ensure the repetition of the very message that makes a fairy tale so deeply satisfying to children. (The struggle against difficulties in life is unavoidable, but if one faces life's hardships and its many, often unjust, impositions with courage and steadfastness, one will eventually emerge victorious.). At the conclusion of both films and fairy tales, parents are generally happy and proud, the princess is won, and the villains are either ruefully contrite or their battered bodies satisfactorily litter the landscape. Evil, too, follows the same course it does in fairy tales; it may temporarily be in ascendance or usurp the hero's legitimate rights, but its failure and defeat are inevitable. Like the temptation to be naughty for a child who is constantly forced to be good, evil in cinema is not quite without its attractions of sensual licence and narcissistic pleasure in the unheeding pursuit of one's appetites. After all, it is usually the unregenerate villain who gets to savour the pleasures of drinking wine and the companionship of sexy and attractive women. The intention in both fairy tales and cinema is to appeal to the child within us, to arouse quick sympathies and antipathies, and thus encourage the identifications that help us to savour our fantasies more keenly.

## THE NATURE OF MOVIES

It is generally agreed that mass media are capable of 'reflecting' society because they are forced by their commercial nature to provide a level of content that will guarantee the widest acceptance by the largest possible audience. Thus, there is a definite tendency to create a product that consists of familiar themes, clearly identifiable characters and understandable resolutions. If the film strays too widely from these conventions, the audience will become confused and the result, especially for a movie made for entirely commercial purposes (as are most movies), will be a low return at the box office. The mass audience will simply not to go to see a movie that it has heard is 'difficult' or that deals with unpopular themes. Attracting an audience to a movie in sufficient numbers is a difficult enough process without having the additional burden of being considered intellectually challenging. It is for this reason that much of popular culture, and movies in particular, consists of the re-weaving of old, familiar, comfortable plot elements.

The movies have always done a remarkable job in creating a type of visual public 'consensus'. The relationship between the content of motion pictures and the role that such content plays in influencing audience behaviour is not easily understood. We do not know that the movies were among the first of the mass media to create a new form of collectivity, the 'mass public'. Mass production and distribution of message systems tend to transform private perspectives into broad public perspectives, and thus create mass publics. The movies, as an entertainment medium, have been a potent 'public message system' for more than a hundred years. Thus, whether reflecting or shaping, movies contribute to the overall perspective we have of our society. Furthermore, they have made a significant contribution to the collective vision we all have of things about which we know very little.

## THE PSYCHOLOGY OF MOVIE VIEWING

Movies provide a vivid visual presentation in which images are already fully established, easily identified (in most cases) and easily followed. While we still grapple with understanding the complete psychological significance of the movie-viewing experience, it does seem clear that movies are conducive to ready comprehension on an elementary level. The ease of comprehension helps the viewer to assume the role of the characters and to identify with them quickly and effectively. If the aesthetic contributions of the close-up and the dramatic form are added to vividness of presentation, it is not difficult to explain why movies are such an effective form of communication. Also, it is the avowed purpose of movie producers to include this absorption or identification on the part of the viewer; and the viewer's basic goal when he or she attends a movie is to have just such an experience. Emotions, passions and sentiments are over-emphasised. It is precisely because motion pictures deal with a mass of individuals of widely varying educational and cultural backgrounds that they find a common responsiveness on this elementary level. This could mean that viewers have paid their entrance fee in order to laugh, cry, be frightened or angered or sexually aroused, or merely to escape from their everyday lives. Thus, when the lights dim and the curtains part, their minds are particularly open to receive the 'message' of the movie. This sets the stage for an unusually strong type of communication process, because the viewer is willing, even eager, to receive what the communicator has to offer. The object of the moviemaker, then, becomes one of persuading viewers to cross the distance that separates them from the screen, and to enter imaginatively the space of the screen world to experience vicariously the events that occur within it.

This is where the emotional aspect of movie-viewing becomes important. The vicarious involvement affects the viewer both physiologically and emotionally. For example, as the unidentified man carrying a knife stalks the unsuspecting woman through the jagged patterns of shadow and light in the deserted city streets, the viewer experiences fear for the fate of the endangered woman. This results in actual physiological changes: the heart rate increases, the palms may become sweaty, and the overall condition would be one of approximating fear. This intense vicarious involvement in the flow of events is brought about because of two principal factors. The first is displacement of attention, which allows viewers consciously to ignore technique and style and focus primarily on the unfolding narrative events. The second is their identification with stars, characters, story types and situations.

The viewers' desire to 'enter' the narrative events of the movie is matched by the moviemaker's desire to create a narrative that would encourage viewers to do exactly that. This explains the attraction the narrative form has for the moviemaker. The narrative form is developed to guarantee unflagging interest by omitting the 'dead spots', and by refining resources of suspense.

The technologies involved in movie-making also help in this by masking the techniques of narration. Camera technology (as exemplified by deep focus in particular) and camera movements (determined by the actions), combined with invisible editing all tend to blur the limits of screen space. The entire movie is constructed in such a way as to rivet attention on the story, allowing viewers to become deeply involved with the characters in the movie and in the sequence of situations in which these characters find themselves. Once inside the theatre, even for the solitary moviegoer the experience becomes essentially a collective one. In sociological terms the audience for movies is "an unstructured group" (Jarvie 1970: 89) in that it has "no social organization, no body of custom and tradition, no established set of rules or rituals, no organized group of sentiments, no structure of status roles, and no established leadership". Of course, as Jarvie (ibid.) notes, "any particular neighbourhood audience, which in suburb or drive-in is likely to reflect some of the characteristics of the surrounding society it is recruited from, is less unstructured".

## THE NATURE OF MOVIE AUDIENCES

The audience is a collectivity of heterogeneous individuals who have come together for the sole purpose of seeing a movie, and even here there is a wide variety of personal reasons behind the decision to attend. However, once the movie begins, the communicative interaction creates an audience from the heterogeneity, and a triadic relationship develops between screen and audience. The message does not just go from the screen to the individual; it is interpreted, enhanced, amplified, diminished, or even misinterpreted by interaction with other members of the audience. This audience interaction is most clearly exemplified by the presence of one or two persons who laugh (sometimes too loudly) in the right places in a comedy, or perhaps in the wrong place in a drama. This sets the mood for the rest of the audience, who sometimes may object to the response if it is not in keeping with the overall mood intended by the moviemaker. A more pervasive type of audience interaction is the hushed, quiet concentration in a dramatic scene or the definite air of tension experienced in a horror film, to be punctuated by screams of fear at appropriate moments. These collective moods contribute to the overall reception of the movie's message.

The spontaneity of response is carefully calculated, for as anyone can see, the audiences always cheer in the same places, interact with applause as the hero wreaks vengeance after suffering a long period of tension-building humiliation, and the final denouncement is always calculated to elicit a warm, self-satisfied response from audiences who obviously have a close identification with the major character and who see his victory as symbolic of the triumph of the little man over an increasingly complex bureaucratic society.

## MOVIES AND MODERN SOCIETY

Exactly what is the function of movies in modern society? Why do people continue to attend what should be by now an almost technologically redundant medium in a world where audio-visual images can be much more easily and cheaply obtained? Several theories have been advanced in response to these questions: Some see movies primarily as 'entertainment' while others are more concerned with their latent effects as a reflector of the stress patterns and the commensurate needs of their audience. Based on the theory that people go to movies primarily to 'get away from their problems', observers have suggested that people attend movies more often, and in larger numbers, during economic crises and wars. Their anxieties must be relieved by some interpretation or form of reassurance. Thus, movie attendance could act as indicator of tensions in society. In addition, as the traditional family structure disintegrates, there is a greater reliance by young people on all the mass media to provide an interpretation of life, which was once the function of family and cultural traditions. A case can be made for understanding movie going as an interaction between audience expectancies and the fulfilment of gratifications. In simple terms, the audience believes that by going to a particular movie, it will receive some sort of satisfaction of its need to be entertained.

## CINEMA AND FANDOM

We all know who the fans are. They're the ones who wear the colours of their favourite team, the ones who record their soap operas on VCRs to watch after their work day is over, the ones who tell you every detail about a movie star's life and work, the ones who sit in line for hours to get front-row tickets to rock concerts. Fans are, in fact, the most visible and identifiable of audiences. The literature on fandom is haunted by images of deviance, with the fan being consistently characterised (referencing the term's origins) as a potential fanatic.

Mark David Chapman's killing of ex-Beatle John Lennon, and John Hinckley's attempted assassination of President Ronald Reagan (to gain and keep the attention of actress Jodie Foster) are frequently brought up as iconic examples of the obsessed loner type. Though not all soccer fans engage in spectator violence, the association between fandom and violent, irrational mob behaviour is often assumed. Fans are characterised as easily roused into violent and destructive behaviour, once assembled into a crowd and attending competitive sports events. But what is assumed to be true of fans — that they are potentially deviant as loners or as members of a mob, can be connected with deeper and more diffuse assumptions about modern life. Each fan type mobilises related assumptions about modern individuals: for instance, the obsessed loner invokes the image of the vulnerable, irrational victim of mass persuasion. These assumptions about alienation, atomisation, vulnerability and irrationality are central aspects of twentieth-century beliefs about modernity. Communities are envisioned as supportive and protective: they are believed to offer identity and connection in relation to traditional bonds, including race, religion and ethnicity. As these communal bonds are loosened or discarded, the individual is perceived as vulnerable — he or she is 'unstuck from the cake of custom' — and has no solid, reliable orientation in the world.

The modernity critique, with its associated imagery of the atomised individual and the faceless crowd, is mostly social theory: it does not directly develop assumptions about individual psychology. Nonetheless, it implies a connection between social and psychological conditions — a fragmented and incomplete modern society yields a fragmented and incomplete modern self. What we find, in the literature of fan-celebrity relationships, is a psychologised version of the mass society critique. Fandom, especially 'excessive' fandom, is defined as a form of psychological compensation, an attempt to make up for all that modern life lacks.

Fandom is often conceived of as a chronic attempt to compensate for a perceived personal lack of autonomy, absence of community, incomplete identity, lack of power and lack of recognition. The literature on fandom, celebrity and media influence tells us that fans suffer from psychological inadequacy, and are particularly vulnerable to media influence and crowd contagion. They seek contact with famous people in order to compensate for their own inadequate lives. Because modern life is alienating and atomised, fans develop loyalties to celebrities and sports teams to bask in reflected glory, and attend rock concerts and sports events to feel an illusory sense of community

Much social analysis gets conducted from this savannah of smug superiority, particularly research on media effects. Whether concerned with media uses and gratifications, or the circulation of ideology, or the reasons for fandom, researchers see viewers, consumers and fans as victims of forces that somehow cannot and will not influence 'us'. The commentator on fandom is protected by reason or education or critical insight: thanks to these special traits, 'we' don't succumb to whatever it is we believe applies to 'them'. What it means to be a fan should be explored in relation to the larger question of what it means to desire, cherish, seek, long, admire, envy, celebrate, protect and ally with others. Fandom is an aspect of how we make sense of the world, both in relation to the mass media and in relation to our historical, social and cultural location. Fandom is a common feature of popular culture in industrial societies. It selects from the repertoire of mass-produced and mass-distributed entertainment certain performers, narratives or genres, and takes them into the culture of a self-selected fraction of people. They are then reworked into an intensely pleasurable, intensely signifying popular culture that is both similar to, yet significantly different from, the culture of more 'normal' popular audiences. Fandom is typically associated with cultural forms that the dominant value system denigrates — pop music, romance novels, comics and Hollywood stars (sports, probably because of their appeal to masculinity, are an exception). It is thus associated with the cultural tastes of subordinated formations of people, particularly those disempowered by any combination of gender, age, class and race.

All popular audiences engage in varying degrees of semiotic productivity, producing meanings and pleasures that pertain to their social situation out of the products of the culture industries. But fans often turn this semiotic productivity into some form of textual production that can circulate in — and thus help to define — the fan community. They create a fan culture with its own system of production and distribution that forms what I shall call a 'shadow cultural economy', which lies outside that of the cultural industries yet shares features with them which more normal popular culture lacks.

## FANDOM IN TAMIL NADU

Fandom seems to be a phenomenon that has a long history in Tamil Nadu. *Chilappathiharam*, a famous epic from Tamil Nadu, supposedly written in the eighteeth century, talks about fandom. *Kovalan,* the hero of the epic, was a fan of a performing artist *Madhavi.* The main plot of the story is built around the attachment between the performer and the audience. The history of film fandom in Tamil Nadu is also a long one, going back to the very beginning of the silent era. However, stage actors and actresses also had a very active fan following. There are various ways in which Tamil fandom was popularly expressed. Even 50 years ago many products in the market were named after actors, actresses and films. Even beggars were singing popular film songs to beg in trains and buses.

Fandom was the result of the growth in popularity of films in Tamil Nadu, and today it is quite common to see fans decorating film theatres and garlanding posters of their favourite actors and actresses. The fan clubs in Tamil Nadu are very active and their presence in the state is very strong. They are involved in social service, hold rallies on the birthdays of their matinee idols and are even ready to give up their life for them. In extreme cases film fans in Tamil Nadu have built temples for their favourite actress (*The Times of India*, 9 March 1993). The cult of M.G. Ramachandran, the film actor who later became the state's chief minister, was started by Mr Gopalasundaram. The followers wear black *dhotis* and abstain from wearing slippers, eating meat and drinking alcohol. They bathe before dawn and pray to MGR for forty days before undertaking a pilgrimage to MGR's *samadhi*. They also claim that many miracles have taken place in their lives. All this has had a strong impact on the political history of Tamil Nadu, where film personalities double up as political leaders. In fact, since 1967, all chief ministers have been elected on the basis of their popularity in films.

However, Tamil Nadu film fans do not limit their affiliation to just vernacular films and the actors and actresses of the Tamil film industry. In Madurai one can come across fan clubs that are devoted to Hong Kong action hero Jackie Chan, Hindi actor Shah Rukh Khan and Hollywood idol Sharon Stone.

## WHY CINEMA IS POPULAR

To what extent is the popular cinema a reflection of society's interests and 'ways of seeing'? More specifically, what does its particular confection of ingredients tell us about the society that supports and sustains it? Though there is no one consensual view of what cinema is all about, yet writers and critics of the genre all affirm that cinema, in telling stories and portraying characters and events, is an attempt to make symbolic sense of the world. Its symbols and archetypes are drawn from society and reflect the classifications, interpretations and inconsistencies that society imposes on the individual understanding of the world. To this extent, the study of cinema — particularly the kind that is widely understood and enjoyed — is a means of gaining access to the organising principles and assumptions with which a particular society attempts to order and conceptualise its experience.

To the question, 'Why is the Bombay commercial film so enduringly popular?' — is offered the explanation that the masses everywhere seek pleasure and distraction from the daily grind, and that they find it in the explosive action and syrupy sentiment of the cinema. Because mass entertainment is manufactured for sale to an anonymous mass audience, its products are tailored to meet an average of tastes.

## CINEMA AND CULTURE

Films are cultural events; but they are not autonomous in that their meaning and significance are derived in large measure from the cultural matrix in which they operate, as well as their relationship to other films. It is important to bear in mind the fact that cinema is never merely the display of objects or the transmission of a message; it is always seen as a contested terrain of meaning where complex relationships between people and class operate. Its sounds and images reflect both the way in which it was produced and the reason for its production. We can thus assert that cinema is a process of social production that situates men and women in specific personalities in relation to film industries, social relationships and cultural discourses.

In the modern world, film constitutes a part of the larger entertainment industry in most countries. In the commercial cinema, film came to be perceived as yet another commodity in which the social relationships of its production are reflective of the capitalist economy in general. Cultural production and commodity production are integrated, and two overlapping domains of activity — the ideological and material — play a critical role here. Commercial cinema generates in the audiences the wants, the fears and the anxieties by which they are situated in the capitalist society. The forms of mass entertainment are cultural products in both the ideological and material senses. The material production process is complete only when the viewer buys the ticket at the counter. As with all other commodities in the market, for film, too, the consumer is all-important. It is generally said by film critics and cultural historians that cinema reflects culture. This is normally interpreted to mean that the content of a film reflects the values, beliefs and the contours of the culture in which it was made. But one has to expand the comprehension of this statement considerably if one is to study cinema as a cultural practice with anything like the thoroughness that it deserves. Film is not merely a reflection of society; it is an active intervention in it.

The statement 'film reflects culture' should be construed to mean that films are active generators of cultural meaning and that a careful examination of them will tell us how and why they come into being. In any consideration of cinema as a bearer of meaning and pleasure, the nature of the audiences, which up until now were treated as inert and undifferentiated, needs to be studied more carefully. During the last decade or so, there has been an increasing — and healthy — tendency to integrate the artistic, social, economic  and technological dimensions of popular entertainment.

British cultural analysts, notably those who, like Stuart Hall, belong to the Birmingham school, focused attention on texts and their diverse modes of reception. According to them, the viewing of a film could be seen as a negotiation of meaning between the viewer and the film. In other words, far from being passive consumers, audiences are active participants in the generation of meaning and pleasure. . As a consequence of this line of thinking, the concept of audience has begun to attract greater attention from film scholars, and the interface between filmic text and the differentiated audience has become even more important.  Film audiences, far from being a passive and undifferentiated mass, are extremely diverse, constantly exercise judgment, and are actively involved in the process of creating meaning. Mass audiences represent a range of social groups and subcultures that are reflective of the social formation of capitalist societies. Audiences are also differentiated along a plurality of interesting axes such as age, gender, race, religion, profession and education. As Fiske (1987) points out, the social position of any one person within this network of axes is nomadic and unstable; hence, the social alliances he or she establishes change as different axes are granted different priorities at different periods.

Film audiences are also extremely discriminating.  How else could one explain the fact that while one film succeeds at the box office, another made by the same director, using the same formula and the same glamorous stars, fails dismally? They are also amazingly productive; the ways in which they derive pleasure and meaning from films and create newer subjectivities in relation to the films that they see are as fascinating as they are complex.

In modern societies cultural meanings are not stable, monological and unitary but volatile, plural and fragmented. Institutional structure, economic forces, material foundations and symbolic constructs all competitors in the process of cultural construction. How certain groups appropriate cultural values and meanings as a way of gaining legitimacy for their actions is a complex and problematic phenomenon. Walter Benjamin once remarked that, "There is no document of civilization which is not at the same time a document of barbarism" (Benjamin 1970: 256). His statement calls attention to the effects of violence and social domination that are endemic to constructions of culture. Cultural meanings are generated by human groups contending with each other in a terrain characterised by domination and inequality. It follows, therefore, that culture cannot rise above or remain untouched by the material forces and relations of production in any given society. This is, of course, not to suggest that culture is a mere reflection of the economic system, as some Marxists would have us believe. What this points to is that the interaction among material forces, relations of production and symbolic meaning have to be examined in their true mutual complexities. The generation of cultural meaning is always already implicated in the political and economic behaviours and social relations of domination. It is only by recognising this fact that we will be able to understand the true nature of culture as one of the sites where the contestation for power, hegemony, dominance, and the establishment of a set of values and ideologies over rival ones takes place.

Moreover, film is not just a reflection of a pre-given experience; rather, it is the creation of it. The making of a film and its subsequent viewing by audiences are interventions in the social production of meaning. Therefore, the more suitable trope for the understanding of cinema and social experience is not the mirror but a field of force, a terrain where forces of textual authority, resistance and subversion meet in unexpected ways.

## MOVIES AS MASS COMMUNICATION

Movies are a facet of mass culture and mass art, or in other words, one type of "mass-mediated culture". The concept of mass-mediated culture has been defined by Michael Real (1977: 14) as encompassing "expressions of culture as they are received from contemporary mass media, whether they arise from elite, folk, popular, or mass origins", and is based on the assumption that "all culture when transmitted by mass media becomes in effect popular culture". Movies are popular culture in the sense that their appeal depends on a skilful combination of familiarity and novelty and often involves a certain degree of empathy between the audience and the creator, with much of the latter's success depending on personal 'style'. In many other instances, however, movies are mass culture products since they are designed to please the average taste of an undifferentiated audience. As with the other media, the pervasiveness of the movies (both nationally and internationally), the nature of the messages they convey, and the role that they occupy in the overall cultural system make them significant objects deserving of attention and requiring a multidisciplinary or interdisciplinary perspective to be fully understood.

With the advent of television, however, the role of movies in the media environment has changed. Movies are no longer perceived as the major social force they once were. The displacement by television of the movie's role as the most important entertainment medium has caused us to devalue its functions and influence. But this attitude neglects the fact that movies are attended, at one time or another, by all segments of society, have immense appeal for a particular age group in society (adolescents and young adults), and occupy a special place in the social ritual of youth at a time when they are establishing patterns for the rest of their lives.

However, the situation in India, particularly in the state of Tamil Nadu, is very different. The advent of television has in no way reduced the popularity of films. The number of films being produced has increased, even as more and more television programmes are being made.

In line with McLuhan's (1964) dictum that the structure of one medium becomes the content of the medium that follows it, movies have drawn very heavily on literary works as source material — more specifically, on the novel's narrative fiction approach, and on stage plays, novellas, short stories and, to a lesser extent, on non-fiction. So strong is this link that film production companies are willing to pay huge sums for the movie rights of best-selling novels —or even for prospective best sellers. Although making money is the primary goal of movies, it is a business that is at the same time an art.

## CONCLUSION

Film is fundamentally a medium of communication that captivates us through its parade of images, movements, light, sound and colour. We tend to invest the filmic image with authority, credibility and legitimacy. The cinema itself constitutes a powerful mechanism for socialisation, and the popular image is a vehicle that propagates the established conventions and dominant meanings of society. At its best, film is an art form capable of delving into the depths of a culture. Although in viewing the film as an art form we privilege its aesthetic dimension, this by no means holds sway over cinema as a social institution, for art and aesthetics are informed by complex historical as well as contemporaneous political and economic forces. Although the dominant conception of cinema in contemporary society revolves around its entertainment value, it is important to point out that the over-attention to cinema as entertainment is primarily a by-product of the concerns of consumer societies. To privilege film as a means of expression which reveals certain formal or deep cultural contingencies governing the lives of the people of third world countries is to shift attention to a fuller understanding of the functioning of the medium in society. This is why a principal concern of Tamil cinema has to do with the nature of the filmic image, the way filmic signification establishes meanings and the manner in which these relate to the system of power or the existing status quo which delineates the scope of social relations.

Cinema and viewers are in a symbiotic relationship. On one side are the characteristics of the film medium as perceived by the viewer — those to which s/he most readily responds. These elements are visual primacy, visual context and relevance of content. On the other side are those characteristics of the viewers themselves, which normally affect perception. These elements are age, sex, intelligence, level of formal education and, above all, one's cultural roots and the shared ethos of a society.

## REFERENCES

Abell, Walter (1966). *The Collective Dream in Art.* New York.

Benjamin, Walter (1970). *Illuminations.* London: Fontana.

Cohen-Seat, Gilbert, H. Gastaut and J. Bert (1954). Modifications de l'E.E.G. pendant la projection cinematographique. *Revue Internationale de Filmologie,* Vol. 5, No. 16 (January-March).

Fiske, John (1987). *Television Culture,* London: Routledge

Freud, Sigmund (1965). *The Interpretation of Dreams.* Translated and edited by James Strachey. New York.

Gernelli, Agostino (1950). Le film, procede d'analyse projective. *Revue Internationale de Filmologie,* Vol. 2, No. 6.

Jarvie, I.C (1970). *Towards a Sociology of Cinema.* London.

Lacassin, Francis (1967). 'Feuillade' in *Anthologie du cinema,* Vol. II. Paris.

McLuhan, Marshall (1964). *Understanding Media.* London: Routledge Kegan and Paul.

Metz, Christian (1965). A propos de l'impression de realite au cinema. *Caniers du Cinema*, Nos 166/16 (May/June).

Real, Michael R. (1977). *Mass Mediated Culture* Englewood Cliffs, N.J.: Prentice Hall.

Silverstone, Roger (1981). *The Message of Television: Myth, Narrative in Contemporary Culture*. London: Heinemann.

Spottiswoode (1965). *A Grammar of The Film.* Berkeley and Los Angeles.

Tyler, Parker (1947). *Magic and Mye Movies.* New York.

## CHAPTER 10

# The Role of Music in Religious Communication: Implications for a Theological Curriculum

## *Hannibal Cabral*

> Music is so powerful a thing that it ravisheth the soul, the queen of
> the senses, by sweet pleasure...and corporeal tunes pacify our
> incorporate soul...And 'tis not only men (sic) that are affected
> ...Fish...as common experience evinceth, are much influenced
> by music. All singing birds are pleased by it, especially
> nightingales... and bees among the rest, though they may be
> flying away, when they hear any tingling sound, will tarry
> behind harts, hinds, horses. Dogs, bears are exceedingly delighted
> with it...And in Lydia in the midst of a lake there be certain floating
> islands (if ye believe it) that after music will dance (Wilson–
> Dickenson 1992).[1]

Music has always been considered communicative, having the
power to touch the senses of not just human beings, but also of
nature and the whole of creation. Music is an art that expresses
the sentiments and emotions of both the composer and the presenter
through either musical instruments or singing. It goes without
saying that the basic nature of any art is to communicate truth to
others. Music too communicates something of one person to
another. Because of its complex nature and effect, discussing music
is a difficult venture. Therefore, in this paper I confine my
reflections to some of the issues relating to the role of music in

---

[1]Quoted by Andrew Wilson-Dickenson (1992), pp. 11-12.

communication, which derive from my experience as a pastor and a theological teacher.

The main policy document of the World Association for Christian Communication, 'Christian Principles of Communication', lists five dimensions of communication from a biblical perspective: *a*) communication it creates community, *b*) it is participatory, *c*) it liberates, *d*) it supports and develops cultures, and *e*) it is prophetic. To a certain extent, even music as a mode of communication endorses these and other dimensions like sustaining and transforming individuals and communities. In our reflection on the role of music in communication and on the nature of religious music, I shall be guided by these principles.

## MUSIC — BUILDING UP AND PARTICIPATING IN COMMUNITY

One of the most basic functions of music is to involve persons in the making of it. Whether it is music that has evolved from the people of the Stone Age or those of the present age, it knits the feelings, frustrations, joys and celebrations of the people in a corporate and collective manner. The value that is central to any music is active involvement rather than passive observation. Whether the songs are sung in paddy fields, in workplaces, in temples or churches, at concerts or by *bhajan* groups, music demands active involvement and thus creates communities. Music brings people together, which is what any communication aims to do: bind people together in a common bond. By expressing the message of togetherness and unity, music breaks down barriers and builds bridges.

Another aspect of music is that it encourages learning and remembering. It therefore acts as a mode of transmitting and carrying forward the traditions and values of the present generation to the future. For example, singing the song 'We shall overcome' in a civil rights march in the 1960s helped the marchers to identify with and strengthen the commitment of each of them to the common purpose of the group. Such music draws attention to the common bond that holds the group together. Lyrics and songs with a liberating dimension are now being used by leaders like Gaddar of Andhra Pradesh and Siddalingiah of Karnataka. But while it is true that music can transmit effectively the tenets, values and traditions of any given community, it can also, on occasion, engender oppression. For example, numerous traditional songs in the Karnataka region have been instrumental in continuing customs and rituals like the sati, the dowry system, the devadasi system and the karma theory.

One of the most basic functions of religious music is to involve persons, i.e., the whole worshipping community, in the making of it. The central aim of this type of worship is to place people as a community before God and connect and bind them to him and to each other.

## MUSIC AS A QUEST FOR THE TRANSCENDENTAL

It is well known that the temple and the church have been the cradles of many forms of art. It is in the courtyard of the temple or of the church that these arts were nurtured, enriched and developed. The music of India, from the earliest times of which there is any record, has been closely associated with religion. In particular, it was associated with the *Sama Veda*, one of the four ancient sacred books of Hindu religion. Most of the songs and hymns that are referred to in Jewish history are related to hymns and music performed in the temple. When the Hebrew Bible describes the arrival of the ark of the covenant in Jerusalem, it notes that a well-trained and official body of musicians led the worship (by heredity the privilege of the house of Levi). Together with the text of a song of thanksgiving, all manner of musical instruments are mentioned — a list more extensive than any other hitherto recorded.

Rabindranath Tagore, the famous poet of Bengal, writes. "For us music has above all a transcendental significance. It disengages the spiritual from the happenings of life; it suggests a relationship of the human soul with the soul of things beyond" (White 1957: 26).

Mention of music in the New Testament is limited to a few comments about congregational singing. For example, there is mention of the hymn sung by Jesus and his disciples at the end of the meal in the upper room (Matt. 26: 30; Mark 14: 36). St Paul advises two of the newly founded churches to "teach and admonish one another in all wisdom, and ...sing Psalms and hymns and spiritual songs with thankfulness in your hearts to God" (Col. 3: 16; Eph. 5:19). According to Robert H. Mitchell, the history of the church shows no consensus concerning the role of music. It was in the monasteries that formal musical styles were developed and musical notations invented. In the Middle Ages Gregorian (or Plain) Chant became the origin of a multitude of people's hymns, some of which are still sung today. It was in the church that music was nurtured as an enriching part of human experience. During the reformation period, music found a life of its own outside the ecclesiastical circle (Mitchell 1978: 77–78).

There is a special place for music in all religions. If religion consists in binding God and humans together and humans with each other, this is expressed through songs, chants and music. If we take away music from any religion, we find it void of expression. All worship comes alive through music, chants and liturgy, which is why so much attention is paid to music in divine worship, particularly in relation to lyrics and hymns. When these three elements are well blended, they can express our inner urge and desire to be united with the divine very effectively.

## MUSIC CREATES IDENTITY AND OPENNESS

There is no country, nation or culture that does not have musical art forms typical to its nature. Music and other arts keep the countries, nations and cultures alive and give cultural and social identity to persons and communities. At the same time, music is also an ecumenical language that does not limit itself to a particular culture or space. That is why a real artist is able to enjoy music in any form and so see in it something deeper and more profound. The fact that music can be composed in various languages by people from different religions, cultures and ethnicities only shows that it can cut across all boundaries — whether religious or any other — and transcend all petty and small minds. It can have an exhilarating effect on one and all.

## Music as Feeling

One of the most powerful usages of music is in drama or in cinema, where it can most effectively communicate the mood or emotional state of the people or the context. When music is used with sensitivity, it can communicate with great richness, and with equal power, the variety of human emotions, from rage to tenderness. The sound produced by certain musical instruments is often used symobolically to represent certain emotions. For instance, the sweet tone of the violin is often as a symbol of love, and the melodious music of the *shehnai* is used to create the feeling of despair, worry, sadness and fear. The situation of war is often symbolised by the music of brass bands with their cymbals, bringing to mind sudden flashes of past victories. These same processes are at work when we use music in worship. As Mitchell says:

> When the derived function of music is to create a *feeling* of reverence or celebration; when the minister says, 'I like good music because it gets people ready for sermon'; when the organ plays quietly beneath the devotional parts of the service such as prayer or communion; when the choir hums sweetly and softly during a time of invitation; then we are in this dangerous and elusive but important territory where music is being used to create mood.

A few congregations of the Church of South India (CSI) in Karnataka have experimented with using music to create certain moods. Instrumental music is played softly at the time of dedication, commitment and prayer. Many of the fundamentalist groups bank on this kind of music in their worship to create a special mood of reverence or celebration or even ecstasy. Sometimes overt and over-use can lead to the "danger of striking attitudes in worship" (ibid. 86), which may lead the devotees to become fanatics. The reason is that in several of the mainline churches, it is expected that certain attitudes should characterise Christian worship. The commonest of these is an appropriate quiet and sobriety. In many Christian congregations worship leaders are expected to act with dignity. Therefore, caution should be taken to avoid any hint of lightness or frivolity that might be incompatible with such expectations. Perhaps separate worship sessions could be arranged to use the mood of celebration and joy for those who are in need of it. At the same time, the pastor or the leader of the worship should be in a position to select appropriate hymns and music to set the tone for meaningful worship. According to Archibald Davison:

> The finest church music suggests the church and nothing outside of it, for that music is not sensuous or emotional as is the music of our secular world.... One need but ask himself, "Is this the music of every world? Is its language familiar to me in many forms? (That's bad). Or is it a speech apart; remote, archaic perhaps, sacerdotal, strange; a language to which the church alone would be hospitable? (That's good)" (Davison 1952: 129).

Music that is associated solely with worship and with nothing else may be desirable to evoke feelings of mystery and reverence. But as a general criterion for religious music it is more than questionable. Can we really restrict the experience of the divine to just this kind of music, without acknowledging the fact that the divine presence and truth can be grasped in ever more fresh and new ways? What is important is that we acknowledge our commitment to God's revelation and reflect this in our music and singing In other words, it is remembering God's mighty acts and what they mean in today's context that can lead to confidence and hope, courage and anticipation, excitement and joy, and true peace.

## Music as Revelation

We live in a world of communication explosion. The messages that we wish to communicate to others no longer need to be limited to the spoken or printed word. We can communicate effectively the same messages through the arts, especially through music, and particularly to the people at the grassroots level. Today, access to a variety of music has become easy with the availability of cassettes, compact discs, videocassettes, the Internet and other technological innovations. But church music has the ability to express the inexpressible. Speaking about the incredible truth of the incarnation — the identification of God with humanity, Karl Barth said:

> Words are hostile to it (the genuine miracle of Christmas), detrimental, always powerless to justify it. The man who undertakes to celebrate in *words* his own "elevated humanity" becomes all too easily confusing and incredible to himself. "All patterns are too stiff for me and all speech too tedious and cold." How fortunate that when we are disturbed and oppressed by the problem of words we can flee to the realm of music, to Christian music and to a musical Christianity! Exactly because of its lack of concepts, music is the true and legitimate bearer of the message of Christmas (Barth 1962: 157).

There is always the possibility that God may break through to us, revealing himself through the ineffable. The description of the dedication of Solomon's Temple (II Chronicles, 5: 13) is a case in point. When the song was raised with trumpets and cymbals and other musical instruments, the house of the Lord was filled with a cloud, so that the priests could not stand to minister because the glory of the Lord filled the house of God.

## THE CHALLENGES AND IMPLICATIONS OF MUSIC FOR THEOLOGICAL EDUCATION

### Contextualising Music

Missionaries have played a major role in establishing and sustaining the churches in India. Their commitment to improve the religious, social, economic, educational and medical fields has been laudable. At the same time, it is a matter of regret that there have been relatively few missionaries throughout the history of Christian missions in Karnataka, who have shown any real interest in indigenous Indian music, not in terms of appreciating it for itself, but for promoting its value and developing it among Christians. As Emmons White very appropriately said: "Had missionaries given equal attention to India's musical culture, there might have been less ground for the charges that Indian converts tend to be de-nationalised and that the church is essentially a foreign institution" (White 1957: 69).

It is high time that the church educates the people to live out their faith, keeping in mind the cultural ethos of our soil.  In particular, our worship and liturgy should be rooted in our own culture and adopting Indian music is part of this.  Bringing about such a change in churches where the music and rituals are still Western is a challenging task, and until and unless sincere efforts are made to create awareness, the necessary transformation will be difficult to achieve. It is therefore extremely important that theological education equips students to create new contextual lyrics and use appropriate music. This would also include the skill of analysing existing hymns in relation to their writing style, translations, melodies and beats, and their general appropriateness for the present generation.

**Encouraging Innovation**

Indian society has passed through many drastic social and cultural changes. Innovative experiments have already been made by many denominations in the field of Christian indigenous worship and liturgy.  Christian musicians committed to improvisation in liturgy and worship need to be encouraged.  In particular, such elements of worship as confession, thanksgiving, praise, the apostle's creed, and the Lord's prayer and benediction should be cast into indigenous religious patterns, including musical composition. Amidst the current media explosion, it is evident that the present generation has developed a tendency to accept whatever is exciting and relevant to the modern context. It is sad to note that they blindly borrow whatever comes from the West, especially in the form of popular pop music. This has eroded the culture of the soil. New songs need to be composed on contemporary issues and themes by Indian lyricists and composers with indigenous charisma and taste. The ultimate goal of producing and performing new, contextualised works is to enrich our understanding and experience of God, bear new witnesses to the Gospel and to nourish the spiritual growth of the kingdom of God. New ventures in music should interpret our faith by reflecting images, issues, struggles and concerns for a just and peaceful society. At the same time, to ascertain our Indian affinity, we have to go back to our roots and find the values and truth embodied in the lyrics written by our ancestors. In many of the churches in Karnataka, lyrics are no longer sung because the members of congregations have forgotten the tunes. But recently, however, when with the support of the Church of South India, the Karnataka Christian Communication Service, Mangalore, arranged a three-day workshop on writing contemporary lyrics for the use in the churches of Karnataka, participants were able to produce and compose a few new lyrics that aimed to raise awareness on issues like HIV/AIDS, cancer, depression, drug abuse, ecology and women's empowerment, as well as songs for house-warming ceremonies, the harvest festival and church dedication. These songs are now available on cassettes and CDs. Amalorpavdass puts such efforts into a wider context:

> Indigenisation takes account of all the realities that constitute human existence today, that shape the life of societies and nations, that mark the history of the world; problems of hunger and disease, ignorance and illiteracy, unemployment and frustration, struggles of humanity for liberation from all forces of slavery and alienation, wars and world peace, social justice and integral development of man, contemporary culture and its all pervading effects (Amalorpavdass 1973: 8-9).

Though contemporary musicians have written several lyrics, they are clearly influenced by Western practices. In addition, in many churches the use of the lyric has become secondary, with hymns being given paramount importance. At present, there is an emotional debate going on about whether sexist language can and should be eliminated from the hymn books. If music is a medium of participation and of building a just human community, then where is the place for hymns like, 'Rise up O men of God' or 'Men and children everywhere'? Thus, there is undoubtedly a need for re-writing hymns from an inclusive perspective, keeping in mind the context of religious plurality. Furthermore, there are many traditional hymns whose imagery is rooted in the concept of the holy war. Though some of it is based on the imagery found in the Scriptures, their use is being questioned today, given that we live in a world where communities are being fragmented because of the war and violence. In addition, the hymn books used in most churches have not been revised for the last several years. As a result, new compositions have yet to be taken on board. In view of all this, there is need to create a forum that could introduce and propagate lyrics written and composed by contemporary writers and musicians. Theological colleges could take the lead in their respective areas for revising, reformulating and re-inventing religious music in our communities.

## Need for Systematic Study on Christian Music

There are several questions regarding the quality and use of church music that need serious consideration. For instance, should particular lyrics or hymns determine the character of worship? Have we alienated the common folk by only using lyrics from the Brahmanical tradition and ignoring the tradition of the village folk song? What about the use of Bhajans in our worship? Which lyrics are used most often by congregations? What is the fate of lyrics that are seldom used in worship? What are the reasons for not using them? What are the contextual issues — such as justice, harmonious living, peace — that need to be dealt with in the production of new lyrics? Is it necessary set lyrics to Western melodies and notes? How can we improve Indian church music? What is our response towards the emerging trend wherein people write lyrics and compose melodies without a proper theological thrust and musical knowledge? Adequate answers to all these questions can only be possible after a careful study has been made of the present use of music in churches in all parts of India.

## Proper Training

An oft-raised issue concerns the variation in the singing of lyrics in different churches. The main reason for this is that the notations for the lyrics have not been preserved or printed systematically as they have in the case of hymns. Since lyrics have been transmitted orally from group to group and from generation to generation, the original *raga* and *tala* have been gradually forgotten or replaced by other tunes. Due to this, in many churches there are quite a number of congregational lyrics that bear little or no resemblance to any known *raga* and appear to be simple Christian folk songs. It is necessary, therefore, to re-set and refresh many of the Christian lyrics, and restore to them their proper tune and *tala*. Furthermore, congregations should be trained to sing them correctly. To do this it is possible that we may have to use some of the resources that are found among people who are experts in this field but belong to other faiths. Along with reviving old lyrics, opportunity and encouragement should be given to young talent with the aptitude and capacity for producing new lyrics and new compositions. Youth should be encouraged to train themselves in using indigenous musical instruments. The new compositions should be made available to the common people either in book form or through cassettes and CDs.

Music and lyric writing should thus form an important component of theological education. For instance, in order to help theological students develop their artistic talents in music, the Karnataka Theological College in Mangalore offers training in singing lyrics as well as hymns. It has also introduced a course on audio-visual methods to help the students improve other methods of communication such as story-telling, drama, innovative liturgical skills and selecting songs and music for worship with the help of experts in these fields. The audio-video studio in the campus has been an added blessing for this venture.

## REFERENCES

Amalorpavdass, D.S. (1973). Efforts Made in the Roman Catholic Church towards Indigenisation. *Bangalore Theological Reform*, Vol. 5. January–June.

Barth, Karl (1962). *Theology and Church*. London: SCM Press.

Davison, Archibald (1952). *Church Music*. Harvard University Press.

Mitchell, Robert H. (1978). *Ministry and Music*. Philadelphia: The Westminster Press.

White, Emmons E. (1957). *Appreciating India's Music*. Mysore: Christian Literature Society.

Wilson-Dickenson, Andrew (1992). *A Brief History of Christian Music*. London: Lion Publications.

## CHAPTER 11

# Freedom Songs, Popular Culture and Subalternity

### Etienne Rassendren

There is an extraordinary scene in Steven Spielberg's film, *The Amistad* (1997),[1] in which an enslaved captive form Sierra Leone recasts the Christ figure as his own mystical liberator from captivity. Simultaneously, white anti-slavery activists protest the practice of the slave trade outside his prison. The captive cannot understand the language of Christian redemption at all. Yet he possesses the language of his captors and makes it speak for his freedom. This film-event is relevant even today because it is about *the manner of speaking* that subjugated peoples employ against oppressive, even racist, authority. Like African-American peoples, Other subjugated communities also speak of a world to which they cannot belong but desire to make their own. This cultural strategy is called 'repetition with revision' and is both a mode of *resistance* and a concept of *self*.[2]

Henry Louis Gates Jr., the African-American theorist —

---

[1]This film by Steven Spielberg (1997) examines in great details the disempowering economic and cultural practice of slavery. It graphically describes the trauma and anguish of dislocated people as also their sense making endeavours in an alien land. This truly is a *middle passage* film in which the problem of cultural forgetting is sympathetically portrayed.

[2]This specific idea deals largely with characterising the intellectual and ritual productions of oral cultures, which both access and redefine usually mutual discourse of white racist culture. Hence something negative is often converted into a matter of prime importance. For a more elaborate analysis, see Gates Jr. (1988).

following Geneva Smitherman's communication theory — explains the complex function of *"talkin and testfyin"* to the oppressing centre of control. She claims that it is employed "to insult" the white man by parodying his speech and authority in order to assert the black person's self.[3] Among the many characteristics that Smitherman identifies as black 'signifyin', she focuses pointedly on the "teachy, but not preachy" nature of the discourse, "pun and play of words" in its rhetorical structure and the "logically unexpected" nature of its semantics.[4] These aspects of black signification are aimed at "making a point", and at making sardonic "fun" of white authority in the civilisational sense of North American racist arrogance. Speaking against white power as an act of discursive protest is symbolised in the figure of the "Signifyin Monkey", who as a ritual "trickster" (Gates 1988: 6) imitates but reverses the language of white authority. Indeed, this trickster-figure, like Spielberg's enslaved Sierra Leone character, takes over the language of civilising power and turns it against itself, making the language of black people a powerful mixed idiom of resistance against white cultural authority. African-American ritual performance of resistance, which includes the signifyin' and testifyin', is a mode of black resistance that informs the spirituals and gospels of the African-American tradition. Their singers inhabit the position of the Signifyin' Monkey speaking to white power.

But over time these songs have been *stolen* by the global culture industry and transported to the rest of world as packaged commodities. Those who receive these packaged products understand neither the context nor the experience of subjugation

---

[3]Geneva Smitherman, the famous linguist, whose analysis of orature and oral linguistics is used effectively by Gates Jr. in his work on the African-American literary tradition. For a further understanding of Smitheman's theory, see Gates Jr. (1988), p. 94.

[4]Across the analysis on signification the critic conceptualises signifying as a re-inscribing process of cultural retaliation. He speaks of it as the one central linguistic and literary method that marks the African-American tradition. This process is satirical in nature and is often critical of white culture. See Gates Jr. (1988), pp. 1-6.

felt deeply by the black people of the American South. These songs not only dramatise the pain and anguish of the African-Americans, but also focus attention on the cruelty and brutality suffered by them. There is thus an empowering double-edgedness to the performances of African-American gospels and spirituals. But the largely white, capital-dominated entertainment industry de-contextualises the resistance and history of the popular resistance songs, universalises them into neat bourgeois entertainment packages, and reduces its reception to a whittled-down experience.

Those who belong to subaltern groups within and outside the Western world thus receive only sanitised silences of disassociation and therefore cannot quite identify with the resisting black communities. As a result, subaltern solidarities between those within and outside the North American world remain elusive. As the knowledge of subjugation is made progressively invisible by the protocols of the culture industry, the coming together of oppressed communities from diverse cultural and political locations is further constrained because of the failure to recognise differing yet similar subjugating cultures.

My interest relates specifically to the politics of appropriation that the slave songs have endured. Apart from exploring some aspects of this appropriation to explain the mediation of obedience and silence among subaltern groups, I also examine the role of the culture industry in this process in an effort to explain its power over communication issues. To do this, I draw upon Adorno's concept of the "popular" and Habermas' theory of the "public sphere". I am aware that the African-American peoples and their specific subjugating condition are not perceived by culture theorists as equal or similar to the experiences of subalternity elsewhere, particularly in South Asia. I therefore explore such a discursive possibility in an attempt to theorise the conceptual discordance from which it suffers, and conclude by some comments on subalternity itself.

## NEGRO SPIRITUALS AND GOSPELS: CONTEXT AND ANCESTRY

The most traumatic experience in African-American slave history is the dislocation of black peoples from their native culture and civilisation. In the new world of slavery, the African-American peoples scrape together their native songs and legends in an effort to preserve their cultural memory (Gates 1988: 4). They mix these stories, rites and legends with a deliberately 'broken' variety of English in order to produce a hybrid language and culture. For the African slave, at the height of the Atlantic slave trade, the most violent experience was the terrifying journey from the African coast to the North-American frontiers. Their experience of white brutality in the hold of the slave ships, the constant fear of being 'unloaded' in the sea as 'excess tonnage' (see *The Amistad,* 1997), the confusion over their languages and cultures — all constitute what is euphemistically called the 'middle passage'. Some thinkers assume that for the black slave peoples this middle passage represents their period of 'forgetting', or of cultural amnesia. Gates Jr. disagrees: "The notion that the middle passage was so traumatic that it functioned to create in the African a *tabula rasa* is as odd as it is fiction, a fiction that has served several economic orders and their attendant ideologies" (ibid. 5).

What Gates Jr. is emphasising here is the near impossibility of cultural amnesia, though a disempowering cultural alienation from ethnic specificities is a real experience for the African slave. Thrown among differing ethnicities, the African slave on his/her journey to the New World is distraught and confused, but is also confronted with the potential of cultural exchange against racism. In such a dynamic new context and despite the trauma of and the anger with slavery, the African in the new environment rallies against the grace of Western linguistic superiority and puts together a new Africanised language that will serve as the very culture instrument of resistance. Therefore, in the new world of slavery, they produce a hybrid culture that marks both their difference and resistance. The distinct cultural forms emerging from this mixed experience carry a characteristic doubleness that W.E.B. Du Bois calls the "two-ness" of the African-American identity. In the 'Souls of Black Folks' (1901), Du Bois explains this two-ness (Gates Jr. and Mackay 1997: 615) as a sense-making endeavour that is both "American" and "Negro" alike (ibid.). The language of African narrative, found in the orature of African peoples, conjoins with the language of white power to yield a new and empowering idiom of black address called the *vernacular* (ibid.: 1). When we speak of the 'vernacular' in the African-American tradition, we are largely referring to 'church songs' and other such oral forms, including the contemporary 'rap', that belong to the tradition of black expression. In its earliest form, the vernacular lives in the Negro spirituals and then in the gospels. Although the distinctions between the two forms are hard to depict, it is important to make the difference particularly in terms of theme and periodisation.

The spirituals belong to the earliest period of enslavement, when freedom and liberation implied a return to Africa. In contrast, the gospels speak of a sense of exile, which captures the conflict between 'here' and 'there'. By the time the gospels come into being, the African-American people recognise both the implausibility of returning to the homeland and the value of indigenisation. Liberation now means coming to terms with exile and freedom from the master's whip on the plantation. These evocative songs are performed not only during black church worship but also in the secular public sphere of plantation life. They are not merely ditties that dramatise African-American suffering and subjugation; rather, they serve as daring calls to revolt and rebellion against white masters. Often the call and response structure of the oral song inspires the people to run away from plantation life or to fight against its brutality and hard labour. Many of these gospels and spirituals led to slave rebellion on the plantation or induced men/women to escape to a more free North.

The African-American speaker in this context and in Roman

Jakobson's (1988: 35) terms is both receiver and inhabitant of white violence and African difference respectively. In his 'Linguistics and Poetics', Jakobson speaks of six different aspects of language within the communication paradigm, the most important being 'the message', 'the code' and 'the context'. The message and code signify the substantive content of a human linguistic transaction and the common linguistic graph of a language respectively. The arrangements between the speakers and the listeners are worked out within a context (ibid.: 35). But Jakobson takes his communication paradigm beyond its rather basic tenets when he shows that developing any linguistic transaction further involves reformulating the code and the message differently. In other words, the subject and object of the code and the message largely order the meaning systems of the linguistic context. When applied as a theory of communication to the function of African-American discourse, we can see that the Negro spirituals and the later gospels are the speech of black Otherness which reformulates the 'message' and the 'code' differently (ibid.: 35, 39). The object of this language is both the white master and the black slave. The principal intent of the Negro spirituals and gospels is to take over the language of 'othering' and revise it in a way that will objectify white authority as a symbol of racist violence. This reversal in the grammar of cultural politics attempts to constitute an otherness for black selfhood in order to construct a counter-canonicity for white self-definition. Therefore the refocusing of message and code in Negro spirituals/gospels reverses the contradictory logic and the politics of self and other. In making the functions of the songs both "emotive" and "exhortative" (ibid. 38), the power dynamics between the speaker and listener is altered. Now the producer and consumer, the speaker and listener of the spirituals/gospels are the African-American communities, their trajectory and object of ridicule and denouncement being the white man (Gates 1987: 3-55).

In this way, Negro spirituals and gospels simultaneously violate and free the language of white authority in order to yield a communication paradigm that is disobedient to the hierarchy of linguistic order (Jakobson 1988: 38). The language of white oppression thus begins to serve an altogether alternative and radical purpose in and through Negro spirituals/gospels. The context in which these songs were born foregrounds the peculiarities of African ancestry and the local American condition. The experience of slavery, exile and alienation jostle with the dynamics of indigenisation, citizenship and colour-pride to mark a discursive conjuncture that is beneficial to and inspires identity-formation and self-representation among the black peoples in North America.

## THE AFRICAN-AMERICAN SINGER: NATIVE INFORMANT AND MIMIC RESPONDENT

The African-American Negro spirituals singer recasts herself as the eternal trickster (Gates and Mackay 1997: 6), consistently combining the American word with her African ancestry. She signifies and deploys a dramatically broken English idiom, appropriating in the process the Judeo Christian salvation story to yield concepts of freedom. She uses the call/response mode accompanied by ritual dance, suggesting a combination of discursive practices that disrupt the white master-language and its cultural control. The concept of divinity in African ethnicity is highly humanist in nature. The ancestors that pass into eternity are those that become the spiritual icons of any ethnic community in Africa, and ancestor-worship is often a powerful social event that mediates between the temporal and the eternal. In a grave reversal of commonsense concepts of divinity that normatively speak of a heavenly *a priori* being or force, the African tradition critically moves the human into the sacred. For them, the sacerdotal is a possibility that human endeavour can dream about and attempt. Therefore, the profane consistently contains the sacred. Jesus Christ as the liberator and emancipator of the African-American peoples is appropriated into *this* ethnic conception of divinity, thereby recasting him as a temporal interlocutor of the evil of racism and enslavement. What, then, becomes of a Westernised religious icon is interesting in that the eternal in Western religious iconography is temporised into an earthy, humanising figure.

Besides this conjuncture between the eternal and the temporal, the African and the American, as they join in spirituals and gospels, constitute a subversive praxis that carries a resisting and revolutionary message to inspire rebellion and revolt. The spirituals sung in Southern plantations during the 1880s often subversively communicated the call to revolt or escape from the white slave driver. There is therefore a 'this-worldliness' about the spirituals (ibid.: 6) that allegorises black struggles on the North American mainland. The 'other-worldliness' of American religiosity is discursively challenged. It is this that in a critical sense marks the difference between church and plantation. As Gates Jr. and Mckay (ibid. 6) put it: "Not surprisingly some of these songs offered not just psychic escapes and veiled criticism but calls for this-worldly attention and direct action."

What these theorists have in mind are the 1800s spirituals like 'Coming for to Carry Me Home' and 'Go Down Moses', in which the singers repeat/celebrate Old Testament figures of liberation and cast them as their own symbols of liberation. The deliberate privileging of Old Testament figures is mediated by a concept that is consistently propagated in the Old Testament: that of the homeland. The Jewish nation in exile and under slavery is an extremely provocative and powerful concept that provides the simulacrum with the American state and the position of black peoples in North America. For instance, in 'Go down Moses' (ibid. 14), one of the earliest plantation songs, the singer calls out:

Go down Moses
Way down in Egyptland
Tell old Pharaoh
Let my people go

This song, the footnotes claim, was banned in the slave plantations because it was considered too revolutionary and inspiring for the white master's racist control and authority. It describes the concept of *the homeland, the figure of the liberator and the status of African-American exile* in a language that is certainly minimal but evocative and metaphoric.

Effectively, the African slave breaks the language of white authority, appropriates it and then revises it to yield meanings to his new condition. In fact, the African-American employs this process to make the epistemological break with the violence of slavery. The use of the Christian figure, the language of the white American, the mythology of salvation — all these Western hermeneutic constructs are juxtaposed with oral narration, rhythmic dancing, repetitive calling and affirming response. The conflict that develops between the Western tradition of knowledge and the African experience of celebration and resistance proposes a critical syncretism that entails power and purpose for the African-American people. Hence this 'double-voicedness' (Gates 1998: 4) is the African-American's sense-making. It is the way in which slave peoples *re-member* their lives, cobbling together memory and environment.

## FREEDOM SONGS: THE POLITICS OF APPROPRIATION

There are at least two ways in which appropriation with revision travels in contemporary cultural practice. In the African-American tradition, Negro spirituals/gospels appropriate from their master narratives a new sense of hope for black peoples. There is in this form of application a clear move to syncretism, often to overcome the problem of cultural forgetting. The black slaves of this period read and interpret the master narratives differently, inserting in the process of revision their own meaning-system, often representing their imaginary of free men/women in the nation of their option. The songs narrate not only the crisis of slavery but also a sense of freedom. Thus the spirituals/gospels become what I provisionally call Freedom Songs; they provide the narrative for black identity-formation. They shift the concept of Christian salvation from the grand narrative of sin and morality to the public realm of secular ethics and justice. The question of race and racism seems uppermost in the minds of African-American communities, who perceive their cultural-political position as being mediated by concepts of race and racism. The theology of white superiority is more an instrument of discursive authority and political control than an experience of self-representation and cultural freedom. Through the gospel/spirituals, the black slave communities begin to represent their view of the world, their sense of reality and their notion of freedom. Thus the language of religious morality yields to the call for black liberation, disrupting the linguistic order of white racism. Freedom rather than salvation marks the discursive shift in African-American culture.

In the 1920s one can see a conceptual shift in the Freedom Songs, particularly with regard to the concept of homeland. In the period when 'Go Down Moses' is popular, home is Africa both culturally and territorially, while exile is the American nation marked by foreignness and alienation. By the 1920s home ceases to be Africa. This is not the hermeneutics of co-optation — an idea that I will return to later; it is more about reinventing one's foreignness in order to belong to the alien American nation. The African-American peoples make their homeland within post-abolition America with their own 'two-ness'.

Among the most popular gospels in the 1920s is the rather lamenting 'Take My Hand, Precious Lord' (1920), in which the African-American performer describes the "storm", the weariness and "the night" of "anguish and slavery" (Gates Jr. and Mckay 1997: 20). The vast and diverse web of symbols that the gospels/spirituals build does not represent the African-American condition. Instead, it is the African-American condition that is represented in the symbolism of these Freedom Songs. In this powerful reversal of cultural perspective, there is a clear epistemic break, a move away from stereotype to archetype.  The African-American performer speaks on behalf of her condition of pain and anguish, as also in terms of self-assertion. The conceptual shift is in terms of *locus*: from slavery to enslavement, from victim to victimisation. In this manner, the African-American performance moves the focus from the white subject to the black other.

Towards this end the singer imagines a new home leading on "to the light" (ibid.: 20). Notice the last verse:

When the darkness appears
and the night draws near
and the day is past and gone
at the river I stand
guide my feet, hold my hand
take my hand, precious lord
lead me *home* (emphasis added).

There lies between the 'darkness' and 'the light' a new homeland. It is a new, unfriendly and 'worn' nowhereness, a culture and territory that are 'drear' and alien. There is a hint of discontent, yet a renewed hopefulness in the Christ-figure (ibid. 20). *Home* now is on the margins of the American nation, to which the African-American peoples must seek to belong in and through their double-ness of alienation and adversity. Home is thus both belonging and exile in the American world. This double-ness, while re-echoing Du Bois' conception of African-American expression, is a way of repetition and revision too. In a sense, the habit of African-American cultural sense-making constitutes its poetics. In this respect, appropriation strategies revise narratives of white power in order to free black self-assertion from its shackles in the slave condition.

But appropriation practices can also travel the way of co-optation into comprador culture. This culture makes resisting thought and expression complicit with conservative political expedience. For all that, the contemporary economics of African-American music is largely a universalised idiom of entertainment, as white capital directs its processes to profit. When African-Americans perform in the universalised network of capital markets and 'seduce' the masses of people the world over, they perhaps also fall into the trap of becoming complicit with white capital. 'Reggae' and 'rap' are the means by which they are co-opted into the mainstream of popular.cultural production. With eminently visible compromises in both their nature and performance, the products of the culture industry, even though they are progressive black music, testify to the unconscious collapse into the universalising entertainment paradigm of showbiz. Indeed, Frantz Fanon's analysis in *The Wretched of The Earth* (1987) is extremely instructive for it holds the native ruling classes responsible for this disempowering process of co-optation. The native rulers smother political urgency for change and demolish critique in the name of law, order and peace.[5] Besides, the powerful systems of regulation earlier set up by the white master continue to exert control over the transforming power of African-American resistance. Added to this is the voluntary nature of white charity and sympathy, which seeks to assuage its guilt over the crime of racism. This robs the people's voice of its power and relevance. It also silences the speaking voice of the displaced native by its charitable liberalism.

Among the many structures of regulation is the highly capitalist and commodifying media industry of the day that Theodor Adorno refers to as 'the culture industry'.[6] For instance, in the case of 'Take My Hands Precious Lord', it is the Jim Reeves rendition that is the most popular today. It is also rendered during church services as another wholesome and assuring hymn. Often the more

---

[5] This particular analysis of Frantz Fanon is not just an efficient study of colonialism in Africa. It is in fact a seminal work on the problematic of nationalism that is based on a traditionalist nativism. My reference here is to the coercive nature of nationalist thought and practice. For an in-depth analysis of these issues, see Frantz Fanon (1960/1987).

[6] I have drawn most of my ideas from Adorno's theories of popular/mass culture. See Max Horkeniemer and W, Theodor Adorno (2001), pp. 126-67; and W. Theodor Adorno (1991), pp. 26-92.

radical verses of the song are abandoned. There is no recourse to either its ancestry or its slave context. Instead, there is a co-option of its social meaning into the zone of cultural niceties.

By romanticising its implications to suit the sentiments of the masses, the culture industry and traditional church worship commodify the Freedom Songs. In the Jim Reeves version of 'Take My Hand', concepts of after-life and death-wish replace the concepts of homeland, exile, alienation and weariness. There is a co-optation of signification here. Indeed, *other-worldliness* displaces the *this-worldly* nature of the gospels. This is truly an example of co-optation that advises obedience instead of resistance to the social conditions of the African-American peoples. Thus one observes an elitisation of radical agency, while silencing the voice of subaltern.

## THE CULTURE INDUSTRY AND SUBALTERNITY

Theodor Adorno, one of the most severe critics of mass culture, distinguishes between popular and mass cultures. The differentiation makes for an interesting shift from his earlier position of denouncing all popular music as 'massifying' people. In *Dialectic of Enlightenment* (2001), first published in 1965, there is no real distinction between popular and mass cultural production, whereas in *The Culture Industry: Selected Essay on Mass Culture* (1991) Adorno argues that we must "distinguish between cultural production arising spontaneously" from the masses themselves, and the culture entertainment packages produced by the culture industry. The latter, according to him, do not belong to the realm of popular art, which he acknowledges does constitute a potential for resistance against upper class art. He argues that the culture industry manipulates 'high' and the 'low' art products to suit its profiteering habits:

> To the detriment of both it forces together spheres of high and low art separated for thousands of years. The seriousness of high art is destroyed in speculation about its efficacy; the seriousness of the

lower perishes with the civilizational constraints imposed on the rebellious resistance inherent within it as long as social control was not yet total (Adorno 1991: 85).

The former, he says, represents 'the seriousness' of the people's voice, and the latter, anti-enlightenment (ibid.). He argues further that commodifying culture only destroys lower culture because it irons out the protest and the rebellion inherent in it.

When applied to the Freedom Songs and its appropriation by the culture industry, one observes the abrogation of subalternity. The Freedom Songs, particularly the gospels, are often, if not predominantly, performed by women. While it is true that African-American music is largely dominated by male performers, there is a constant insertion of women's voices that recreate an alternative perspective to the rendering of these songs. This also alters the double-ness of the African-American experience. In the performance, women's experience is represented not merely as dramatisation of ideas but as a critical bias that raises questions about the maleness of revolutionary black movements within the American nation. Thus, the internal critique in the context of gender problematises the politics and practice of the ritual performances of the spirituals and the gospels. If women displace their male counterparts ever so often, they will insert an alternative space for African-American women through a revision of the male meaning-systems of African-American cultural productions, i.e., the Freedom Songs.  But the culture industry replaces the woman performer with a suave and sophisticated white male star, indirectly but hegemonically denying and restricting African-American women from constructing the cultural space required for self-assertion and self-definition.  Instead, there is an imposition of white, sellable authority that is not only racist but also patriarchal. This replacement shifts the focus from the *specific* condition of the African-American women to a universality of other-worldliness and sentimentalises the African-American women's experience.

When women singers speak of home, they associate that space

with much more than their African roots. For them, it includes an escape from the sexual slavery they often experienced as house slaves on plantations, as well as a resistance to the sexual objectification of their black men. In the process of performing these songs, they make public their double burden as black people and as women — as publicly racialised and as domestically gendered people. With the control of the culture industry and the sanitisation of pietistic worship, this empowering critique of universal patriarchy and racism is silenced, and an empowering discourse becomes the rhetorical prerogative of white male patriarchy. In this respect, the culture industry is anything but free. It is an essentially ideological and gendered apparatus in the service of white male power, which subtly but surely steals away the otherwise radical narrative of black female subjectivity. In this manner the gendered subaltern emerges.

Here I must pause to explain what the term 'subaltern' could include. Except for Spivak's theorisations, the *subaltern* does not specifically include women in its conceptualisation, though it is perhaps among the otherwise most inclusive terms. According to Ranajit Guha (1982: iii), it simply means *of inferior rank*. It covers the experience of the subjugated class and caste, but tends to subsume gender. For Spivak, however, this definition is limiting and hence she includes "the aboriginal" and women within the category of the native informant.[7]   While Guha reserves this definition only for the South Asian peoples, Spivak chooses this frame of reference and spreads the definition to include the native informant everywhere, simultaneously theorising the position and space of the gendered native as well (Spivak 1999: 404).  This term runs counter to the term 'elite' that Guha proposes, which includes international industrialists, mercantile classes and comprador rulers (Guha 1982: 8). It is Spivak's re-theorisation of

---

[7] I have drawn this concept of the *native informant* as woman from Gayatri Spivak's perspective of the gendered subaltern.  For a more incisive analysis, see Spivak (1999).

the concept of subaltern that we may need to deploy to reconstitute the politics of location. The term becomes useful and instructive in that it covers the otherness of the inferiorisation process as it reassembles the subjugation of that location as resistance. Thus, if anything, the subaltern is the counter-hegemonic informant to liberal elite classes.

## CULTURAL PRODUCTS AND THE PUBLIC SPHERE

Over time the culture industry of late capitalism has become a transnational global system, constructing its own markets for popular music. The prime target for popular culture products like black music is the youth. The gospels/spirituals are further marginalised because they are seen merely as artefacts of African-American cultural history. They bear anthropological significance but appear to have no relevance to the realities of the African-American condition. This is because the culture industry socialises the implications of the Freedom Songs as entertainment packages that are exotic and of the past, though not because of any inherent weakness that prevents the gospels/spirituals from informing contemporary African-American life. They continue to remain well-honed packages that reify the history of rap and the underground as they travel into the Indian context (Gates 1997: 1). What is absent however is the elemental ethos of the African-American experience. There is a cultural whitewash here that smacks of sanitised universalism. The cultural impetuses, the sufferings, the dilemmas, the momentary joys and the celebrations — all are lost in the exotic sophistry of star-value and cultural co-optation. The contemporary listener ceases to hear the pulsating, libratory perspectives of these Freedom Songs. The native South Asian informant cannot identify in solidarity with the African-American peoples, or recognise the subalternity of the African-American tradition. Thus the inferiorised of the world remain divided and insular as the co-optative practices of culture enable the culture industry to become an institution of hegemonic power.

The public sphere continues to be constrained by the power of the culture industry, as there can be no true democratisation of public spaces. Juergen Habermas's formulation that the public sphere exists outside both the formal state and private authority implies a public realm in which independent people gather together to raise public issues (Habermas 1991). Somehow, with the culture industry and transnational capital everywhere, it seems as if this realm can never be actually free. Therefore radical music like the African-American Freedom Songs may yet interrupt the hegemonies of that public space which global capital attempts to occupy.

As a case in point, one can see that popular music of the African-American variety lives with the elite classes. In India today, listening to pop music itself is a leisurely activity belonging to the language, economy and politics of class. A recent study in Bangalore[8] shows how rock music is the pleasure and precinct of elite youth culture. Subaltern groups do not have access to this kind of music because of the economic demands that it entails. How, then, can we expect subaltern communities to engage with the radical and revolutionary politics of African-American music? The power and the relevance of African-American questioning in the spirituals/gospels is thus further distanced and marginalised. By and large, music of this nature remains a status symbol rather than an informing agent. The capitalist economies of popular culture co-opt marginal communities, native informants and women's groups as part of the masses. Their narratives fail to build progressive projects of social transformation and do not help with identity-formation.

---

[8] I have drawn this idea from variety sources, including some theorists mentioned above. But the more specific and empirical analysis and findings are to be found in an unpublished dissertation submitted by Siddharth Naidu to the Communications Department, Bangalore University. The student is a practising musician and was a student of the Communications Department between 2000 and 2002. For a more elaborated and revealing perspective of youth culture in Bangalore, see Naidu (2001-2002), pp. 43-57.

## CONCLUSION

In conclusion, I wish to raise a few issues related to the question of communication theory and subalternity. Communication theorists may need to re-examine the whole practice of repetition with revision, either as aspects of the message and context or as material of reception. In this regard, the field may need to interrogate what Jakobson's 'figuring' and 'refiguring' in *Linguistics and Poetics* (Jakobson 1988: 53) entail. In doing so it may have to account for the constant elitist encroachment and occupation of both the context and the message within the communication process. Simultaneously, it will have to engage the intrusiveness of the culture industry and controlling power of travelling capital in the communication project. In a sense, the core question may well be: what is the actual place and position of the message and the context in the communication grid? Who then owns the communication process itself?

Communication systems may have to address the complex terrain of subalternity and provide a differentiated approach to conceptualising subaltern subjectivity. For that, the present universal category of the subaltern may have to be disentangled to re-examine the twice-marginalised of subjugated cultures. In other words, we must account for the universal/specific category of gender enmeshed in issues of class and caste, race and religion.

Theories of the public sphere itself may require critical attention from the field of communication theory. There is need to differentiate between the ideologies of democracy and the practices of freedom in civil society.

Another very significant question relates to the politics of recasting cultural and religious figures to articulate issues of justice and equality in contemporary social formations. In the peculiar case of the Christ-figure in the African-American tradition, the recurrent refiguring of the historical Christ as against his traditional pietistic counterpart may have to be sustained. It may often seem an insufficient intervention to repeat the Freedom Songs without subalternising the Christ-figure itself. Yet it may well be the insertion of the African-American Christ-figure and the subaltern performance of the spirituals/gospels that might revise and assert a this-worldliness to the otherwise awe-inspiring religious Christ figure. We may therefore have to theorise not just issues in communication, but the entire politics of the public sphere and the scope and relevance of subaltern reformulations and transgressions. It is often assumed that since the object of address of African-American music is the English-educated *intermediate petit-bourgeois classes,* its influence on subaltern solidarities may be extremely minimal as it could alienate and distance those who do not belong to the upwardly mobile class. This may not be entirely true as revolutionary narrative and discourses have been known to impact on cultural activism in India. A powerful example of this cultural potential is the influence of Malcom X and his Black Consciouness Movement, which directly impacted on Dalit cultural politics in the Dalit Panthers Movement. If anything, the power of the gospels and spirituals as narratives of struggle is bound to be felt among cultural activists. In this way the Freedom Songs will make the upwardly mobile petit-bougeoisie suspicious of itself. Consequently, these songs will intervene to make their comfort-driven audience *self-reflexive*  and *self-critical.*

Perhaps, then, the subaltern will be able to speak herself to power.

## REFERENCES

Adorno, Theodor W. (1991). *The Culture Industry: Selected Essays on Mass Culture.* London: Routledge.

Du Bois, W.E.B. (1901). 'Souls of Black Folks' in Henry Louis Gates Jr. and Nellie Mackay (eds.) (1997). *The Norton Anthology of African American Literature.* London/New York: W.W. Norton and Company.

Fanon, Frantz (1960/1987). 'The Pitfalls of National Consciousnes' and 'On National Culture' in *The Wretched Of The Earth.* Harmondsworth: Penguin Books Ltd.

Gates Jr., Henry Louis (1987). *Figures in Black.* London/New York: Oxford University Press.

_____. (1988). *The Signifyin' Monkey: A Theory of African American Literary Tradition.* London/New York: Oxford. University Press.

Gates Jr., Henry Louis and Nellie Mackay (eds.) (1997). *The Norton Anthology of African American Literature.* London/New York: W W Norton and Company.

Guha, Ranajit (1982). 'Preface' in Ranajit Guha (ed.) *Subaltern Studies I: Writings on South Asian History and Society.* New Delhi: Oxford University Press.

Habermas, Jurgen (1991). *The Transformation of the Public Sphere:An Inquiry into a Category of Bourgeois Society.* Trans. Thomas Burgen and Frederick Lauren. Boston: MIT Press.

Horkeniemer, Max and W. Theodor Adorno (2001). *Dialectic of Enlightenment.* New York: Continuum.

Jakobson, Roman (1988). 'Linguistics and Poetics' in David Lodge (ed.) *Modern Literary Criticism and Theory.* London/New York: Oxford University Press.

Naidu, Siddarth (2001-2002). The Impact of Rock Music on Youth Sub Culture in Bangalore City. Unpublished dissertation. Bangalore: Bangalore University.

Spivak, Gayatri Chakravorty (1999). 'Culture' in *A Critique of Post Colonial Reason: Toward a History of the Vanishing Present.* Calcutta: Seagull Books.

# PART III
## BIBLE STUDIES

## CHAPTER 12

# 'Ephphatha': Opening Channels of Communication (Mark 7: 31-37)

*Marlene Marak*

Then he returned from the region of Tyre, and went by way of Sidon towards the Sea of Galilee, in the region of the Decapolis. They brought to him a deaf man who had an impediment in his speech, and they begged him to lay his hand on him. He took him aside in private, away from the crowd, and put his fingers into his ears, and he spat and touched his tongue. Then looking up to heaven, he sighed and said to him, "Ephphatha," that is, "Be opened." And immediately his ears were opened, his tongue was released, and he spoke plainly. Then Jesus ordered them to tell no one; but the more he ordered them, the more zealously they proclaimed it. They were astounded beyond measure, saying, "He has done everything well; he even makes the deaf to hear and the mute to speak" (Mark 7: 31–37).

The deaf man, whose disability was doubled by an impediment of speech, literally lived incommunicado, watching others speak but not hearing what was being said. He lived in a world of absolute silence. This underprivileged man did not have the faculty to hear the chirping of birds or be captivated by enthralling music, nor the ability to wish his friends 'good day' or admonish his children.

That is a taste of what the deaf experience all the time. A speech impediment is something equally awful. I believe that in the encounter of Jesus with the deaf man, we have a design for what should characterise Christian communication. 'Ephphatha', the exciting word Jesus spoke, is powerful and symbolic of the collapse of communication barriers.

Conversation is the most fundamental constituent of human interaction. Those who can converse regard it like a pair of sandals, which they use regularly but never truly notice, or like a door they open and close everyday oblivious of the task. But if our need for expression by conversation is curtailed, we sink into a pit of morbid hopelessness. The opening up of communication channels, the enabling of 'conversation', is a lease of life to the hopeless and helpless in society.

Jesus was taking a hiatus from his ministry in Galilee. So instead of coming directly back into Galilee from Tyre, he took a long and circuitous route through what is presently the country of Syria, and reached the region of the Decapolis. The Decapolis was a league of 10 Greek cities clustered on the eastern side of the Sea of Galilee, and the event described in the passage quoted above took place in that area.

The passage (Mk. 7: 31-37) records a miracle in which Jesus re-establishes blocked or interrupted communication.[1] The account of the healing of the deaf man can be broadly sorted into four movements: the description of the deaf man (v. 32a), petition for healing (v. 32b), Jesus' use of body language (vv. 33-34), and the miracle and its consequences (vv. 35-37).

1.  The condition of the deaf man is stated very briefly in a few words, but we cannot fail to notice that he was in a desperate situation. Mark describes him as suffering from hearing impairment using the Greek word *kôphos*, which carries the sense of being 'blunt' or 'dull'. The man's aural handicap affected his oral faculty, and he apparently spoke with great difficulty. The word 'mute' that appears in some English

---

[1] I have adopted many biblical insights from from Carlo Maria Martini, *Communicating Christ to the World*, trans. Thomas M. Lucas, Kansas City: Sheed and Ward, 1994.

versions of the Bible is a mistranslation; the Greek word used is *mogilalos* (*mogis*, with difficulty, scarcely, and *laleô*, to speak, to utter), meaning 'a stammerer' or 'one who speaks with difficulty'

2. The deaf man had friends who not only took him to Jesus but also implored Jesus to heal him, interceding on his behalf. Their intentions were good, but they were looking for an 'ordinary' miracle, indicated by their request to Jesus to 'lay his hand on him', which was the 'usual' way that Jesus and his disciples healed people. What they did not realise was that healing does not depend on formulae and can take place in unusual, striking ways. What they did not realise was that they would get more than what they had asked for.

3. In response to the appeal of the deaf man's friends to 'lay his hand on him', Jesus embarked on a strange routine. He took the deaf man aside, in private, away from the crowd and began to use what can best be described as sign language. Taking people aside for healing was not the customary practice of Jesus, although he had acted in a similar way a couple of times (Mark 5: 40; 8: 23). The only plausible reason why Jesus took the deaf man aside might be that Jesus intended to 'converse' with him in a language he could understand. The man was still deaf, and words would have been meaningless to him. In such a situation, action, literally, speaks louder than words. Then Jesus performed two symbolic actions. He put his fingers into the man's ears and then he spat on his finger and touched the man's tongue. These crude, corporeal signs may appear appalling to modern sensibilities. But how else could he communicate with someone locked up in his very own world? How else can one communicate love to those who are trapped within themselves if not by some kind of physical signs? (Martini 1994:7). Why did Jesus do this? Jesus was communicating to the man through physical touch that he was going to heal his hearing and cure his speech impediment. Jesus was preparing him for a great miracle. Had the crowd

been present, they would probably have thought that this was a magical rite, after the manner of magicians, particularly since spittle was an ancient symbol used for healing.

Still using sign language, Jesus turned his gaze upward to heaven, as if to say to the man in pantomimic terms, 'What is going to take place is by the power of the One above, in answer to my prayer.' Then he sighed, as if to say, 'I have compassion for you, I share in your afflictions.' These visual messages would have rung hollow if not for the fact that these actions were the outward manifestations of what was actually taking place — Jesus was praying to the Father and was moved with compassion for the painful condition of the afflicted man.

Jesus then said, "Ephphatha," which is Aramaic for 'be opened'. 'Ephphatha' — a word that would have been easy to lip-read on the man's part. One word. It was the only word spoken by Jesus. An imperative, a divine injunction that bespeaks the enabling of communication, its ordination, its restoration, its bestowal, to those marginalised, excluded, denied and silenced.

4.  At the command of Jesus, healing was instantaneous; the word used is *eutheôs*, 'immediately'. In an instant, his ears were opened, his tongue was released, and he spoke plainly. The fact that he spoke plainly demonstrated beyond doubt that a healing miracle had indeed taken place. Physical disorder, disease and defect were believed to be caused by moral lapses. In healing the deaf man Jesus restored him to the community. He would no longer be considered an outcast. Indeed, the healing ministry of Jesus signifies a community where there would be no outcasts.

The charge for secrecy that follows conforms to and underlines the motif of secrecy as found in Mark. It is meant to safeguard the identity of Jesus; to prevent making him appear like a commonplace Jewish or Greek healer. Mark insists that Jesus was more than a healer, and that his identity is fully realised only in the light of the cross and the resurrection. The command to keep quiet about the miracle was brushed aside by the tide of a huge, enthusiastic public response. The more Jesus commanded them not to tell anyone about the miracle, the more they talked about it. People were exceedingly amazed. Their acclamation that, "He has done everything well," indicates the overarching impact, the far-reaching consequences, of the work of Jesus. Finally, they said, "He even makes the deaf hear and the mute speak," which is an allusion to Isaiah 35:5. The glorious future which the prophet Isaiah foretold, "The eyes of the blind shall be opened, and the ears of the deaf unstopped," became a reality in the ministry of Jesus. Christ's restoring and enabling of genuine communication is a mark of God's Kingdom. Communication, establishing community and leading to communion are also tasks of every Christian and the church, God's privileged instrument of the Basileia. We may take the actions of Jesus as a paradigm for communication. In this instance, we may say that the healing of the deaf–mute and breaking the barriers of communication was a prophetic action.

## QUESTIONS:

- Who are the people around us that cannot 'hear' and 'speak'? What has been our attitude towards them? Embarrassment, indifference, apathy?

- How can we demonstrate our friendship to those who cannot 'hear' and 'speak'?

- What role can we play to open their ears, release their mouth, and restore them to community?

- As the church, Christ's agent for his Reign, how can we get involved in the redeeming activity of Jesus Christ?

In this task, it would help us to define for ourselves at least some of the obstacles that confront us today: obstacles of education, literacy and illiteracy; of economic disparity; of caste, ethnicity and age; of discrimination based on gender, such as using sexist language and having an anthropocentric attitude; and the obstacles created by disinformation and misinformation: the deceptions wrought by the slanting of information in the mass media, and in the advertisements that they carry.

In the milieu of confusion and ambiguities that plague communication, in a world symptomatic of the Babel syndrome, the need to find authentic communication, in which coherent conversations can take place, is real and pressing. In the text that we have discussed, we also realise that it is God who meets us: His communication is able to heal our failed/broken communications and to fill us again with the grace/blessings of a healthy and constructive give-and-take in relationships. May the Lord "who made the deaf hear and the mute speak" (Mark 7: 37) help us overcome ourselves and our differences on the way to authentic communication.

## CHAPTER 13

# Learning to Tell the Authentic
# Story of God

*Dhyanchand Carr*

The main aim of this study is to establish the connection between story and the many statements of faith and ethical exhortations in the Bible, and from there proceed to show the link between doctrines about God and the human story. In other words, the doctrines of God as creator, provider and sustainer of creation, ruler of the world and redeemer of the world all tell stories about God, but the authenticity or otherwise of these stories depends on their linkage with authentic human stories. We shall take two statements from Paul and a saying of Jesus' to show that without taking note of the stories that gave rise to these statements, their original meaning will elude us. In addition, some stories in the Bible itself have lost their original significance due to the *editorial* changes that have been imposed upon them over the years. If we recover the original stories and the identity of the original storytellers, very important insights could emerge. In order to demonstrate this we shall take the story of Cain and Abel to show how its interpretation depends on the story behind the story. Having gone through this exercise, we shall then be in a position to try and recover the authentic story of God to elucidate the real meaning of important Christian doctrines.

## THE STORIES BEHIND TWO STATEMENTS OF FAITH

Two short excerpts from Paul's letter to the Romans are, what would appear, simple statements of faith. But behind them are two stories, which illuminate these theological statements. The first text deals with justification and salvation, the second with Paul's vision of the Jewish people.

## Relationship between justification and salvation

> If you confess with your lips that Jesus is Lord and believe in your heart that God raised him from the dead, you will be saved. For man believes with his heart and so is justified and he confesses with his lips and so is saved. (Rom.10: 9 & 10).

What must be made emphatically clear at the outset is that believing to be justified and confessing to be saved are not simply tautological synonymous statements. Exegetes have noted that in Paul's thinking there is a difference between justification and salvation. Justification marks the beginning of Christian life, whereas salvation is achieved at the end. Justification is God's free gift appropriated through faith, but to reach salvation one has to work with fear and trembling, without assuming that one has reached it at any point in one's life (see Rom. 13: 11). What is intriguing, however, is that in this text Paul seems to reduce that hard and persistent effort required for achieving salvation to mere confessing with lips. This gross misunderstanding arises because we are not aware of the church's situation at the point when Paul wrote his letter to the Romans. With the increase in the number of gentile believers, Imperial Rome began to get suspicious of the loyalty of Christians to the Emperor. For some time it believed that the Christians were only a sect of Judaism who, with Rome's permission, were exempt from saying, 'Caesar is Lord'. But Rome soon began to wake up to the reality that the majority of Christian believers were gentiles. Their confession of Jesus as Lord was scandalous, for it meant that they were claiming they had another king. In such a context, Roman officials would often demand that Christians say, 'Jesus is cursed, but Caesar is Lord'. So when Christians, even under the threat of the sword, insisted that only Jesus is Lord, it provided clear proof that they had already renounced the world and its powers in a radical manner and had totally transferred their loyalty to Jesus as Lord, not just personally but also on behalf of the entire world. Without the story of the church, which gave rise to Paul's statement of faith, his words have often been grossly misunderstood and reduced to mere pious platitude (see also 1 Cor. 12: 3).

## Paul's conversion to accept the Jewish people as People of the Covenant

> I want you to understand this mystery, brethren: a hardening has come upon part of Israel until the full number of the Gentiles come in, and so all Israel will be saved (Rom. 11: 25-32).

While Paul vacillated between his belief that unbelieving Jews should be totally rejected and his intuitive conviction that they would ultimately be saved, two factors helped to strengthen his faith in his intuition. The first relates to how, without the long history of Judaism and its specific contribution to the diaspora in terms of creating a large group of gentile God fearers, who were the most responsive to Paul's Gospel, gentile believers would not have come into existence at all. Their continuing nurture also depended a great deal on an understanding of God's involvement in the history of Israel, the chosen people of God, and accepting Abraham as the father of all the faithful.

Secondly, and in all probability, Paul was reminiscing, without clarifying this in so many words, over all that had happened with regard to the circumcision controversy. Had the Jewish people, at the very outset, responded to the Gospel in large numbers, gentile believers like the God fearers of the diaspora synagogues would have been under pressure to seek circumcision before getting baptised. The fact that more gentiles became Christians in the diaspora inevitably forced the Jewish leadership to concede that the gentiles need not be brought under the purview of the Mosaic Law. It therefore became necessary that, to maintain the truth of the Gospel, Jewish people, the very sap of Christianity, be kept at bay until such time as 'the fullness of the gentiles' was brought in. However, the faithfulness of God to the covenant made with Israel was inviolable. This belief, together with the principle that the first fruits offered sanctify the whole harvest, i.e., the fact that Peter, James and Paul and a host of other Jewish people had accepted the Gospel as 'first fruits', made Paul reach the conclusion that, in some mysterious way, all Jews would be included in the final summing up.

Without realising that Paul had undergone a second conversion with regard to the ultimate status of the Jewish people through calm reflection on his mission story and the story of God linked firmly with the people of Israel, many have thought that God had rejected Israel outright, and many Christians wrongly thought that they themselves were a replacement of Israel.

## ETHICAL INJUNCTION OR MISSION STATEMENT?

We now take up a well-known saying of Jesus: "Blessed are the meek for they shall inherit the earth."

Matthew's beatitudes have been understood as ethical exhortations. This beatitude is therefore taken to mean that we must try hard to be meek persons if we are to inherit the earth. Quite apart from the fact that nobody explains what is really implied by the promise that the meek shall inherit the earth, such an understanding introduces a strange element of eschatological hope that is present nowhere else. But when we understand the saying as an assurance of God's intention to restore to people their land, which had been taken away from them forcefully, and that therefore meekness refers to the powerlessness of the people, which had rendered it impossible for them to retain their land as their cherished and legitimate possession, a completely new hermeneutical horizon opens up for interpreting Matthew's beatitudes. And if we also take into consideration the possibility that these words were remembered by a people who were 'in exile', having been driven out as despised Galileans suspected to have become terrorists by Rome, and for whom the question of how and when they were going to get back their land was paramount, we can then grasp the real significance of this beatitude. Similarly, we can obtain important insights on Jesus' understanding of his mission if we set all the beatitudes against the backdrop of the story of the despised, mournful and 'exiled' Galilean Christians.

## A STORY OF ORIGINS OR AN ONGOING STORY OF TWO COMMUNITIES?

Having seen the importance of understanding statements of faith and exhortations only in the context of stories that gave rise to them, we now turn to see how some stories in the Bible themselves need to be re-read in the light of the original storyteller's intention.

The story of Cain and Abel is a classic example of how stories themselves are either naively or deliberately misinterpreted. This story is not about sibling rivalry; nor is it the story of the first murder. It is a story told by Abel's community about the steadfastness of their faith in the face of the fact that God, despite being a God of justice, in the end seems to protect the powerful and the wicked, i.e., Cain and his descendants. And how, in spite of this seeming injustice, they would rather stick with God than adapt the ways of the wicked. This is the real message of the story of Cain and Abel. So even for understanding stories we need to know the story of the people who told these stories in the first instance. Once we know the real meaning of 'The Story of the Abel Community', we can easily understand what James means by his statement that God has granted to the poor to be rich in faith.

## A RETELLING OF THE STORY OF GOD AS CREATOR AND PROVIDER

We are now in a position to attempt to tell the story of God interlinked with the human story and understand the real significance of the tenets of Christian belief.

The tenets of the Christian creed — such as God is the creator, provider and protector of life, the one who elects a people for salvation, the one who saves them through the giving of his own Son — are some of the most important creedal affirmations constitutive of the Christian church. The church's worship and programmes of nurture have deeply instilled these beliefs in the hearts and minds of the Christian people the world over. As we all know, these beliefs comprise the basic formative influence in shaping the church's values, its self-understanding as a peculiar people of God and its sense of mission. But what we also know only too well is that while the entire church confesses a common creed, there is an almost infinite variety of convictions about how God relates to creation, how he carries out the work of providence, how he is at work redeeming the world, and what exactly Jesus did in this work of redemption. One reason for this is because while the same creed is confessed, the stories behind each of the tenets have been told and retold differently.

Take the stories of creation and providence for example. The standard Christian belief is that God created the world *ex nihilo*. For many people, therefore, the heavens are literally the work of God's fingers. Many firmly believe that God created the first human like a doll out of clay, and literally blew into the nostrils to give life to the first man, Adam. As God made woman out of Adam's rib, many naively believe that all men have one rib less than women! The implications for popular theology arising from such a story of creation are that (*a*) the relationship between God and the creatures he created is that of a potter to clay. The creature cannot and should not question how and why God made one person blind, another deaf, and yet another a dwarf... Ultimately, all such deformities are also meant to glorify God the creator. (*b*) There is absolutely no room for evolutionary forces to have had any influence on creation. Further, the Bible affirms that God ensured that everything that had been created was good. Despite this, without theologically squaring their logic with this belief, many people hold human sin has some effect on various aspects of creation. (c) The integrity of creation or of human participation as co-creator is an unthinkable heresy for many pious Christians. Today, it is well recognised that couples have the right to decide the size of their family and/or exactly when they will have children. Further, countries like the People's Republic of China have proclaimed that its citizens will be allowed to have only one child. In such a context one might well ask, 'Exactly what role is played by God the Creator?' This question becomes even more serious when we take into account the thousands of children who were born deformed to Hiroshima survivors or the victims of the Bhopal gas disaster due to exposure to radiation. Can we attribute these disastrous and tragic creations to God the creator? Such questions are dismissed as blasphemous. The pious seldom realise that the real blasphemy lies in attributing to God deformities, which, as in Hiroshima and Bophal, have been caused by human wickedness or negligence. How we talk about God being the creator thus needs to be thought about carefully. The theological problem, however, is how to tell the story of God as creator without prejudice to God's sovereign prerogatives, and at the same time accept the role that human freedom and the laws of genetics play in the process, albeit by God's own arrangement. The only way to get around this problem is to formulate God's story as interlocked with the story of human freedom and the God-given integrity of creation. In such a formulation, the story of creation would have to account both for the theological necessity of affirming God's sovereignty, as well as for the reality of human freedom and the interplay of the laws of creation.

Next, let us briefly examine our belief that God is the provider and sustainer of life. Jesus, our Lord, assures us that we are more precious than the animal world and the world of nature, and so God is bound to take care of us. Not even a sparrow falls to the ground without God's will. The tragic reality of the world, however, is that millions are starving through no fault of their own and many are killed in wars and in accidents. Are we to hold God responsible for the starving millions and for the many tragic and untimely deaths? Even more important is the nature of relationship between God the provider and the millions of underpaid workers in the field and in the garment industry through whose labour we are fed and clothed. As provider, God seems to provide only for the well off and seems to have no care for the already exploited labourers that, having produced food, remain ill fed. In the face of this, how are we to affirm faith in the goodness and fairness of a God who is supposed to care for every human being?

In both cases we first need to affirm the primacy of story over concept and admit the inadequacies of the traditional stories that are based on the assumption that God is the only actor in creating and caring for the world. This primacy is clearly reflected in the fact that the doctrines are based on stories contained in the Bible. The willingness to admit their inadequacies is therefore hard to achieve. In what follows I attempt a retelling of the story of God as creator and provider, taking into account that it is intertwined inextricably with the human story.

The God of the universe is the sovereign Lord. This sovereign God is perfect in love and has a consuming passion for justice. His love drives him to give up his sovereign prerogatives out of deference to the laws, principles and processes he himself brought into being while creating the universe. God also respects human freedom. Therefore, even when that freedom is grossly abused, the only option open to God is to be in solidarity with the victims of such abuse and suffer together with them.

However, there seems to be yet another player in the field — an intelligent evil power. From time to time, this evil power seems to incite the natural forces into misbehaving and inspire humans to wantonly abuse their God-given freedom. This is why human rebellion and nature's erratic behaviour are interlinked. The way God has chosen to redeem humankind, restore nature and overcome the power of evil is by suffering together with the victims of abuse, of famine and flood.... God is indeed concerned to provide for all and protect even supposedly insignificant creatures like sparrows. It is another matter that this concern cannot become a reality until nature has been restored and humankind redeemed. Belief in God's impartial and perfect care for every human person, indeed the whole of creation, is thus the real affirmation of faith, which needs to be qualified with the reality that the power of evil, the source of all falsehood, often infiltrates the religious psyche to make the pious believe that they alone are the objects of God's providential care and redemptive purposes. This, of course, is manifestly false. Just as God enlists the cooperation of the humans in God's work of creation and in God's work of providence, God also seeks and enlists human cooperation in God's work of redemption. All humans, especially those who are victims of injustice and oppression, or of the erratic forces of nature, should therefore be regarded as God's partners in his work of redemption.

The reader may quite legitimately think that this retelling reads more like a stringing together of concepts rather than a story. This is admitted without apology. For the main purpose of this brief reflection is to show that behind every precept and aphorism, exhortation and statement of faith, there lurks a story. If these stories are recovered, then a whole world of lost meaning may be revealed.

We set out to show the primacy of story over doctrine. Only when the story behind any particular faith affirmation resonates authentically with the real story of God and his intentions will that affirmation lead to the right values, convictions and ortho-praxis. Otherwise we shall end up legitimising many unjust beliefs, values and practices.

## CHAPTER 14

# Listening to the Cries of the People

### Kuruvilla George

I remember watching a Hindi movie on the television (I forget the title) in which that thespian stalwart of yesteryears, Utpal Dutt, played the role of a mean *zamindar* (landlord). He had exploited and tortured to death many poor people of his village, and in the course of his rampages even managed to bury alive a number of small children. Towards the end of the movie, he becomes deranged and restlessly roams the streets of the village muttering, *Dharthi ke neeche, rone ki awaz!* ("Listen to the voice of weeping rising from the ground!") The voices give him no peace until he is driven by the pangs of his conscience to his miserable and gruesome end. It was many years ago that I watched the movie, but the panic-stricken face and the grating voice of the *zamindar* still haunt my dreams: *Dharthi ke neeche, rone ki awaz!*

I believe that if we searched our hearts and listened to our conscience, we would also hear voices of weeping, of muffled cries, of mourning and lamentations of other people rising from the depths of our being. When we consciously or unconsciously deny life or livelihood to others, don't we share the character of the evil *zamindar*? Can we deny the fact that we are also unkind human beings who make life difficult for others by the choices we make every day? In our blind pursuit to meet our selfish ends, don't we callously trample on the rights and privileges of our fellow beings? Is not the bread we eat (and the bottled water we drink) snatched from the poor and the hungry? Are not many 'religious' edifices and 'cultural' landmarks in our society built on the victims of oppression? As a community, could we wash our hands of the suffering and torture of the innocents that characterise our self-seeking culture? The victims of the six bomb blasts in Mumbai cry out; Marad and Gujarat raise their voices; Kashmir mourns its dead. *Dharthi ke neeche, rone ki awaz!*

The Bible is full of the cries of the oppressed. In fact, blood drips from my Bible and if I hold it to my ears like a transistor radio, I can hear unmistakable voices of weeping, mourning and lamentation. And God listens to the cries. In the very first book of the Bible we read about Cain and Abel. Cain murdered his brother in cold blood and thought that he could get away with it – – until God said to him: "Why have you done this terrible thing? Your brother's blood is crying out to me from the ground, like a voice calling for revenge" (Gen.4: 10). The Israelites were slaves to the Pharaoh of Egypt, but God was paying close attention to them. "The Israelites were still groaning under their slavery and cried out for help. This cry went up to God who heard their groaning and remembered his covenant with Abraham, Isaac, and Jacob. He saw the slavery of the Israelites and was concerned for them" (Exod. 2: 23–25).

The Book of Psalms is full of the cries of the oppressed. "God remembers those who suffer, he does not forget their cry, and he punishes those who wrong them" (Ps. 9: 12). "The helpless call to him, and he answers; he saves them from all their troubles" (Ps. 34: 6). Psalms 44, 60, 74, 79, 80, 83 and 89 are all laments of people in great pain and distress. Rachel, Hagar, Hannah, David and Job are among those who weep and lament without comfort. There is even a book of Lamentations in the Bible, which bewails the collapse of religious and political systems. All these references show that weeping, lamenting and keening are all acknowledged in the Bible. They speak a language that God 'understands' and is moved by.

The voice of weeping is a language that is common to the Jew and the Gentile, to the villager and the city dweller; it is a language that communicates itself across national boundaries. It is a universal language that can never be mistaken or go unheeded anywhere in the world. It is not just the language of humans either; the Bible says that it is the language of desecrated nature as well: "For we know that up to the present time all of creation groans with pain, like the pain of child birth" (Rom. 8: 32). *Dharthi ke neeche, rone ki awaz!*

It would even appear that the language of crying and weeping is the only language that can catch God's attention. Take, for instance, our efforts to communicate with God by means of feeble prayers and perfunctory worship, which the Holy Spirit has to convert into a language that God can understand. See, for instance, Rom. 8: 26: "For we do not know how we ought to pray; the Spirit himself pleads with God for us in *groans* that words cannot express. And God, who sees into our hearts, knows what the thought of the Spirit is."

God understands. God responds. God in Jesus Christ becomes a partner in communication with the world he has created. But how does God communicate? In human experience, to communicate effectively one needs something more than language and media. Husbands and wives quarrel and wring each other's neck not because the mobile phone is not good enough; they would quarrel nevertheless. They do not quarrel because they do not understand each other's language; they would quarrel nevertheless. To communicate effectively with one another we need something more than common language and effective media. We need to listen. We need to develop a positive attitude and interest in the other person, an attitude that translates into respect and consideration for the other person: "God exhibits his positive attitude in his steadfast love" (John.3: 16). We also require the ability to respond ("...in Jesus God sees and is moved with compassion"). We also need a theory or a rationale for our positive attitude and behaviour: in other words, a philosophy of communication (in the Gospels it is enshrined in the message of the Kingdom of God). Furthermore, we need to develop a commitment or a willingness to take pains, to give of ourselves and what we have (as uniquely illustrated in the cross and resurrection of Jesus Christ).

God engages in communication with the world by responding positively to human misery; God in Jesus Christ affirms his solidarity with the suffering and the oppressed, the tortured and the exploited millions of this world. For Jesus, given his human limitations, such communication does not seem to be an easy proposition. So we see him under severe duress and anguish in the face of human pain or loss ("Jesus wept") or the prospect of human devastation which he foresaw (Luke 19:41). In the Garden of Gethsamane "his sweat was like drops of blood falling to the ground" (Luke 22:44). The writer of the Letter to the Hebrews says: "In his life on earth Jesus made his prayers and requests with loud cries and tears to God, who could save him from death. Because he was humble and devoted, God heard him. But even though he was God's son he learned through his sufferings to be obedient. When he was made perfect, he became the source of eternal salvation for all those who obey him...." It is likely that Jesus' prayer of anguish was not limited to Gethsamane; Jesus must have always prayed in that way. That was the language God understood. To participate in the human predicament of pain, misery and destitution was a struggle for Jesus, a life-long agony. But by means of his personal suffering, Jesus overcame his selfhood and became part of humanity. Jesus emptied himself so that he could take in the whole gamut of human suffering in his own person. He was willing to give up his personal identity so that he could identify with all those who suffered. In doing so he was offering God his full obedience and fulfilling God's will to perfection, refusing to submit to the will of his tormentors. Therefore, the dark forces that caused his suffering could not get the better of him. Jesus suffered and died, but he rose again and emerged victorious. Thus, in Jesus, we can see both suffering and victory over suffering.

The early church was a persecuted community ("The blood of the martyrs is the seed of the church"), a community that shared the suffering of the world. The church is still being tortured in some parts of the world and its tears flow intermingled with the tears of the poor and the oppressed. I must ask myself why my church does not experience any pain or grief except in its little inconveniences? Why don't I feel any pain except my own or that of my family? Why don't I respond to the grief of the world? Am I not guilty of causing pain by my inconsiderate attitudes and actions? What shall I do in recompense of my sins of callousness and insensitivity? According to the prophet Joel, God tells us: "Repent sincerely and return to me with weeping and mourning. Let your broken heart show your sorrow. Tearing your clothes in not enough" (Joel 2: 12-13).

*Dharthi ke neeche, rone ki awaz!* Weep, cry out, lament! Recognise the fact that we are not full-fledged members of the human community until we break down and weep.

## PRAYER :

O God of all life, who is all eyes and ears when we call upon you: open our eyes and ears to see and listen to the cries of all who are being tortured and persecuted in our world. Help us to share the pain of all who suffer unjustly and to fight alongside those who care for the oppressed and the exploited. Help us to confess our own guilt in being oppressors ourselves by choosing and enjoying an easy and selfish lifestyle at the expense of others whose rights and privileges we have denied. Forgive us, Lord, and enable us to transcend our pettiness and self-centredness, and to choose the way of your Son who emptied himself so that we may become filled with the riches of your compassion. In his name we pray. Amen.

# The Seoul Manifesto on Communication in Theological Education

*WACC, with the support of the Lutheran World Federation and the World Council of Churches, held a meeting of 17 people who have taught communication in theological colleges. It took place in Seoul, South Korea, on 20-24 March 1989. One outcome of the meeting was a declaration in which the need for and salient features of communication education in theological studies were highlighted.*

## WHY ARE WE INTERESTED IN SECURING THE PROPER PLACE FOR COMMUNICATION STUDIES IN THEOLOGICAL EDUCATION?

1.  The purpose of theological education is to make it possible for the Gospel to be heard in our time. For this reason, we believe that the study of communication must begin to play a much larger role in theological education. Critical communication theory today challenges many of the ways we do theology. It illuminates and affects our understanding of the church, revelation, knowledge of God, community, Holy Spirit, and the scripture. It provides us with the tools to understand the power of the mass media, with both its dangers and potential. It clarifies our approach to intercultural mission. It guides our homiletic task in a world essentially informed by the media of mass communication. Without an adequate grasp of communication, those who would bring the Gospel to our

world may uncritically accept the powerful but largely hidden power of the media and their worldview. On the other hand, an adequate understanding of communication can lead to a revitalisation of Christian communication, through the rediscovery of older forms of communication and the proper use of new ones.

2. The Christian assessment of the mass media is a complex matter. We recognise that the modern media have dehumanising and destructive power. The media are often abused by oppressive forces as a technique of social control and the dissemination of ideology. But we also know that the media may play a significant part in strategies that work for justice, transmit culture, encourage participation and build communities. We are confident that the media, rightly utilised, could make the church more bold, effective and faithful in its mission.

3. Communication theory has rediscovered the value of the story and of image. While theological education during the past 300 years has focused on extracting and distilling what the Christian stories 'mean', secular communication has understood the power and importance of telling stories in ways that the people hear gladly, and which they have integrated into their lives. Communication can help theological education recapture the power of story and image to help people once again hear the Gospel.

4. Communication by Christians that is authoritarian, monolithic and individualistic is inauthentic and discredits mission and evangelism. Authentic communication builds communities. Its dialogical and communal nature is an integral dimension of evangelism. Establishing authentic communication, both genuinely receptive listening and faithful speaking, is an essential part of mission.

## WHAT ARE COMMUNICATION STUDIES?

5.  We see communication as an increasingly well-defined and distinct field of study. It has an important contribution to make to the doing of theology. It is essentially a multi-disciplinary area, ranging from communication skills and techniques through critical analysis of communication to reflection on the theology and ecclesiastical implications of communication. The topics that might be considered are various: from learning how to write a press release, through skills of attentive listening and analysis of communication order structures, to rethinking how we do theology and understand God's word and action.

6.  We do not wish to prescribe a curriculum of topics which may be studied everywhere. But we must affirm that it is not enough to treat communication studies as simply a matter of skills and techniques. We advocate the widest possible exploration of communication, in its broadest cultural expressions both within the church and in society and between cultures, always aware that it is the Holy Spirit who enables all communication.

## IMPLEMENTATION

7.  Communication studies hold the promise of overcoming monological and authoritarian structures of education. The authentic pedagogy of communication must always be a genuinely dialogical process.

8.  In theological education we teach those who are already themselves communicators within the context of their culture and their church. The task of the teacher of communication is to help people to identify, clarify and develop their existing skills, insights and potential so that they may become more confident and effective communicators in their various contexts. The teacher should also seek to increase awareness of the ways in which the media are influencing the values and worldview of the culture, and how this influence affects religious communication.

9.  A major contribution of communication studies to theological education is the insistence on relevancy. For example, communication theory understands that many different environments are required for education; thus seminaries should consider alternative forms of education in addition to the traditional three-year, in-seminary context. Also, communication theory insists that people, especially the poor, need to speak for themselves, and this concept has significant implications for those in the church who prefer to 'speak for' others.

10. To establish a recognised place for communication studies in the seminary or theological faculty requires the support of the staff. To win that support involves extensive reflection and orientation. This, of course, takes time and persistence. Not only space and resources for communication studies are required, but also the introduction of a communication perspective into all major theological disciplines. What is entailed is nothing less than a re-ordering and reconceiving of how theology is understood and taught.

11. We believe that communication studies deserve and require a more significant place in theological education than simply appearing as choices for the few, or modules concerned with skills. We advocate that not less than 10 per cent of time be allocated to communication studies, and that the subject be offered at advanced as well as introductory level.

12. Nothing is more encouraging to the spread of communication studies than the knowledge that the subject is widely taught in other seminaries. A strategy for the future must include the regular exchange of information about the development of courses, increased facilities for research and advanced work to prepare teachers, and a network to provide encouragement for active teaching.

# Roman Catholic Guide to the Training of Seminarians in Social Communication (Extracts)

It will make good sense to begin the course of instruction in media matters and to continue it along three different levels.

At the first, or basic level, attention is to be focused on the receivers, which is to say, all readers, viewers and listeners of mass media. Since every student must be classified as a receiver, training from this aspect must be given to all of them without distinction.

The formation given at the second level is 'pastoral', and is to be given to all future priests, since it has to do with their future priestly ministry. In that ministry, they are going to require to be able to train the faithful, in their turn, in the right use of *mass media;* they will also need to know how they can themselves use the media to the best advantage for the purposes of their apostolate.

On the third level is 'specialist' training, and it will affect those who already work in the *mass media,* or who, giving evidence of special talent, are being prepared to work in the field. Also to be considered on this third level will be those who are preparing to teach and give training in mass media on the first two levels.

It will be well, at each level, to be quite precise about what is being studied. Clear distinctions are to be made between the questions which have properly to do with the instruments of social communication, and other questions which do not touch these instruments directly. The following advice is offered:

Close attention should be paid — in so far as the differences in languages allow — to the correct use of terms; and the different accepted meanings authorised by the various authors and schools will have to be kept in mind...

Keeping in mind the accelerated evolution, worldwide, of the social communications technology in the direction of telechronics and telematics, of which the mass media are at once the object, vehicle and mirror, it is clear that no one medium should be treated in the training course as if the others did not exist (e.g., cinema alone or television alone, with no mention of the printed word). Similarly, it would be a mistake to deal with some particular aspect of a medium in isolation (e.g., the culture and civilisation of 'the image'). The media ought to be treated all together and as a whole, and all the questions and angles dealt with by the best-known authors should be looked at, such as the word 'dialogue', 'the global village', 'one dimensional man', 'computer-conditioned man [humans]'....

Finally, among these and other socio-cultural macro-phenomena, it will be necessary to give most space to the questions concerning information, propaganda, advertising, public opinion, and the use of leisure, in so far as these have specific connections with the media.

At the first two levels of formation especially, the basic and the pastoral, care will have to be taken to give the students a formation to mass media which is all of one piece, with its limits and content clearly defined, and the appropriate attention devoted to didactic practice. Thus:

a)  What is to be attempted in every case is to form and conserve a fully human personality in the receivers, making them receptive of those psycho-sociological and ethico-cultural values with which the mass media involve themselves so unremittingly, providing occasion for the growth or withering of that personality. The students are to be assisted towards

Christian maturity, so that, by using the mass media responsibly, they will then know how to live the whole of their priestly lives in a rich and productive way.

b) Side by side with the teaching of theory there must be provision of practical experience in the use of the tools of social communication. This will help the students to acquire, as they mature, a knowledge of the cultural and political, religious and moral trends in the current productions and programming. It will also enable them to evaluate, critically and realistically, the modern techniques. To make all this possible, the seminaries and institutes of instruction need to be supplied with the proper equipment.

The above text is an extract (S 9-11) from *Guide to the Training of Future Priests concerning the Instruments of Social Communication*, issued by the (Vatican) Congregation for Catholic Education in 1986. The full text is published in Franz-Josef Eilers (ed.) (1997). *Church and Social Communication. Basic Documents*, Manila: Logos Publications, 181-198.

# On the Introduction of Communication Studies in the Serampore affiliated Colleges

*Samuel Rajkumar*

From 1983 to 1986 five joint workshops of theologians and communication specialists were held mostly at the United Theological College, Bangalore. Their broad aim was to lay a basis on which communication curricula could be developed for both the levels of the Bachelor of Divinity (BD) and Master of Theology (MTh) at colleges affiliated to the Senate of Serampore university. Another aim was that participants would sensitise other faculty members of these colleges, who were not participants at these workshops. The coordinators of these workshops were CRW David, Fr. Joe Naidu SJ (both deceased) and Dr Henry S. Wilson. Seven modules were worked out and tested, in full or in part, in some of the Serampore affiliated colleges.

The most important tangible result of the five seminars was the publication of *Communication in Theological Education: A Curriculum* in 1988, edited by CRW David (now out of print). This enabled the Senate of Serampore to proceed with introducing communication studies into the general curriculum of its affiliated colleges in 1991. The BD communication curriculum contains eight subjects. But at most colleges only three are compulsory: a theoretical paper (introduction to communications), a mixed theoretical/practical paper (media awareness) and a course in skill development. Communication is thus taught to well over a thousand students every year in over 40 theological colleges under the umbrella of Serampore.

Around the time when the revised Serampore BD Curriculum of 1991 came into effect, there were a few intensive workshops conducted in Bangalore for teachers (particularly those with a flair for teaching communications) from Serampore affiliated colleges; they were awarded certificates recognising them as teachers of communications. This was done at a time when graduates with a MTh degree in communications studies were still few in number.

Tamilnadu Theological Seminary (TTS) in Madurai was the pioneer in communication studies. It started its MTh programme in communications already in 1988 (the year the *Curriculum* was published) with a focus on Alternative Communications and Development Communication. Gurukul Lutheran Theological College in Chennai followed suit in 1995, with an emphasis on Information Technology. At the United Theological College in Bangalore the Master's level syllabus was first taught in 1996 with 'Gospel, Cultures and Communication' as focus. It was partly, but not only, the need for teachers of communications in seminaries that prompted the three theological colleges to introduce communications on the MTh level.

In 1999/2000 a new curriculum for MTh was worked out. It is far from perfect. It has some major omissions that are badly in need of correction. Its most important aspect, perhaps, is the fact that the mass media are only a small *part* of the total communication environment of the majority of people in India, and that this is likely to remain so for some time. The MTh curriculum thus emphasises the inter-relatedness of all human communication, mainly through interpersonal and group communication, and the continued use of 'traditional' media. The mass media, therefore, are seen from a broader theoretical perspective than is normally the case in communication studies. At the same time, the curriculum incorporates many of the changes that have taken place in information and communication technologies before the start of the new millennium.

## SOURCES

CRW David (ed.) *Communication in Theological Education. A Curriculum.* Bangalore: Board of Theological Education of the Senate of Serampore College & Asia Trading Corporation, 1986, 272 pp. The book gives a list of the participants at the workshops and a brief description of the work process by H.S. Wilson, pp.ix-x

Another publication (also out of print) gives the papers presented during the first two workshops. It is entitled *Communication Workshops I & II, 1983-84.* Bangalore: BTESSC, 1985.

# Contributors

**A. Suresh Kumar**, is a presbyter of the Tiruchy-Tanjore Diocese of the Church of South India. He has a post-graduate degree in Mathematics and a MA in Mass Communication from the University of Leicester (UK). Since 1990 he has been teaching post-graduate communication courses at the Tamilnadu Theological Seminary, Madurai, and has served on the Board of Studies (Communication) of the Senate of Serampore College.

**Dhyanchand Carr** is a pastor of the Church of South India. He holds a doctorate in New Testament studies, which he taught for many years. He was awarded the William Paton Fellowship at Selly Oakes Colleges, Birmingham, and later served as Executive Secretary, Mission and Evangelism, at the headquarters of the Conference of Churches in Asia (CCA), Hong Kong. For many years he was Vice Principal and then Principal of Tamil Nadu Theological Seminary, Madurai. He is now retired. Dr Carr was one of the participants of the Summer Workshops 1983-87 in Bangalore, at which the first curriculum for communication studies in theological education was worked out.

**Daniel J. Felton** obtained his Licentiate in Theology and an MA in Social Communication from the Gregorian University in Rome in 1989. He has had a long association with the Catholic Telecommunication Network of America (USA), of which he has been Director of Media and Affiliate Affairs.

**Etienne Rassendren** teaches English and English studies in St Joseph's College, Bangalore. He has a PhD in South African Poetry and his interests include race, caste and gender questions, popular culture, subalternity, cultural studies and nations and nationalism issues. He is also Adjunct Faculty and Student Advisor at the South

Asian Centre of the Friends World Program, Long Island University, USA. He is also a Consultant on their Curriculum Committee.

**Hannibal (Honey) Cabral** is a presbyter of the Church of South India, Karnataka Southern Diocese, and professor of communication at the Karnataka Theological College, Mangalore. He is also the director of the Karnataka Christian Communication Service and Kalaa Sangama Digital audio-video recording studio in Mangalore. He has composed more than five hundred Christian devotional songs in Kannada, English, Tulu and Hindi. He has worked for radio FEBA and All India Radio. Rev. Cabral got his DTh from the Senate of Serampore College.

**J. Daniel Kirubaraj** completed his MTh in Communication Studies at Gurukul Lutheran Theological College and Research Institute, Chennai, in 1998. He pursued his doctoral studies at the same college, and in 2004 completed his thesis entitled 'Communication for Community Action: An Explorative Study of Communication in Theological Education in South India'. He is now teaching communications at the Tamilnadu Theological Seminary, Madurai.

**Joseph Palakeel** has a Diploma in Social Communication and a Doctorate in Theology (1995) from the Gregorian University in Rome. Since 1997 he has been Dean of Studies and professor of Fundamental Theology and Communication at Ruhalaya Seminary, Ujjain, MP. He is co-founder and executive editor of *Jnanatirtha, Journal of Sacred Scriptures.* Dr Palakeel is the editor of *Towards a Communication Theology,* Bangalore: Asian Trading Corporation, 2003.

**José M. de Mesa** is a Filipino lay theologian and a member of the Asian Communicators' Network (ACN). He is on the faculty of De La Salle University, Manila, where he teaches Applied Systematic Theology. Dr de Mesa obtained his MA and PhD in Religious Studies from the Katholieke Universiteit Leuven in Belgium, where he was a Senior Fellow in 1996. He has published, among others, *In Solidarity with the Culture* (1987), *Marriage is Discipleship* (1995), *Following the Way of the Disciples* (1996) and *Why Theology is Never Far From Home* (2003).

**Kuruvilla George** is a pastor of the Church of South India. He is a former teacher of theology, and was principal of the Kerala United Theological Seminary, Trivandum, for many years. Dr George was also chairperson of the Federated Faculty for Research in Religion and Culture in Kottayam. He is now head of a diocesan higher secondary school. Kuruvilla George is a drama specialist and holds degrees in communication studies from Manila (Philippines) and the University of Edinburgh (PhD).

**Kavito Zhimo** obtained his MTh in Communication Studies from the Tamilnadu Theological Seminary in Madurai (1992). He was principal of Trinity Theological College in Dimapur, Nagaland, from 1993 to 2000. He was reappointed principal after completing his doctoral studies in communications at the United Theological Seminary, Bangalore (2004). His thesis is on 'The "Naga Communal Labour Force" as an Alternative Model of Communication for Participatory Development'.

**Marlene Marak** did her MTh in Communications at the United Theological Seminary, Bangalore, with a thesis on 'Ethical Norms of Communication in select Garo Oral Literature' (1999). Since then she has been teaching communication studies and homiletics at Eastern Theological Seminary in Jorhat (Assam).

**Michael Traber** has been visiting professor at the United Theological College in Bangalore since 1996. He worked as a journalist and book publisher in Africa (Zimbabwe and Zambia). For almost twenty years Dr Traber, a Catholic priest, was the editor of the international journal *Media Development* (published in London by the World Association for Christian Communication). Among his books is *Communication Ethics and Universal Values* (co-edited with Clifford Christians), Sage Publications.

**Pratap C. Gine** is a New Testament scholar with a PhD from Melbourne University. He has been seconded to the Senate of

Serampore College for three years to serve as Deputy Registrar. Rev. Gine has taught at Eastern Theological College, Jorhat, and is Visiting Professor (New Testament) at the North India Institute for Postgraduate Theological Studies (IIPGTS), Kolkata. He is the author of two books and of several articles on biblical themes.

**P. Solomon Raj** is an ordained minister of the Evangelical Lutheran Church. He is painter of religious themes and has held exhibitions, particularly of his Batik work, in the USA, UK, Japan, Germany, the Philippines and other countries. From 1978-83 he lectured at Selly Oak Colleges, Birmingham, and also obtained his PhD from the University of Birmingham. Dr Raj is the author of *Living Flame and Springing Fountain* (1993), *Palm Leaf Prayers: Woodprints and Linocuts from India* (1995) and *Fiery Wheels: Art Works and Meditations* (1994).

**Pradip N. Thomas** is the Director of the Global Studies Programme of the World Association for Christian Communication (WACC). He holds a PhD in Mass Communication from Leicester University. From 1988–1990 he taught communication studies at Tamilnadu Theological Seminary in Madurai, where he also organised the first MTh programme in Communication and Theological Education. He has written widely on communication and development, the right to communicate, intellectual property rights and the political economy of communication. His latest book (co-edited with Z. Nain) is *Who Owns the Media? Global Trends and Local Resistances* (ZED/Southbound), 2004.

**Samuel Rajkumar** obtained his MTh in communication studies from Tamilnadu Theological Seminary in 1990. He subsequently taught communications at Serampore College, Kolkata, and since 1995 at the United Theological College, Bangalore. Rev. Rajkumar, a Lutheran minister, also holds an MPhil in Christian Studies from Madras University (2000). He is currently working towards a PhD at Madras University. He is also Faculty Advisor of the Friends World Program of the Long Island University.

# Index